HIDE AWAY BY THE SEA

AN OAK ISLAND NOVEL
BOOK 1

L.P. DOVER

Hide Away by the Sea by L.P. Dover

Edited by: Yvette Rebello at YR Editor
Cover Designed by: Letitia Hasser at RBA Designs

Created with Vellum

1

EVERLEIGH

I awoke with a gasp, my hand covering the spot over my erratically beating heart. My skin was burning hot as if I'd just finished sunbathing out on the beach. In my dream, that was what I was doing, but I wasn't alone. Jensen was beside me, his hands caressing my skin as we lay on the soft blanket in the sand with the sound of the waves crashing nearby. I have never dreamed of him like that before, not until . . .

I slowly turned my head to the side and there he was, lying on his stomach with his glorious bare back on display. The breath hitched in my lungs, and I quickly covered my mouth with my hand to cut off another gasp that was desperate to break free.

Memories of last night came flooding back, making my head spin. There was too much eggnog, too many laughs, and too many innocent touches here and there. Not to mention I was on a high from getting my pre-med degree. There was a lot to celebrate. I was home and I'd missed it so much.

Many things had changed over the past five years. I wasn't the same and neither was Jensen. Yes, we still kept in touch through phone calls and texts, but I hadn't actually *seen* him in over two years. His once smooth baby face now had stubble and his chest and arms were chiseled with perfectly sculpted muscles I never knew he had.

Growing up, I always thought he was cute and sweet; my best friend. Of course, he had his girlfriends and I had my boyfriends, but there was one thing for sure, we could always count on each other. He was the one I shared my secrets with, the one I thought would always be a constant in my life. However, last night I didn't see him as just my fun-loving best friend who I used to spend every waking moment with. That was who he was in the past, but the tides have changed. We weren't kids anymore.

One thing led to another, and . . .

Oh my God. What have I done?

Biting my lip, I glanced around the room. We were in Jensen's childhood home, in the same bedroom we used to play video games in, no less. We were too drunk to drive to his house across town after last night's party, so we decided to venture over here. Luckily, his parents were in Barbados for Christmas. I couldn't imagine the awkwardness of having to walk past them or worse . . . try to sneak out and get caught.

My grandmother lived just next door, which was where I was supposed to be right now. I had no doubt my grammy knew precisely where I was. She always said something would happen between Jensen and me, but I never gave it much thought.

Carefully, I inched my way to the end of the bed,

trying my best not to jostle the mattress. The hardwood floor was cold beneath my feet as I tiptoed across the room. In the dim light from outside, I could make out my red dress, crumpled and discarded on the floor alongside one lone red high heel. I searched frantically for its matching partner, but it had disappeared entirely.

With a heavy sigh, I gave up and crept toward the door, desperate to escape before Jensen woke up. The stairs creaked as I went downstairs, and I cursed under my breath with each step I took. I wasn't ready to face him, not after what we did last night. Even though Jensen was my best friend and I wanted more from him, it would never work. All it would do is complicate things. His life was in Oak Island and there was a time when mine was too, but not anymore. I just got accepted to medical school. Trying to juggle that and a long-distance relationship was not feasible; we would never see each other.

Once I made it down to the main level and out the back door, I breathed a sigh of relief as I hurried over to my grandmother's quaint blue house named Hide Away by the Sea. It was precisely what I wanted to do—hide away.

The sun wasn't far from rising, illuminating the sky in shades of deep orange and pink. It was beautiful, but it was a ticking time bomb for me. Jensen was an early riser, and the first place he'd come looking for me would be at my grandmother's. I had to leave before that.

Keys in hand, I ran up the stairs to the back deck of my grandmother's house, desperate to disappear behind its walls. However, the second I stepped foot on the deck, I found my grandmother there, dressed in the doughnut-covered nightgown I got her when I was in seventh grade, and sitting in her favorite red rocking chair with a steaming cup of coffee in her hands. Her long, white hair fluttered in the wind as she rocked back and forth with a knowing grin on her face as she looked down at my feet.

"Good morning, Grammy."

She snorted out a chuckle. "Good morning to you, too, my dear," she said, lifting her twinkling emerald and honey-colored eyes back to mine. "Judging by your haste and the lack of one of your high heels, I'm assuming Jensen doesn't know you left?"

There were no secrets between me and my grandmother, but it didn't stop my cheeks from burning with embarrassment and guilt. Grammy loved Jensen like a grandson. She may be smiling, but I knew she wouldn't approve of what I was about to do.

I quickly glanced over at Jensen's parents' house, hoping like hell he wasn't about to walk out the door. "Last night went a little too far, Grammy. I don't have the words to deal with Jensen this morning."

Her gaze narrowed. "So, basically, you're scared."

She said it more as a statement than a question. I huffed out a sigh and hung my head. There was no lying to her; she could always see right through me.

"Fine," I gave in, letting her see the turmoil I knew was evident on my face. "I'm scared. Jensen and I crossed a line that never should've been crossed. We can never go back to the way things used to be."

My grandmother stood and set her cup down on the small distressed wooden coffee table Jensen had made her when we were in high school. Then, she walked up to me and grabbed my hand.

"That line should've been crossed a long time ago, Everleigh. You and Jensen have always been made for each other. I knew it the moment you both were born."

It wasn't the first time she had said things like that. I've always known she wanted me and Jensen to be together. Grammy was a romantic at heart, and it was one of the things I admired about her. She was always so optimistic and full of life.

I squeezed her hand and let go. "I just got accepted to medical school, Grammy. Focusing on my career is what I need to do right now. I can't juggle my love life and that at the same time."

Her face fell as if I'd just broken her heart. She cupped my cheeks. "I understand," she murmured, "it's just . . ."

"It's just what?" I replied, feeling the guilt weigh me down even more. Her eyes misted over, and she looked away as her hands slid from my face. She turned toward the horizon, where the waves crashed against the shore. It was as if something was on her mind, weighing her down. There was a sadness on her face that I'd never seen before.

"Grammy, what's wrong?" I asked.

She shook her head and closed her eyes. "I don't want you to have regrets, Everleigh." When she focused back on me and opened her eyes, not only could I see the emotional pain she tried to hide, I could feel it, too. Before I could speak, she held up a hand, halting me. "If you leave without working things out with Jensen, you *will* regret it, child. Last night was the beginning of something amazing for you two. I don't want to see you give up that kind of happiness. Not everyone gets the chance to be with the one they love."

Crossing my arms over my chest, I laughed but there

was no humor to it. "Love wasn't a part of last night, Grammy. It was too much alcohol and no self-control."

All she did was stare at me with her lips pursed as if I was a child who had no understanding of how the world worked. People made stupid decisions all the time and last night was one of them for me. Finally, my grandmother reached behind me to slide the glass patio door open.

"If that's what you believe, then go. Just don't say I didn't warn you. Running away from what you truly want will only lead to more pain and heartache. *You* have to be the one to decide what's most important right now."

I couldn't let a one-night stand stop me from returning to Boston. Yes, I could transfer to a school closer to home to finish my medical degree, but I wanted to be more than just a general doctor and take over my father's practice; I wanted to be a surgeon. I couldn't achieve that by staying in Oak Island.

I turned toward the door and stepped inside, before glancing back at my grandmother. "I do love Jensen, Grammy, but there's still so much I have to do in life. I can't give that up."

My heart hurt just thinking of leaving without saying goodbye to Jensen. But unfortunately, there was no other choice. I was afraid of what would happen if I saw him. The wall I had built between my heart and him was thinner than an eggshell. Just one tap would make it crack. I couldn't afford to have those feelings ooze out.

Swallowing hard, I took one last look around my grandmother's living room. It was my second home growing up, and I sure as hell was going to miss it. After what happened last night, I didn't see myself coming back anytime soon.

My grandmother had followed me inside and I hugged her hard, squeezing my eyes against the burn. "I love you," I whispered.

She embraced me back. "You're leaving, aren't you?"

Tears fell down my cheeks. "I think it's for the best. I'm going to pack up and run to Mom and Dad's to say goodbye." And then, I was going to drive my rental car back to Wilmington and get on the first plane back to school. I let her go and quickly wiped the tears away. "I promise to video chat with you every day. Then, maybe you can come to visit me this spring in Boston?"

She smiled and nodded. "I would be happy to."

There was no time to waste. I had to get out of there before Jensen stopped me.

BEFORE GOING to my parent's house, I changed clothes and threw my suitcase in the back seat. I intentionally left my cell in the car while I said my goodbyes to them. The calls began when I got back in my vehicle and was on my way to Wilmington airport.

Every time it rang, it felt like someone was jabbing a pin in my heart. What was I supposed to say to him? I rubbed a hand over my chest, afraid that my grandmother was right. I already regretted leaving, but there was no turning back. The decision was made.

My phone beeped with a text, and I drew in a shaky breath, knowing I needed to read it. A gas station was up ahead, so I pulled in and parked. If I was going to call Jensen back, I didn't need to be driving.

When I looked at my phone, there were three messages.

Jensen: Where are you?

Jensen: Please call me back. Your grandmother said you left.

Jensen: What's going on?

There was never a time when I couldn't confide in Jensen or just be brutally honest with him. Why was it so different now? How did one night change everything between us? I stared at my phone, my finger hovering above the call button. Before I could press it, Jensen called again.

It was now or never.

I took a deep breath then let it out slowly. "Hey," I answered, biting my lip so hard it hurt. The second I heard the worry in Jensen's voice, I wanted to cry.

"Everleigh, where are you? Are you seriously leaving town without saying goodbye to me?"

Closing my eyes, I leaned my head against the steering wheel, my throat thick and tight. "I didn't know what else to do."

"What do you mean? Did I do something wrong?"

"No," I replied quickly, lifting my head. I wiped my tears away and sighed. "You were perfect. I can't begin to describe how amazing it was to see you for the holidays."

He huffed. "Then why did you sneak out on me? I thought you weren't going back to Boston for another few days."

I wanted to tell him the truth, that I was scared of what last night meant to me, of what it would mean for our future. Could I see us being together? Yes, but not right now. Unfortunately, things were never going to be the same between us. It already hurt to leave him.

Getting attached and going months without seeing each other would be unbearable. It was best to cut things off before they could progress any further.

"I got a call this morning from one of the doctors I know at the hospital," I said, hating myself for lying to him. "She asked if I could shadow her for the next three weeks. It's too good of an opportunity to pass up."

I waited for him to say something, but there was only silence; it was deafening. Jensen wasn't stupid. Even though it was a good lie, he could always see right through me. I wasn't the type of girl to run from a sticky situation. Usually, I bolted headfirst into them, but I couldn't do that this time. I didn't want to deal with my feelings, not when I had more important things to worry about.

Jensen let out a sigh, and it made my chest tighten. "You do what you have to do, Everleigh," he said. "But I want you to know I don't regret last night. I'll be here when you want to talk. Just call me when you're ready."

"I will," I whispered softly, barely able to get the words out. "Goodbye, Jensen."

I couldn't bear to hear him say goodbye to me, so I hung up before he could. But then, the tears started flowing freely as an avalanche of emotion came crashing down on me.

Was I ever going to be ready to talk to him?

One day, I would be . . . but it wouldn't be anytime soon.

2

EVERLEIGH

TWELVE YEARS LATER

Sunlight.

Warmth.

The sun glinted off the ocean's surface, glimmering like a million tiny diamond shards. I stepped onto the beach and felt the granules of sand move beneath my feet as the waves lapped against my toes.

A gentle breeze blew back my hair and carried with it the distinctive smell of saltwater mixed with the sweet fragrance of honeysuckle from my grandmother's garden. It was a scent that had come to represent home to me. I breathed it in deeply, feeling nostalgia wash over me.

Standing by the water's edge, I took a moment to take in the sight before me—a vast blue expanse shimmering under the rising sun. I couldn't help the smile that came to my face as I thought about how amazing it was going to feel to walk in my grandmother's garden again soon, to see the beautiful flowers and enjoy the tranquility.

When I was a kid, I spent hours helping her with all the planting she wanted, including digging the massive hole for the man-made pond she just had to have. I was happy to do it, though; I cherished the memories with my grandmother and our talks about love and life while sitting by the honeysuckle bushes. It won't be long until I am able to see my family again.

"Dr. Abbott?"

I was lost in thought when the sound of my name jolted me back to reality. I didn't even realize I was standing by the sink with the warm water running over my hands. I had been yearning to escape the four walls of the hospital locker room, an area I had spent many days and long nights in. This was where I changed into my scrubs, prepped for surgeries, and sadly mourned when some patients didn't make it. Despite knowing that death was inevitable, it still hurt deeply. I hadn't allowed myself free time to contemplate anything except my job as a doctor for years—until now. Thoughts of vacations had slowly crept in and captivated my mind, preventing me from realizing where I truly was.

"Dr. Abbott?"

The voice reminded me that I wasn't off the clock yet. I stepped away from the sink and shut off the water, stealing a glance at my surgical tech as she gazed upon me with amusement in her crystal blue eyes.

Mera was thirty, only four years younger than me, with deep chocolate-colored hair that she always wore up in a bun. Her light blue scrubs matched her eyes perfectly. We had just completed a pituitary tumor removal—the last of my surgeries for the day—and it was also the last one I'd be doing for two months. I had requested the entire summer off, and that vacation was set to begin tomorrow morning.

Mera tried to mask her smile, but it was no use. She wasn't just a nurse, she was a friend. The way we moved together during surgery felt like magic; I swear Mera could read my mind sometimes. During critical moments, we were quick and efficient, which was what you needed when someone's life was on the line. When Mera and I first met, an instant connection was born between us. Mera stepped closer to me, her lips twitching in suppressed laughter.

"I turn my back for one moment, and you're already off in la-la land," she said, releasing her bun and running a hand through her short curls.

"What can I say? That's the life of an overachiever," I replied with a laugh.

Drawing out a paper towel from the dispenser, I dried off my hands and thought about my path so far. I had never taken a truly long vacation since I finished high school sixteen years ago; it had been college straight into residency and then working as a neurosurgeon at Massachusetts General Hospital. It was a dream come true—just like my dad had always hoped for me.

Feeling a surge of excitement within me, I met my gaze in the bathroom mirror. My caramel-blonde hair had grown past my shoulders, framing my heart-shaped face, and there was joy sparkling in my hazel-green eyes.

"And now I'm taking the whole summer off to show my grandmother around the world," I added happily.

I barely had time to spend with her since I finished my residency two years ago. Even my parents see very little of me due to the long hours I worked each week. However, they did make it a point to fly up and visit occasionally.

The moment I returned home, though, I was ready to take Grammy on an adventure to the Caribbean. My parents planned to join us in Aruba in a couple of weeks.

Mera watched me with sadness in her sapphire-colored eyes as she tucked her curls behind her ears. "I'm so jealous of you right now. I still have one grandmother, but she can barely move around anymore. Seeing her now breaks my heart; she was always so active when I was growing up."

My heart ached for Mera, and I couldn't imagine what life would be like without my grandmother. I reached into my locker and pulled out my purse before turning back to her.

"I'm sorry, Mera. I didn't know."

She shrugged. "No worries. She still has a sharp mind. The woman can beat anyone in a poker game," she said with a wry smile. "Don't know how she does it."

At that moment, the sound of my cell phone ringing pierced the air, and I knew who it was going to be; Dr. Nyla Clark, a close friend of mine and one of our hospital's best ER doctors. I grabbed my phone from my purse, and sure enough, saw Nyla's name on the screen.

"It's Nyla. She wants to meet me for lunch."

Mera snorted and hugged me warmly. "Lunch? It's almost six o'clock."

I gently pulled away from her embrace and nodded solemnly. "Exactly. I was in surgery all morning and afternoon. There was no time to eat."

A sympathetic expression crossed Mera's face. "Don't

know how you do it. But, one thing's for sure—you're dedicated to the job," she said with admiration.

I smiled at her words, but there wasn't any hint of boasting in my reply. "Someone has to be," I insisted simply before making my way toward the door. "See you in two months! Don't get into too much trouble while I'm gone." Mera's laughter echoed in the hallway as I walked away, juggling the phone to my ear.

"Hey," I said into the phone.

Nurses moved silently through the hallway, their strides full of purpose as they went about their work. Time never stopped here; there was always something going on.

"Ready for lunch?" Nyla asked, her voice slightly breathless.

I turned the corner and pressed the button for the elevators. "I am. Where are you?" A faint ding came through the phone; the ER was on the floor just below me.

"Waiting for the slowest elevator in the world to open. That's my luck."

Memories of the first time we met flooded my mind and I smiled. We were both racing to get our food from the cafeteria before our break ended, and Nyla had slipped on a pile of peach cobbler someone had dropped on the already slick floor. She went sliding across the cafeteria, covered in salad dressing and cobbler. I rushed over and helped her up, both of us laughing so hard that tears sprung from our eyes. Ever since then, we've become great friends.

I chuckled as I hung up the phone and stepped into the elevator. Its doors groaned open a few seconds later, and there she was. Her auburn hair was pulled back in a wild ponytail, her freckles standing out against her pale complexion. The hunter-green scrubs clung to her curves under a white lab coat that billowed out behind her as she rushed toward me.

"Can you believe it?" she said, her voice laced with exasperation. "The whole city seems to be here today!"

I smiled, shaking my head. "They just want to see you."

We stepped further into the elevator to let more people in and headed down to the next floor. As we descended, Nyla turned to me with a mischievous glint in her eye. "If only there was one hot guy in the hospital I could fix up . . ."

Smiling, I rolled my eyes playfully. "You're too much."

As soon as the elevator doors slid open, we stepped out and walked briskly down the hall. A few nurses nodded in acknowledgment as we passed by, but I barely had time to return their greeting before focusing back on Nyla.

"How long has it been since you went on a date?" I asked, racking my brain for any potential suitors she may have gone out with since her divorce, yet coming up empty-handed.

Nyla let out a heavy sigh. "It's been so long I don't even remember. You've probably been on twice as many."

I couldn't help but snort at that response. When it came to dates, I was well aware of my failure record.

"I went out with three guys," I informed her. "And none of them led to second dates."

The first guy was a lawyer I met while picking up a latte at my favorite coffee shop. Conversation between us quickly dwindled to him talking about himself, so I excused myself as soon as my fresh-baked blueberry muffin arrived without batting an eye. The other two men I met were doctors rotating through my hospital, but all they wanted was a good time while they were in town. I wasn't interested in that. I wanted something that would last.

Maybe I didn't deserve love after what I did to Jensen all those years ago. Even though it was just one fantastic night, I knew what we had was real, and I let it slip through my fingers. Jensen told me to call when I was ready to talk, but I never did.

He called and left messages for a while, but I never got the courage to return them. The days turned into months, then the months into years. Eventually, I gave up the thought of ever calling him back, especially after hearing a couple of years ago that he was engaged to Michelle Short—a girl we went to high school with. I haven't been back to Oak Island since hearing that news. The last thing I wanted was to see him around town with her. They were probably married already with two kids and a dog. I wouldn't know because I've intentionally avoided discussing him with my family; it was best not to know. But sadly, I've tried to find someone who could make me feel a fraction of the desire I had with Jensen. No one else could compare with him, but part of me hoped I'd find it one day.

"Still," Nyla said sadly, drawing me back to the conversation, "it's better than nothing."

The cafeteria buzzed with the sound of people chatting and dishes rattling, but as soon as Alice—our favorite cafeteria worker—noticed us, she waved us over to the salad station. She was in her late sixties with short white hair and a little shy of five feet tall, but her kind eyes were like beacons that easily cut through the din of the room.

A warm smile crossed her lips, and I couldn't help but smile back. Alice reminded me of my grandmother with her gentle mannerisms.

"Hey, Alice. We'll take our usual," I called out.

Alice winked. "I'm already ahead of you, Dr. Abbott."

With sure steps, she walked over to the refrigerator behind her and pulled out two salads—one chicken Caesar for me and one grilled chicken salad with extra pine nuts and strawberries for Nyla.

Nyla breathed a sigh of relief. "Alice, you just gave me a few extra minutes to relax. Thank you so much."

Alice beamed with happiness. "You're welcome, sweetheart. I knew you two would be down here sometime. Figured you wouldn't have much time to eat."

I held a hand over my heart in appreciation. "Thank you, Alice. We really appreciate it."

We carried our plastic salad packages to the checkout line and hovered over a scanner. The gadget beeped, signaling permission to enter the café's dining area. Nyla bolted for the nearest table with her salad container open before I had even unzipped my purse. It was then that I noticed how much weight Nyla had lost; her cheeks had sunk in more than usual, and her skin lacked its characteristic rosy glow.

Nyla shoved a forkful of lettuce and chicken into her mouth while talking. "Don't forget about me when you're sunning your buns on some tropical beach island. I want to go with you!"

I chuckled while opening my salad container. "Why

can't you? After all the hours you've put in at this hospital, you must have accrued at least a year's worth of vacation."

Nyla nodded slowly, pausing mid-chew. "True, but you know I can't just up and leave like that. Besides, my passport expired months ago. So even if I wanted to go to the Caribbean with you . . ." she trailed off.

I placed my hand on top of hers and looked directly into her eyes. "Nyla, I love you. You are one hell of a doctor and my best friend, too, but you need to take care of yourself first. How else will you be able to help others?"

Nyla's eyes began to mist over as she looked away from me. Her voice cracked when she spoke next. "Why are you always right?"

I squeezed Nyla's arm. "I want to make sure you're okay, and a vacation isn't far-fetched. I'm taking the summer off, and I have no doubt the hospital will survive without me here. We both need some time away from it all."

Nyla returned my gaze and wiped her tears away with her sleeve. "All right, I'll see what I can do."

I swallowed a bite of my salad, hoping Nyla would agree with my next proposal. But, of course, there was always an alternative if she couldn't use her expiring passport for international travel.

"You know, my grandmother's beach house is the ideal spot for rest and relaxation. You can take strolls by the shore, catch some sun, or explore my grandmother's gardens in peace and quiet; you'll have it all to yourself."

Her face brightened and it pleased me immensely.

"Seriously?" she breathed in surprise. "From what you've said before, it sounds like heaven! I've been dying to go there!"

I couldn't help but smile widely. "It's settled then. Go ahead and take the time off that you need. We can only work so hard before we break down; I was nearing my limit."

Nyla tried to look away, but I saw the exhaustion in her eyes. She shoveled a few more bites of food into her mouth and looked at her watch, which had started beeping.

"My time's up. I have to go."

She started to stand when I grabbed her wrist. "Promise me you'll take some time off. Oak Island is the perfect place to get away. I need to know you're going to be okay before I leave."

A sad smile tugged at the corner of her lips. "I promise. A beach vacation does sound like a good idea." I stood, and Nyla wrapped me in a warm hug. "You'll have your phone on your travels, right?"

"Yes," I replied, returning the embrace. "We can talk anytime. I'll make sure the beach house is ready for you whenever you decide it's time to go down there."

She squeezed me tightly before releasing me from the hug. "Thanks, Everleigh. Guess I've been putting this off for too long, huh?"

"Just a bit," I teased with a grin. "But we can fix that easily enough."

The beeping of Nyla's watch grew louder before she groaned and let go of me. "I really have to go now. I'll call you soon!"

She hastily threw away her half-eaten salad and rushed out of the cafeteria. Usually, I would have to rush out with her, but not today. However, a part of me did feel slightly guilty for leaving the hospital for two months.

I had almost finished my salad when my phone rang; it was my mom. She's been calling numerous times over the past couple of weeks to make sure I was still coming home, so I smiled as I answered it.

"Hi, Mom. And before you ask, yes, I'm still coming home. My flight leaves at seven-thirty tomorrow morning and nothing has changed." But instead of hearing her boisterous laugh, there was just silence on the other end. "Mom, you there?"

She cleared her throat and sighed in a nasal tone that caused me to tense up in dread. "I'm here, sweetheart."

My heart sank as I heard her muffled sobs on the line. My mother rarely cried, so whatever this was must have been gut-wrenching for her. Her cries grew even more distressing, and all I could do was listen until she'd hopefully calm down. I pressed the phone to my ear, my heart racing.

Panic clawed at my throat, making it hard to breathe. Quickly, I flung my purse over my shoulder and dumped the rest of my salad in the trash. Something was wrong; terribly wrong. I rushed out of the cafeteria, searching for a place to hide. The first supply closet I found was dark and musty with a sharp scent of disinfectant and cardboard boxes. It made me nauseous, but I didn't care; anything was better than being surrounded by people who were oblivious to my pain.

"Come on, Mom, tell me what's going on. Is it Dad?"

I begged for answers, desperation creeping into my voice. My mother hiccupped through her tears.

"No," she said quietly.

I swallowed hard and closed my eyes tightly, afraid of what she would say next. Images of loved ones flashed before me. Grammy? No, please, no. I wasn't even going to ask if it was her; I couldn't. Jensen? It had been eleven years since we last spoke, but there wasn't a day that went by when I didn't think of him. If anything happened to him, I'd never forgive myself for never returning his calls, for being an idiot and letting fear take over.

"Is it Jensen?" I whispered shakily.

"No, honey," she replied softly.

Relief flooded through me like a balm, but it was short-lived. There was only one person left it could be. My throat constricted, and I sucked in a shallow breath. Tears stung my eyes, and I leaned heavily against the closet door.

"Is it Grammy?" I whispered.

She was my last living grandparent, and she was like a second mom to me—the one who knew all of my hopes and dreams, fears and secrets that no one else did. In my heart, I wanted to believe she was invincible, that nothing bad could ever come close to touching her. But deep down in the depths of my soul, I knew death lurked around every corner.

My mother let out a gut-wrenching sob. "She's gone, sweetheart," she said between cries. "I couldn't get hold of her this morning, so I went to her house. I found her sitting in the chair in her room with a book in her lap. She passed away sometime during the night."

I gasped, my hand clutching at my chest where I could feel the heart-shaped locket my grandmother gave me for my sixteenth birthday. A searing pain spread through me like flames licking a dry field. I tried to suck in air, but it was as if I was drowning deep beneath the ocean's surface.

My knees buckled and I crumpled down to the floor.

Everything around me became distorted, twisted, and darkened until there was only agony left. The fear of losing my grandmother had always been my greatest terror, and now I was living through it.

A low, keening wail rose from the depths of my soul; no words, just raw grief. There were no miracles or happy endings here—just an ending that shattered all that came before it.

My voice barely rose above a hoarse whisper when I finally found words. "What are we going to do?"

My mother swallowed audibly before speaking, her voice gentle yet fragile with emotion. "I don't know yet, sweetheart."

Tears blurred my vision as rage flared within me. "Why did you wait all day to tell me? I could've caught a flight earlier to be with you."

It hurt to think of her being alone in this moment of utter devastation. She had my father, but there was a special bond between mother and daughter. My mom's voice shook with sorrow.

"I'm sorry, honey. I didn't want you to have to worry."

The world kept spinning on its axis even though everything within me had crumbled away into nothingness. As much as I had witnessed death over the years in my profession, nothing had prepared me for this —for losing my grandmother—for watching my mother lose her own mother.

My breaths came in ragged gasps, and I clutched at my chest once more as the agony ebbed and flowed like waves crashing against a rocky shore.

"I knew you had surgeries today, Everleigh," my mother murmured. "Your head needed to be clear."

I didn't know what to say or think, but I knew I would've left everything behind if my family needed me. Family was important. My mother was the backbone of the family, but my grandmother was the heart and soul. Without that, nothing was ever going to be the same.

She cleared her throat again. "Everleigh, are you okay?"

Tears burned my cheeks. Usually, I was strong and nothing could get me down. My skin was thick. It had to be in order to be a doctor. During my residency, patients yelled at me, threw things at my head, and even threatened my life if I didn't help them. It was something I knew could happen, but also something I was prepared for. Never once have I regretted my choice to be a doctor. I could work a double shift and still have the energy to go for a run. My whole career had been dedicated to taking care of others and making them better. That was why I coerced my grandmother to take the summer-long trip to the Caribbean. I knew it was way past due and something she had wanted to do for years.

Now it was too late.

I'd waited too long to fulfill my grandmother's wish, and that regret will weigh heavily on my shoulders for the rest of my life.

Was I okay?

No, not at all, but my mother didn't need to hear that.

"I'll be fine, Mom," I lied.

"When you come home tomorrow, we have a lot to discuss. There are some things you don't know."

Using my sleeve, I wiped the tears off my face, but more followed. "I'll be there as soon as I can."

"Be safe, sweetheart. I love you and I'll see you tomorrow."

"I love you, too," I whispered.

I hung up and covered my face with my hands. My legs were so weak I didn't know if I could stand. All I knew was that my heart had been ripped out, and the pain was unbearable. Nothing was ever going to be the same again.

3

EVERLEIGH

I drove the thirteen hours down to Oak Island in my little Honda CRV, desperately trying to ignore the tears still streaming down my face. My eyes were red and swollen from sorrow, and it felt as if I'd kept them open during a sandstorm. Blinking only made it worse.

The thought of food made me nauseous, but I forced myself to eat a pack of peanut butter crackers, or else I wouldn't make it to North Carolina. With every mile closer I got to home, the more regret and guilt filled my gut. Grammy was so excited about the Caribbean trip we were supposed to take together; she'd even bought a skimpy red bikini to wear on the beach just to embarrass me. Little did she know I was looking forward to seeing her in it, to see her not have a care in the world.

All that excitement was gone, replaced by painful emptiness at the thought of what could have been. I had waited too long. If only I'd planned the trip years ago. Now my grandmother was gone, and nothing could bring her back. That regret would hang over my head for the rest of my life. It made me second-guess all my life choices. If I'd done things differently and stayed in Oak Island, I would've had more time with my family. Maybe I would be married to Jensen and have kids of my own instead of being a single thirty-four-year-old that worked over sixty hours a week. Having a family of my own was a happiness I feared I'd never feel.

When I reached my parents' house, no car was in sight. It was what I'd secretly hoped for, but unfortunately, it also meant that no one was here. I pulled into the driveway and parked, hoping the time alone would help compose myself. My mother didn't need to see how distraught I was. She was the strong one, the one who could handle anything. Or so I thought. I've performed critical brain surgeries without breaking a sweat. But the loss of my grandmother ripped straight through my heart. I didn't even feel like myself anymore.

I got out of the car and looked up at my childhood home. It was a two-story yellow structure on stilts with teal shutters and an open deck on the front side that overlooked the beach. My parents had named it Sunshine and Cupcakes because its bright colors reminded my mom of, you guessed it . . . sunshine and cupcakes. Although I'd had many memories here, I had even more at my grandmother's place.

I took a deep breath and closed my eyes as the emotions came flooding back in. No amount of time would ever heal the pain from Grammy's passing away. I returned to my car, and reversed out of the driveway and onto Beach Drive. I tried calling my folks, but neither picked up their phones, so I assumed they were at my grandmother's house. I wasn't supposed to arrive for another three hours, so they didn't know I was here yet. I wasn't sure if I could handle stepping into Grammy's house without breaking down, but I knew eventually I would have to face it.

Taking a deep breath, I inched down Beach Drive. With its white sand beaches, crystal clear waters and bright beach houses of every shape and size, Oak Island was where everyone wanted to be. I smiled as the sun shone brightly through my windshield, its rays twinkling off the ripples of the sea. Our street hadn't changed much since I left for college, but a few more houses had been built.

Ahead of me, in the distance, was my grandmother's house. It overlooked the point, but I couldn't see much of it yet. Despite exuberant amounts of money being offered for it, she was always adamant about never selling her beloved home. Most of the homeowners on our street lived here all year long, so we never had too many run-ins with tourists. However, many small businesses in town relied on tourists to stay afloat. My father's medical practice had always been busy during summer months with jellyfish burns or allergies from people finding out they're allergic to seafood—interesting, yet predictable, cases that I used to help him with when I was younger. Even so, I couldn't ignore my dreams of pushing further in my medical career—something my father wanted, too, even if leaving Oak Island was surely not part of his vision.

The closer I got to my grandmother's house, the slower I drove. I wasn't ready because I knew I'd feel the pain of my grandmother's loss even more when I stepped foot in the house. She'd died there, alone in her room. There was no warning, no indication she was sick. Or was there and I just didn't see it because I wasn't around? What if I could've prevented it? I had just talked to my grandmother on the phone the night before and she was so happy. Never did I imagine she would be gone a few short hours after that.

I pulled over to the side of the road to catch my breath. Up ahead, I could see a tiny sliver of the house. It was steel blue with white trim and white shutters that always stayed pristine. My grandmother refused to let the white discolor. That home was her pride and joy. What my grandmother loved even more was the tin roof, especially when it rained. The sound always relaxed her.

Closing my eyes, I laid my head back against the seat. Being utterly exhausted had caught up to me. One minute, I was wide awake and the next . . .

A sudden, sharp knock jolted me awake. My heart raced in my chest as I scrambled to find the source of the sound. Through half-lidded eyes, I spotted Mrs. Georgia Hopkins, a good friend of my grandmother's, standing outside with her beloved golden retriever, Martin. She held one hand on his head and the other clasped over her mouth in shock at what she had done. Her short white hair was disheveled, and lines creased her sun-worn skin.

At eighty-five years old, Mrs. Hopkins still looked every bit as sweet as she did all those years ago. The poor woman had gone through her fair share of family tragedies. Her only son had died of a heart attack at thirty-six, and her husband died about ten years ago from esophagus cancer. After all that, Georgia and my grandmother made sure to see each other daily. They were kindred spirits; that was what my grandmother always said.

My body was exhausted, but I tried my best to smile as I wound down my window. "I'm sorry, Mrs. Hopkins. I can't believe I fell asleep."

Mrs. Hopkins placed a hand over her heart. "Oh, honey, it's my fault. And please call me Georgia. You're Rachel's granddaughter, for goodness' sake. You're practically my family."

I could agree with that. After all, I *did* feel as if we were family. Georgia was my grandmother's best friend.

"Okay," I said, "Georgia it is. I just got so used to calling you Mrs. Hopkins over the years."

Georgia laughed, but there was a sadness to it. "And it makes me feel old when people call me that. Your grandmother was the same way. The townspeople knew to call her Rachel, or they'd get the famous Rachel Holt glare."

Hearing that made me snicker. "Ah yes, I know that glare very well."

Georgia sighed and nodded over at the house. "I knew your parents would be at Rachel's, so I dropped them off some food. They were just talking about how they were going to pick you up in a couple of hours. As I was walking by, I saw your car and recognized you. Thought I'd see what was going on." Her gaze narrowed as she took in my car, which was covered in smashed bugs and dust. "You had a long trip if you drove all the way down from Massachusetts. Your parents still believe they're supposed to pick you up from the airport."

Martin leaned his head against the doorframe, tongue lolling out of his mouth in a friendly smile. I ran my hand gently over the top of his smooth head, trying to keep myself from breaking down.

"Nobody knows I'm here." My voice wavered, and I paused briefly, not wanting to admit why I had chosen to drive instead of flying back home. "I just needed some time away."

Georgia's chin trembled, and fresh tears pooled in her eyes. "I don't blame you, darling. Nobody should be on a plane during times like this." She closed her eyes briefly before re-opening them and looking away; her face was distraught with anguish. "Rachel was my best friend, and it doesn't feel right knowing she's gone." Georgia's gaze returned to mine as she spoke softly, "But you were so close to her—having you around will make it feel like she's still here with us."

My throat tightened and I blinked multiple times, attempting to suppress my emotions that threatened to burst through. Hot tears spilled from my eyes and streamed down my cheeks as I inhaled deeply, struggling to compose myself again.

"Thank you, Georgia," I said sincerely. "I'll be here for you too—just like my grandmother always was."

Georgia smiled warmly at me and wiped away her tears with the back of her hand before responding. "That means a lot to me, Everleigh—if you don't mind visiting every now and then, it would be nice to have your company."

I nodded. "Of course. I'd be happy to."

I glanced down the road at my grandmother's house. It was a one-story building on stilts, painted blue, and was surrounded by lush green grass and rose bushes. A light breeze carried the strong scent of honeysuckles to me from her garden.

"Before you go, how's my mother doing?"

When I focused back on Georgia, she solemnly shrugged. "As good as can be expected. She's at the house sorting through your grandmother's things with your father while your aunt Sandy hovers nearby like a fly trying to land on honey."

The mention of my aunt provoked a nagging feeling in my gut that didn't settle well. I had never liked my aunt Sandy and hadn't given her a second thought in years until now. So, it figured she'd only show up if she thought she would get something out of it. With my grandmother gone, Sandy would no doubt want her cut of the inheritance.

"Of course she is," I scoffed.

Georgia nodded, but there was a twinkle of something behind the pain in her blue eyes; mischief rather than sorrow this time. "I wouldn't worry about her, Everleigh. Even though your grandmother had two daughters and an amazing granddaughter like you, she got enough love from you and your mother to make up for what she didn't get from your aunt. That much is certain."

"Yes, she did," I said softly.

My hand was resting on the door, and Georgia patted it reassuringly. "Take care of yourself, dear. Do you plan on staying for a while? I know you were supposed to leave for vacation tomorrow."

I didn't know what to say, so I shrugged. Everything was up in the air. Was I going to stay for a while? Should I go straight back to Massachusetts after the funeral? Those were questions I didn't have the answers to. But I had a feeling my mother would need me around for a while.

"I don't know," I answered honestly. "I have the next two months off but don't know what to do with everything going on."

A sad smile spread across Georgia's face. "Either way, I know I'll see you again. Your mother said the funeral's going to be in two days."

The thought made my heart hurt. In two days, we would be saying goodbye to my grandmother forever. I wasn't ready. My breath quivered as I slowly exhaled.

"I will see you there, then."

Reaching out, I patted Martin's head again before Georgia stepped back and waved and continued her journey down the road. She lived just six houses down from my grandmother.

After pressing the button to roll up my window, I pulled back onto the road. When my grandmother's house came fully into view, it was as if I'd stepped into a different time—a time when everything was perfect. Her house wasn't as huge as others on the street, but that made it unique. My mother had grown up there, and it was where I spent my summers and then some. Everything was much more fun at my grandmother's house.

For the briefest of moments, I stared at the house and thought my grandmother was going to run out onto the porch and wave like she used to when I would stop by. But unfortunately, that wasn't ever going to happen again. I rubbed that aching spot on my chest that felt like someone was using a dull butter knife to reach my heart.

All I wanted was for the pain to disappear, but I knew it wouldn't be anytime soon.

After taking a deep breath, I pulled into the driveway. My mother's white Toyota Camry and a black BMW i8 were there. The BMW, no doubt, belonged to my aunt. Sandy loved showing off her money and talked about it even more.

I parked behind my mother's car and got out. A gust of wind whipped by, drawing my attention to the ocean. The waves were bigger than usual, almost as if they were also in pain. It was as if they knew my grandmother would never step foot in their waters again.

I walked up the stairs to the porch, and around the back to the door my grandmother always used. You could count the times she went out her main front door on one hand. My parents were inside, looking through photo albums on the couch. I watched them through the window to get a feel of what to expect. My father was dashing as always with his perfectly coifed gray hair, wearing a green polo shirt and khakis as if he was about to play at the golf course. However, the outright concern on his face as he consoled my mother worried me.

My mother was strong, but I couldn't help but remember how devastated she was when my grandfather died twenty years ago. Her cheeks were red, and her eyes were swollen from crying. She was the younger version of my grandmother with her silky-smooth blonde hair and face like an angel. Like mother, like daughter, like grandmother. Everyone on the island used to say that to us since I looked just like my mother, and she like hers. All three of us had the same blonde hair and green eyes with a golden ring around our pupils. My aunt Sandy used to hate hearing people dote on us; she was the one who wanted all the attention.

When my aunt came into view, I could feel a wave of hatred wash over me. Sandy busied herself by looking through the kitchen cabinets and drawers, probably searching for something she could take. I have never known anyone to be as self-involved and selfish as her.

She left Oak Island to pursue a modeling career when she turned eighteen, but it was really my mother who had the beauty in the family, both inside and out. Sandy knew it and resented her for it. She was two years younger than my mother, with the same blonde hair, but her eyes weren't hazel green. Instead, they were brown, just like my late grandfather's. Sandy was also a former Miss North Carolina who happened to marry a man who later became a state senator. They lived in a multimillion-dollar mansion in Durham with their twin twenty-year-old son and daughter, Bradley and Hannah. I've only seen them a handful of times. That was how disconnected Sandy was from the family.

I was about to open the door and walk inside when my mother saw me and jumped to her feet.

"Everleigh," she cried, rushing toward me. I opened the screen door, and she flung her arms around me. "What are you doing here? Your father and I were going to pick you up."

I clung to my mother, inhaling her raspberry-scented perfume. It was a special concoction my grandmother had put together. I never left home without putting on the honeysuckle perfume my grandmother had made for me. Thinking of it now made my chest tighten. Once my bottle ran out, that was it. My grandmother wasn't here to make any more.

My father came up beside us and draped his arm around my shoulders. "We were getting ready to head to the airport," he murmured softly.

My mother let me go, and I turned to my dad and hugged him. His strong arms held me protectively as any father would do. I missed him and continued to hold onto him as I spoke.

"After Mom called yesterday, the last thing I wanted to do was get on a plane with strangers. The drive helped clear my head."

He kissed my cheek and whispered in my ear. "Glad you're here, pumpkin. Maybe you can keep your mother from killing your aunt."

"Great," I groaned as he let me go.

When I turned toward the kitchen, Sandy was nowhere to be seen. But then she reappeared, sneaking out of one of the bedrooms. Unfortunately, it wasn't just any bedroom . . . it was my grandmother's. Even though my grandmother was Sandy's mother, I didn't like her snooping through her things.

"Well, if it isn't my favorite niece," Sandy chirped, her voice high-pitched and nasally. It was the kind of sound that made you cringe. I raised my eyebrows, trying to keep a pleasant expression on my face.

"I'm your only niece," I reminded her firmly.

Sandy waved away my comment and offered me a halfhearted embrace. Feeling obligated to reciprocate, I hugged her even though her hug felt limp and uninterested.

"I couldn't help but notice the CRV outside," she said

begrudgingly as I stepped back. The slight edge in her tone was not lost on me.

My jaw tightened, and I frowned slightly. "What's wrong with it?"

My aunt rolled her eyes and put her nose up in the air. Her words were patronizing yet laced with envy. "You're a doctor now, a highly trained surgeon at that. You can afford something better."

I crossed my arms over my chest and glared at her incredulously. Didn't she have something else to worry about? Her mother had just died.

"Maybe you should concentrate on other things instead of worrying about what I do and don't do with my money."

Sandy scoffed again and raised one eyebrow disdainfully before shifting the conversation to another uncomfortable topic. "You're still single, too, aren't you?"

Her statement felt like more of an insult than an inquiry. A burst of rage surged through my body. My fists clenched, and I felt heat on my cheeks while I held back the torrent of words I wanted to spew at her. But my mother stepped between us before I could find the right ones to say. Her voice rose like a crescendo in a symphony as she shouted.

"What is wrong with you? We're all here mourning the loss of our mother, and all you've done since you arrived is nitpick and belittle everyone." She took hold of my hand and pulled me toward the door. Halfway there, she spun around to address Sandy again. "Why are you even here? It's not like you care about anyone other than yourself."

Sandy's mouth hung wide open with shock, but before

she could utter a response, my mother yanked the door open sharply and dragged me out with her. Once we were outside, she propped her elbows onto the balcony railing and exhaled heavily.

"I still cannot believe that woman is related to me," she said, shaking her head. "It breaks my heart that she doesn't understand how much our mother longed to be in her life."

I gently touched her arm and spoke softly. "Every family has a Sandy."

A small smile appeared on Mom's face as she nodded in agreement. "You're probably right. It hurts me to think that she never gave a damn about spending time with our mother. Her being here makes me so mad. After everything my mom did for her, she deserved so much more in return."

I draped an arm over her shoulders, feeling her tremble under my touch. Her long, blonde hair blew around us as the wind picked up.

"She had *us*, and our love was stronger than anything Sandy could ever give her."

Tears welled in my eyes as I rested my head on hers, and we watched the waves crash against the shore until the sky turned a gentle shade of pink and purple with the dying sun. It felt like my grandmother was standing with us.

My mother broke the silence. "There's something you need to know, Everleigh."

The second I looked at her serious face, dread filled me. I couldn't tell if she had good or bad news for me.

"What is it?"

She wouldn't meet my gaze as she stared out at the sea.

"I read your grandmother's will. In fact, I've known what was in it for many years."

"O-kay," I replied unsurely. "I'm pretty sure she left everything to you, right? Or at least that's what I'm hoping." She shook her head slowly, and my heart sank into my stomach.

"Not me . . ." she answered.

My mouth dropped open. "So, help me God, please tell me not Sandy, Mom."

Smiling sadly, she turned back to me and cupped my cheek. "Not Sandy, sweetheart. *You.* Your grandmother left the house, her belongings, and everything to you."

Eyes wide, I stared at her in complete and utter shock. Grammy never gave me any indication that she was leaving everything to me. I didn't know what to think. "Why wouldn't she leave it all to you?" I cried.

A tear fell down her cheek. "She loved you so much. And she knew this house meant a lot to you."

And it did.

My whole life was spent here. While my parents worked, I stayed with my grandmother, and it had been that way since I was a baby. The same went for Jensen. With Jensen and his family living right beside my grandmother, it was how we became such good friends. We were together almost every day of our lives. After school, there would always be some kind of treat waiting for us, whether it be my grandmother's famous ooey gooey chocolate chip cookies, which were my favorite, or her milk and dark chocolate brownies with extra chocolate chips that were Jensen's.

The Hide Away by the Sea house was full of bittersweet memories. It was not only my second home with a woman who was basically a second mother to me, but it was also where mine and Jensen's relationship grew. He was always helping my grandmother fix things around the house, whether painting the siding, changing light bulbs, or fixing the kitchen sink that constantly got clogged up. Thinking about it now, those memories were so long ago that none of it seemed real. Those days were long gone.

My gaze was fixed on the horizon, my chest tightening with confusion and despair. A part of me wanted to leave my life in Boston and flee to the sea, but I knew I couldn't. My career demanded too much of me, and years of hard work hung in the balance.

Tears stung at the corner of my eyes. "What am I going to do?"

My mother's warm fingers gently moved up and down my back in a soothing rhythm. "Only you can answer that, Everleigh. You'll make the right decision, I'm sure of it."

But how could I decide when all I felt was a vast emptiness that seemed to consume me completely? If this were eleven years ago, I would've had Jensen by my side. He always knew what to say to make me feel better. Leaving him had created an irreparable void inside me, but now instead of one gaping hole, there were two, with no hope of them ever being filled.

4

EVERLEIGH

The past two days went by in a blur. People came in and out of my parents' house to offer condolences and leave baked goods for the family. It was now time for the funeral, and I was nowhere near ready.

I chose a simple black dress and curled my hair because my grandmother liked it that way. As I looked around the congregation, I recognized every single face. However, there was one person I dreaded seeing, but luckily, he wasn't here yet. Jensen would never miss my grandmother's funeral. She loved him as if he was her own grandson. She spent just as much time with him as she did me.

A long time ago, I loved him, too; a part of me still did. It took me finding out about his engagement to realize how stupid I was for letting him go. I had missed my chance at true happiness. My grandmother made it a point to remind me of that every time I saw her. I kept hoping that maybe Jensen had changed over the years, that I made the right choice in leaving and never looking back. He could easily have become an arrogant ass I wouldn't get along with now. It was those thoughts I tried focusing on to make me feel better about my stupidity. Then again, I couldn't imagine that being the case with Jensen. He always had a big heart, was loyal to his friends and family, and sure knew how to have fun. What I loved about him was that he had a way of making things interesting. We once got in trouble with the law when we vandalized the main road by painting a picture of our school's mascot on it during graduation week. We got caught after the police found traces of the exact red paint on our hands. They told us the infraction wouldn't go on our permanent record if we cleaned up the mess. It took two weeks to get the paint cleaned up. It was an experience I was never going to forget. It was also something the community made sure not to forget either. Everybody knew everyone. We were just like what you see in those small-town romance movies.

It wasn't like that in Boston. The hustle and bustle of the city life was exciting, but there was something about the slow pace of my seashore town that I missed. Mostly, it was the people and the way of life; it was wholesome, pure, and safe. Nothing bad ever happened here.

As I sat on the front pew with my mother, father, and aunt Sandy, we listened to the preacher, James Tomlinson, honor my grandmother with stories of her life and accomplishments. But honestly, it would take countless hours to mention everything the infamous Rachel Holt was known for. She was an Oak Island legend, a woman of many talents.

"Rachel Ellen Holt was an amazing mother," James began. "She was a caring grandmother and a loyal friend. Many would say she was gifted beyond belief. She was an artist, an inventor, and she even had a knack for plants. She'd been approached numerous times by companies wanting to get her perfume recipes, but Rachel wouldn't have any of it. Those were her secrets. The people of this town knew how special Rachel was."

Murmurs of agreement echoed throughout the church. Even James had his own stories to tell. My grandmother had babysat him when he was a little boy. Now he was sixty-two years old with a head full of white hair. It was amazing how many lives my grandmother had touched. Hearing all the stories was just what I needed. There wasn't a single dry eye in the crowd.

I held my mother's hand, and we laughed and cried as others went up to the podium to regale everyone with their tales of the famous Rachel Ellen Holt. Instead of a burial, my grandmother wanted to be cremated. Her picture sat on display beside the urn my mother had picked out to hold the ashes. It was made of pewter and had butterflies engraved all around it. My mother planned to keep the urn on her fireplace mantle. If my grandmother were around to see that, she'd roll her eyes and tell my mom to stop being ridiculous and just toss her ashes into the sea. The ocean had always been the love of her life besides my grandfather. Now they were together again. That thought brought me comfort.

Once the choir finished singing "Amazing Grace," Preacher Tomlinson returned to the podium.

"Thank you, everyone, for joining us today in

celebrating the life of Rachel Ellen Holt. She played a huge role in our community, and I know she'll forever be missed. We all loved her." His attention then turned to me and my family. "If you'd like to come up, I know there are many people who'd like to offer their condolences."

My mother stood first and took my hand in hers, the warmth of her skin calming my racing heart as she led me up to the front. My father stepped beside us, his suit jacket stretched at the shoulders as he placed a gentle hand on my mother's shoulder.

Standing next to me was Sandy, dressed in a stylish black pantsuit with an exaggerated bow tied around her neck, her heels added a few extra inches to her already tall frame. I watched her closely for any sign of emotion, yet not even a single tear emerged from beneath her dark eyelashes. I had known my aunt all my life, but the only thing that mattered to her was money. After she heard she only inherited a small sum of my grandmother's fortune, she didn't attempt to hide her true feelings. Instead, she became even more rude and selfish to my mother and me. I was way past ready for her to leave town. The longer she stayed, the harder it was for me to bite my tongue.

I glanced over at Sandy and grumbled under my breath. "I see your family couldn't be bothered to show up today."

She huffed in irritation and answered with a forced calmness, "Bradley and Hannah are still away at college, and my husband is in Washington DC."

I shot her a stern look of disbelief before responding. "That's shameful. I don't care about your husband, but your kids should be here. Their grandmother just died."

Sandy snapped back quickly, her voice low and controlled. "It's not like they knew her really well."

"That's bullshit and you know it," I hissed.

My gaze shifted up to the church's high ceilings, and I silently prayed for God's forgiveness for my language. I'd said what I needed to say and was done with it all. Sandy had to hear it, even if this wasn't the right place. My mother cleared her throat, attempting to keep a smile on her face as people began forming a line around the pews.

"Was that necessary?" she hushed through gritted teeth.

I glanced over at Sandy, and she rolled her eyes before quickly turning away. "Someone had to do it," I muttered under my breath.

By now, the congregation had started drawing closer with Georgia Hopkins in the lead, wearing a canary yellow dress. As Sandy stepped up first in line, the façade of sorrow appeared on her features as she received each person's condolences. Anger and disgust boiled within me, but I pushed it away as best as possible. Seeing Georgia's smiling face helped.

She walked up to me and hugged me tightly. "I just got some fresh pecans shipped to me. I was thinking of making you my famous pecan pie you always liked." The thought of Georgia's homemade dessert made my stomach rumble with anticipation.

"That would be amazing," I replied with a grin, "I could totally go for a pecan pie right now."

Letting me go, Georgia winked at me. "Done. I'll make one for your parents, too, so you don't have to share."

"Thank you," I whispered to her softly as she passed.

Once she moved on, I hugged and shook hands with

what had to be over a hundred people, all of who I've known for most of my life, including some of my old friends from school. There was still that one guy I had yet to see, but then my eyes caught a glimpse of his parents toward the end of the line.

Martha and David McLean.

Martha hadn't changed a bit. She still had the same dark brown curly hair, only now there were wisps of gray on the sides. Jensen's father, however, was a different story. David had just a little bit of gray hair on his head, but most of it he'd lost in his chemo treatments. There was still a lot of life in his grayish-blue eyes, though. I've visited Oak Island a handful of times over the years and had only seen them . . . not Jensen. Whether it was intentional or not, I didn't know. I could only imagine how angry Jensen was at me for letting our friendship go. Of course, it was a relief not to see him, but a part of me always hoped I'd run into him somewhere.

Jensen was always away at sea, earning a living for the family business, McLean Charters. When Martha and David finally reached me, Martha burst into tears.

"Oh, Everleigh, we're so sorry. We found out last night when we got back into town."

I had managed to control most of my tears until now. "I'm just glad you're here."

Martha hugged me. "What happened to her? Was she ill?"

Sniffling, I let her go. "Old age, I guess. That's what the medical examiner said. As far as we all know, nothing was wrong with her."

Martha's eyes glistened with a combination of tears

and affection. "We never know when the Lord will call us home."

She was right; I had seen too many families grieving for loved ones who had left this world too soon. I gave David an encouraging smile. His scalp was sparsely covered with wisps of hair, but he still looked dignified.

"Looking good," I said to him.

He ran a hand over his head. "Thanks. I miss my hair, though."

Martha elbowed him in the side, her voice tinged with amusement. "It's not like you had much before your treatments."

They were always able to lighten the mood, even in the worst of times; it was one of the reasons why I loved Jensen's family so much. David enveloped me in an embrace and kissed the top of my head.

"I wish Jensen were here, but he's at sea. I tried calling to give him the news but never got through."

I opened my mouth to say something, but all that came out was a sigh as I pulled away from him reluctantly. "It's okay," I said softly. "He's working; I understand. Cell service out in the ocean has to be pretty spotty."

With reverence in his voice, David spoke up once more. "I don't know what happened between you two or why you lost touch, but he always asks about you."

My heart skipped a beat at hearing this, yet I felt hollow knowing how much time apart stretched between us now. It was apparent that Jensen didn't tell his parents that we slept together and it scared me enough that I ran away from the only guy I ever cared about. I wanted to ask about Jensen to see if he was married and how that was going, but my heart couldn't take it, not today.

Martha grabbed my hands, clearly picking up on my discomfort as she quickly glared at David. "We're all so proud of what you've become," she said, focusing back on me with admiration and pride in her eyes. "You've worked so hard."

"Thank you," I answered quietly.

I gave Martha's hands a gentle squeeze before releasing them. "As soon as Jensen gets back from sea, I know he'll want to stop by," she said, her expression showing concern.

David might not know what happened between me and Jensen, but I had a feeling Martha had an idea. My heart raced as I nodded in response.

"That's fine. He's more than welcome." And I was nowhere near ready to see him.

David and Martha moved across the room to speak with my parents while I moved out of the way to stand alone in front of my grandmother's photo. I picked it up and it felt heavy in my hands as I held it against my chest and closed my eyes, wishing she was here to tell me what to do with all her things. Of course, taking it all back to Massachusetts would be impossible, but getting rid of her belongings didn't feel right either.

So many decisions were left for me alone to make.

A lump formed in my throat as I whispered to myself. "I'm going to miss you, Grammy." I clutched the photo tighter. "So much."

MOMENTS AFTER THE CHURCH EMPTIED, Sandy rushed to her car and drove away. She left without a goodbye or a promise to return. The money my grandmother had left her would be in her bank account in a few weeks; that was all she wanted. *Greedy bitch.* I may have been a surgeon with a decent salary, but I enjoyed a modest lifestyle. I did not need a fancy house or car to be content; I worked too many hours to enjoy them anyway. My mother drove me back to my grandmother's house as I had left my car there.

"Are you sure you don't want to come home with me and your dad?" she asked as we climbed the steps up to the door.

I looked out at the ocean before gazing back at her. "I'm going to stay here tonight," I said. "I need some time to clear my head."

She worriedly touched her forehead with her fingers. "Have you decided what you're going to do with this place?"

I've already decided to keep the time off from work and stay in Oak Island for the two-month vacation I requested, or at least until I decide what to do. What happens after that? I have no idea.

Shaking my head, I blew out a sigh. "I don't know, Mom. For now, I'm going to stay so I can be close to you."

Her eyes watered. "You don't have to stay here just because of me, but if you want to, I would be more than happy to spend every day with my baby girl. Your father would, too. You can always help him at the medical office if you need something to do."

I had always wondered what working full-time with my dad in his clinic would be like. I'd help out occasionally when I visited home, but never for long stretches.

"Real subtle, Mom," I joked with a laugh.

She waved off my comment. "What can I say? I want you to stay. It could be good for you; a slower pace of life might be what you need this summer. Then, when things die down, you can figure out what you want to do about the house."

My gaze went through the glass door that led to the living room, where all my grandmother's trinkets and souvenirs were displayed in various places. My heart was heavy at the thought of getting rid of them all.

"It's hard to believe that it's all mine," I mumbled dejectedly as I looked away from the old home toward the sea. A part of me wanted everything to remain unchanged forever, but I knew realistically that I couldn't manage the upkeep being so far away in Boston—my grandmother wouldn't forgive me if I didn't take proper care of her beloved house.

"Everleigh," my mother murmured. "Look at me."

With a heavy sigh, I met her gaze. There was so much regret plaguing me that it was hard to breathe. I wished I had spent the time with my family when it mattered. No one was promised tomorrow, and I'd learned that the hard way. I would never get back the time I lost with my grandmother.

My mother gently placed her hands on my face. "If you decide to sell the house, just know I support you no matter what, okay? I know that's what's weighing on your mind right now."

"That's not the only thing," I confessed.

Her brows furrowed. "What else is there?"

Her hands slid from my face, her expression

concerned. My stomach clenched as I tried to ignore the rock forming in my stomach.

"I feel guilty about the house, Mom, but I have so much regret building within me that I honestly don't know if I can handle it." Tears poured down my cheeks, and my stomach hurt even more. "I should've taken time off a long time ago. That way, Grammy could've seen the world as we planned. But, instead, I worked and sacrificed all that time I could've spent with you, Dad, and her. And for what? I'm thirty-four and single, with no hope of starting a family anytime soon. All my old friends from high school are happily married with kids."

Jensen was no doubt one of them. My only single friend was Nyla, but she had been married once before, so that put her way ahead of me as far as life experiences. My mother placed a comforting hand on my shoulder.

"You can't compare your life to others, sweetheart. We all have a path, and you chose yours." She squeezed my arm reassuringly. "Your grandmother was so proud of you, always rambling on to others about your success. You visited as often as you could, and she understood that. Curing people has always been your dream. Don't ever regret what you've done. You've saved tons of lives. That right there is a miracle."

"Still," I cried, "I'd give anything to be in the Caribbean right now with Grammy."

My mother nodded. "So would I."

Her attention shifted to the glass door, and I followed her line of sight to the living room. My grandmother loved every shade of blue there was. The living room walls were a soft cerulean, and the couch and two love seats were in sand and stone shades, with azure-colored accent pillows decorated with starfish. It was a typical beach-style living room with my grandmother's personal touch. The fireplace mantle was filled with starfish, sand dollars, and unique seashells Grammy had found over the years. I opened the door but couldn't yet walk in. All I wanted was to hear my grandmother's voice just once more.

"Everleigh, I'm going to go," my mother said softly. "Several people have mentioned stopping by the house, and I should probably be there. I'm sure many of them would love to talk more with you."

Turning to her, I shook my head and hugged her. "I think I'm just going to stay here. I'm not up for being around a bunch of people."

She kissed the side of my head. "I understand. I'll see you tomorrow, right?"

"Of course," I answered back, letting her go. "You're going to see me every day."

Her eyes brightened and she smiled. "Perfect."

I could tell she was hesitant about leaving by the concern on her face, but I smiled, hoping it would assure her that I was okay. I watched her walk down the stairs and get in her car. The second she disappeared down the street, a stark realization hit me straight in the heart. It was the first time being at my grandmother's house by myself since I've been in town.

Everything was quiet except for the sound of the waves and the seagulls flying overhead. I walked through the patio door but kept it open so I could still hear the ocean. Then, taking a deep breath, I glanced around the living room. It was the central part of the house, and the kitchen was just beyond it.

Down the hallway, my bedroom was the first door on the left; it used to be my mother's room growing up. Sandy's was on the right, but it eventually got changed into a library. So that left the last closed door, the bedroom beside mine. I didn't dare walk down the hall toward it; it was my grandmother's room . . . the place she took her last breath. I wasn't ready to go in there. I didn't know if I ever would be.

5

EVERLEIGH

I was so drained from the past couple of days that I had nothing left in me. Everyone kept coming to my grandmother's house and delivering food, offering their condolences. Some people would stay and tell stories of the times they shared with my grandmother, which was nice; however, I was desperate for some peace and quiet. All I wanted was the space to process what I wanted to do with the house and my grandmother's belongings without any interruptions.

Luckily, yesterday was a blessedly quiet day—no visitors, no distractions. However, I did go to my parents' house, but as soon as I left them, it was hard to keep the grief from taking over.

The sun shone brightly through the large windows overlooking the sea, drenching the room in a warm golden light. I glanced at the starfish clock above the mantle and sighed. The morning had flown by without any visitors to occupy my time. I could feel my body longing for activity, having become accustomed to long work hours over the years.

My gaze drifted to the remote on the coffee table, but I didn't want to watch TV. I've walked on the beach several times during the morning, making me think more deeply than I cared to.

With a heavy sigh, I laid my head against the back of the couch and stared up at the ceiling. The silence felt oppressive. Suddenly, it hit me like a cool ocean breeze—it was summertime at the beach. The area would be buzzing with people and positive energy. That was precisely what I needed.

Jumping off the couch, I paused in the hallway at my bedroom door, glancing over at my grandmother's that remained shut. I had promised myself I would go in there today, but I still wasn't ready.

Tomorrow.

I will do it tomorrow.

Quickly, I changed into an old favorite dress of mine that had been sitting in my closet untouched for years: a pink sundress. Then, I took the short drive to downtown Southport and parked on the main strip.

Joy spread throughout me as memories of past experiences surfaced. Memories of my parents taking me for ice cream every Friday night when I was young and of Jensen and I walking around with our friends, talking about life and college.

Holly Rafferty was my best friend at the time, but we lost touch over the years. Later, I discovered she had died in a car accident eight years ago while driving back home from a dental convention in Myrtle Beach, SC—she had been texting while behind the wheel. It made me sad to know that she left behind a husband and two sons.

I pulled into a spot and exited my car, taking a deep breath of the salty ocean breeze. The bright sun shone hot on my skin, but the wind served as a relief from the heat. I meandered up and down the bustling downtown streets, watching with a smile as tourists laughed and soaked in the atmosphere of their beachside retreat.

Up ahead, an empty bench in front of a candy store beckoned to me, so I sat down for a while and listened to the sound of joyous children screaming in delight over their sugary treats. Then, finally, one little boy with blond hair came closer, holding out a piece of peppermint candy before leaving with his family. My heart melted at his kind gesture, but it also stirred within me an ache that reminded me that my biological clock was ticking. There was still time to have children of my own, but finding love was going to be the problem.

"Everleigh? Is that you?" a voice called from behind, and I recognized it immediately.

We weren't close, but I knew who she was—Michelle Short, or Michelle McLean, as I guess she'd be known as now—Jensen's wife. She was pregnant and dressed in a cute floral dress with flat brown sandals, her diamond wedding band sparkling in the sunlight as she held her belly.

I stood and she threw her arms around my neck, catching me off guard. "I am so sorry about your grandmother. She was an amazing lady."

I hugged her back, even though it felt a bit awkward since we didn't really know each other.

"Yes, she was," I replied before she pulled away again.

Her smile stretched wide across her face as she gazed at me with beautiful blue eyes. Anyone would be drawn to her beauty; unfortunately for me, it ended up being Jensen.

"You look amazing, by the way," she said. "I was going to come to the funeral but had a doctor's appointment." She put her hands on her stomach. "I found out I'm having a boy."

The envy I felt stabbed at my gut—I wanted to be happy for her and Jensen, yet I couldn't help but be envious of their joy.

"Congratulations," I said sincerely. "I can't imagine the excitement you must be feeling."

She beamed. "It's unreal, let me tell you." Her gaze drifted to my hands as if looking for a wedding ring. "How have things been going for you? I heard you're a big-time surgeon now."

I scoffed, forcing out an awkward laugh. "I wouldn't say that. But Boston has been good to me. I like it there."

She bit her lip, her expression now filled with inquisition. "Are you married?"

Laughing again, I shook my head from side to side and shifted my weight from one foot to the other. "Nowhere close to it. Sadly, I haven't had much time to date."

Michelle frowned and stepped closer. "That's not good. How long are you staying in town for?"

I shrugged, feeling a surge of emotion at the thought of leaving this place that felt so familiar, yet distant at the same time.

"Not sure yet. I have some big decisions to make about my grandmother's house. Luckily, I have two months to figure it out."

Her face lit up with excitement, her freckles becoming more visible than before. "Hey, that's two months you can stay here. It'll give you time to catch up with old friends. I'm sure Jensen would love to see you again."

The breath hitched in my lungs, and my stomach dropped as images of Jensen flooded my mind—our special moments together, his warm embrace, his infectious smile . . . If Jensen had told her what happened between us, I highly doubt she'd want me around her husband.

"We'll see," was all I could say. "But it was good talking to you. I'm sure I'll see you around town again."

She tilted her head back and laughed. "I have no doubt." She pointed at the candy store behind us. "I'm always here stocking up on chocolate cake pops. I've been craving them like crazy."

We said our goodbyes, and she waved at me before disappearing into the shop. Seeing her made me really think about Jensen. Would he *want* to see me after I threw away our relationship? Either way, I had no doubt I would see him at some point when he made it back on land. I just had to be ready for it.

6

EVERLEIGH

The sound of birds chirping outside my window was peaceful, but I had to turn away from the sun beaming in through the blinds. With a groan, I opened my eyes and focused on my cornflower-colored walls. All the bedrooms in the house were different shades of blue; it was what my grandmother wanted. Thinking of her brought a smile to my face. She always had a way of making things magical for me.

I looked up at the light blue canopy above me, remembering how I used to feel like a princess sleeping underneath it.

Tossing the covers to the side, I slid out of bed and my muscles ached. To keep my mind off Jensen, I spent all night cleaning my grandmother's house, except her bedroom and the library. There were too many books to dust, so I put that off until today.

I used every ounce of strength I had to scrub the floors and make sure there was no speck of dust anywhere. But, even though the house was mine now, I couldn't bring myself to claim it. It would always and forever be my grandmother's; everything in it belonged to her.

My stomach started to growl, so I rummaged through my suitcase until I found a pair of shorts and one of my college T-shirts. Once dressed, I stopped in my doorway and glanced down the hall at my grandmother's room where the door was still shut. Even my mother hasn't wanted to go in there yet. The only person who had ventured inside was my Aunt Sandy.

With a heavy sigh, I made my way into the kitchen and opened the refrigerator. It was full of food, so I grabbed the carton of eggs and bacon before setting out some pans to prepare breakfast. I grabbed a couple of slices of bacon from the package, laid them into one of the pans, and then cracked an egg on the other. I remembered when my grandmother used to make her eggs—sunny side up so she could mix them into her grits—but I preferred mine scrambled until they were dry as toast. She'd always let me bust the yolks of hers, though.

Once everything was cooked, I poured myself a glass of orange juice, piled everything up on my plate, and grabbed a blueberry muffin that one of my grandmother's friends had made for me.

The counter was packed with muffins, cookies, Georgia's pecan pie, and two pound cakes—one lemon and the other chocolate. There was no way I could eat it all.

I sat down at the kitchen table and peered out at the ocean. The water sparkled against the sun, beckoning me to take a swim. I had yet to get into the sea since being back.

As I ate my breakfast, my thoughts drifted to

yesterday. It felt good to spend time in town, but I couldn't stop thinking of Jensen, especially after seeing Michelle. I even dreamed of him last night, which didn't help matters. The dream was so vivid it almost felt like reality. I was with Jensen in an exotic bedroom; it was like one you'd find in one of those bungalows in the Maldives. He had a look of desire in his eyes as he stared at me, and I felt myself getting lost in them. His warm breath tickled my neck as he whispered my name. But just as things were getting heated, I woke up.

What am I going to say when I see him again? Maybe I could avoid him for the next two months. That was wishful thinking. With how close he was to my family, I highly doubted that was even possible. Still, I could try.

Once I finished tidying up the kitchen, I grabbed a duster and the furniture spray before going into the library. My grandmother had replaced Aunt Sandy's bed with a heavy mahogany desk that dominated most of the room while custom-made bookshelves filled with hundreds of romance novels spanned along the walls. Of course, a few of my old medical textbooks were also mixed in.

I began to dust over each book's spine, pausing when I spotted some of my grandmother's favorites. They were worn around the edges; some even had folded pages where she had left off reading. It made me smile; I always said I'd get around to reading some of them one day. I pulled out three of her favorites and shuffled them around before dropping them on the desk.

Closing my eyes, I reached out randomly for one and picked it up. When I opened my eyes, I couldn't help but chuckle at the cover of a handsome pirate with long hair embracing a brunette beauty.

"This is going to be interesting," I muttered, pulling the desk chair out so I could sit down. I figured I might as well read a few pages. However, my phone rang in the living room the second I sat down.

I sprinted into the hallway and spotted my phone glowing on the coffee table. Nyla's name was flashing on the screen.

"Hey," I answered, walking back into the library and taking a deep breath.

"Hey, girl. You doing okay?"

"For the most part," I said, eyes drifting to the doorway of my grandmother's room. A tingle of trepidation prickled my skin. One way or another, I was going to find the courage to go in there today. "What are you doing right now? Figured you'd be running around the hospital like a mad woman."

Nyla chuckled from the other end of the line. "Believe it or not, it's slow today. I thought I'd call you and let you know that I'll be heading down to see you next week. I took the summer off, too. So, you can sell the house after that if you want, but keep it for a little longer so I can see this amazing place you've always talked about."

A gasp escaped my lips; this was the best news I'd heard in a long time. My heart leaped joyfully as I lifted the duster, swishing it enthusiastically across more bookshelves.

"Seriously?" I squealed, unable to contain my smile. "This is going to be awesome. I'll be able to take you to all my favorite spots. You'll love it here." Having her around would make things so much easier to bear.

"What all have you been doing the past few days?"

I set the duster on the desk and sat in the chair. "Well, I think the visitors have stopped coming around. I cleaned the house yesterday, and today, I'm actually going to go into my grandmother's room for the first time. I just don't know when yet."

Nyla sighed. "You can do it, Everleigh. Who knows, maybe it'll comfort you to be surrounded by her things."

That's what I was hoping.

"Yeah, you're probably right," I agreed.

"Have you caught up with any of your old *friends*?" she asked curiously, emphasizing the word "friends."

I knew who she was asking about. She knew about Jensen and what I did as far as running away from him. Other than that, I haven't spoken much about him. My goal for the past few years had been to forget about him, but of course, that was never going to happen.

"I've seen a few," I told her, tracing my finger around a circular stain on the desk.

"O-kay," she drawled out. "Like who?"

I snorted. "I haven't seen Jensen, Nyla. I know that's what you're asking."

She chuckled. "Hey, I was just curious. He's your long-lost love that you let slip away."

"I swear, you and my grandmother would've gotten along perfectly. She loved throwing that in my face all the time."

Nyla's laughter faded away. "I'm sorry. I shouldn't give you a hard time right now."

"It's okay," I said, hoping she could hear the truth in my voice. "Jensen is still on his boat. I'm a little nervous about seeing him, which I know is inevitable."

"What are you going to say to him?" she questioned.

Visions of his wife came to mind, all glowing in baby bliss. "Probably congratulations," I revealed. "I saw his wife yesterday."

"Congratulations? What for?" Then she gasped. "Oh my God, is she pregnant?"

I stood and grabbed the pirate romance book off the desk. "Yep. And she's as gorgeous as ever."

My chest tightened with regret, a feeling I thought I'd be used to by now. "She said Jensen would love to catch up with me, but I have a feeling she doesn't know our true past."

"Oh wow. That has to be awkward."

"Just a little," I said, walking to the door. I stared at my grandmother's room across the hall, knowing it was time to go in there.

In the background, Nyla's pager went off. "Well, damn, there goes my break. I'll call you back later, Everleigh. Just know I'm thinking about you, and I wish you luck when you see Jensen."

"Thanks," I laughed. "Don't work too hard."

We hung up and I shut the door behind me, holding my grandmother's book to my chest. The entrance to her room haunted me every time I let my gaze linger that far down the hall. I had just started feeling like I had control over my grief, and I was afraid that would disappear once I opened her bedroom door.

Taking a deep breath, I let it out slowly and walked to her room. "I have to do it."

I didn't know what I was going to see, but I placed my hand on the knob and turned, letting the wooden door swing open. The breath left my lungs as I peered inside; it was as if everything had frozen in time. The old chair my grandmother had died in was in the corner; floral pattern was something that would have been popular decades ago. She loved reading in that seat. The blue quilted comforter on her bed had no wrinkles, and the sunlight filtering in through the open blinds seemed almost magical. I took a step inside and instantly smelled my grandmother's rose-scented perfume.

Tears filled my eyes. On the bedside table was a picture of us together, taken the past Christmas when she and my parents visited me in Boston. I had made her an ugly Christmas sweater to match my own. She loved it and promised to wear it every Christmas.

I traced a finger over the photo, barely able to see it through the tears. "Don't worry, Grammy. I'll wear mine for you."

My heart swelled with all the memories flooding into me. It was as if my grandmother was right there by my side, and for the first time since returning to Oak Island, I felt a sense of calm wash over me. Even though she was not here physically, I knew my grammy would remain with me.

7

JENSEN

The skyline of the marina slowly grew more prominent as we approached. The sun was setting, and its glow lit up the horizon in a beautiful mix of oranges and pinks. A sigh of relief escaped my lips; it felt good to be back on land again. I knew my guys would be anxious to get home after being away for two weeks. Seth Hampton, my first mate and one of my best friends since elementary school, hopped off the boat with his bag slung over his shoulder. He stopped and waved in my direction.

"Talk to you later, brother," he said. "I gotta go. The wife is probably angry at me by now."

His phone had taken a dive into the ocean earlier that week, rendering him unable to stay in touch during our journey out at sea. That was the risk we all took when heading out—no communication with those we left behind for a while. It was part of life on McLean Charters, which was started three generations ago and passed down to me.

I watched as Seth sprinted off down the dock toward the parking lot before returning my gaze seaward for one last look. There was nothing on the schedule for a while, so I was going to take some time off.

Once I did my walk-through on the boat to make sure everything was secure, I grabbed my bag and was about to climb off the boat when my phone continuously dinged with incoming texts and missed phone calls.

"Took you long enough," I grumbled as I reached into my bag for my phone. It was probably time I got a new cell service.

When I glanced down at the screen, there were over a dozen phone calls from my parents and a couple from Michelle. Before I could call any of them back, I noticed someone walking down the dock toward my boat: it was my father.

"Hey," I called out, watching him come closer with more energy in his step.

I was happy to see the improvement, especially since he'd been battling pancreatic cancer. However, judging by the trepidation on his face, I knew something had to be wrong. I jumped off the boat and hurried up to him.

"Dad, what's wrong?"

He sighed and nodded toward Henry, who waved from his boat a few docks over. Henry was retired and spent most of his time on the water. My father and Henry also grew up together. "I figured there was something up with your phone, so I had Henry keep a lookout for you. When he saw you sailing in, he called me," he said, his voice guarded.

"I'm sorry about missing your calls," I apologized.

My father waved me off. "It's probably best you didn't find out until now."

It felt as if a rock had formed in my stomach. The only thing it could be was bad news.

"What happened?" I asked.

He closed the distance between us and placed his hands on my shoulders, his eyes growing sadder. "Rachel passed away while you were gone, son."

I thought I had steeled myself for any possible outcome he'd tell me, but the revelation of Rachel's passing felt like a physical blow. She was the closest thing to a grandmother I ever had; her presence in my life was reassuring and supportive and it was as if she were a part of my own family. The last time we spoke, she was so enthusiastic about her upcoming trip with Everleigh. They were going to be gone by the time I got back.

The certainty of the news hit me like a wave, leaving me speechless. I ran my hands over my face, feeling the shock and grief settle in my chest.

"When? How?"

My father shrugged and pulled me in for a hug. "She passed a week ago, and the funeral was Monday. They said it was old age, and nothing was wrong with her."

He let me go and my chest tightened. "Did Everleigh come into town?"

He nodded. "Of course. Your mom and I talked to her at the funeral. We told her you were working and that we'd let you know as soon as possible." He squeezed my shoulders. "She understood."

It's been years since I've seen or talked to Everleigh, but a huge part of me wanted to be there for her, even if she didn't need me. I had no doubt it was too late; she was probably already back in Boston.

I released a heavy sigh and looked down at my ripped jeans, stained T-shirt, and scuffed boots. "I'm going to run home and take a quick shower. Do you think it'd be okay if I went by and visited Everleigh's parents?"

My father smiled warmly, and his grayish-blue eyes twinkled in the sun. I've always been told I looked just like him.

"Becky and Greg would love that. You might want to swing by and see Everleigh as well."

My whole body tensed up like a coiled spring. "She's still in Oak Island?"

His laughter boomed around us. "You've missed a lot, son. Rachel left the house to her. Everleigh's staying in town while she decides what to do with Hide Away by the Sea."

My brows creased together. "What do you mean? She's not going to sell it, is she?"

That place had been so special to her growing up; I knew she wouldn't want to part with it. But, then again, she probably wasn't the same girl I knew all those years ago. Maybe she didn't care anymore.

My father shrugged his shoulders. "I don't know. Greg told me yesterday that Everleigh still hasn't decided yet."

A wave of anger surged through me at the thought of Everleigh selling. Selling the home her grandmother had left her should never have been a choice. Was life in Boston so much better than here? I was sure it had to be since she'd up and left me without ever looking back.

I felt my chest tighten as thoughts of Rachel came into my mind. Whenever I returned from a voyage, she'd leave a plate of my favorite dark chocolate brownies on the kitchen counter; she knew where the spare key was kept. I shook my head and huffed in frustration. I wasn't going to let Everleigh give away her grandmother's house and legacy just to anyone. If that was what she wanted to do and return to Boston, then fine, but I'd be damned if I watched somebody turn Hide Away by the Sea into an impersonal rental property. One way or another, I'd find a way to buy it myself.

"Uh-oh, I know that look." My father pointed out. "What's going through your mind?"

I met his gaze and sighed. "I'm about to do something crazy." I slapped a hand on his arm and hurried up the dock toward the parking lot.

"Good luck," my father shouted.

I was going to need it. For the first time in eleven years, I was about to see the one girl who had shattered me completely.

WHEN I ARRIVED HOME, I rushed inside and was about to head straight to my bedroom when something on the kitchen counter caught my eye. I froze and stared at the pan of wrapped brownies with a folded letter on top. How was that even possible?

Slowly, I closed the distance and reached for the note, my chest tightening when I saw Rachel's handwriting.

Jensen,

Welcome home! I had to make your

brownies a little early this time since I'll be on vacation when you return. Hopefully, they'll still be good. If not, I'll make you more when Everleigh and I get home. Maybe it'll give you both a chance to talk? Eleven years of silence is just about ridiculous. I'm just sad you and Everleigh both inherited my stubbornness. Through hell or high water, I'm going to get you two in the same room again.

Love always,

Rachel

Wiping the tears away with my sleeve, I sighed heavily. "You're about to get your wish, Rachel," I said, setting the note on the counter. "I'm not about to let your granddaughter sell your place. She's not going to hide from me anymore."

I hurried into my bedroom and tossed my bag on the bed. Once showered and dressed in clean jeans and a plaid flannel shirt, I ran back out to my Bronco. Rachel lived next door to my parents, and it was how she became a grandmother figure in my life. I was closer to her than I was to my own grandparents. Now I had none left . . . Rachel was the last.

Heart racing, I turned the key in the ignition and set on my way across town to Hide Away by the Sea. In ten minutes, I was about to see Everleigh for the first time in years. There was so much that needed to be said. But was it the right time? I exhaled and reached for my phone in the center console. There was a voice mail from Michelle saying that I needed to call her back. I pressed her number, and the line rang a couple of times before she picked up.

"Hey," she answered. "I'm assuming you're on land?"

"I am. I'm sorry I couldn't call you back sooner. What's up?"

"Have you heard the news?"

My stomach clenched with grief. "Yes. I can't even believe it."

She sighed. "Same. I know you were super close to Rachel."

I clenched the steering wheel. "I just wish I was here. It kills me to know it happened a week ago and I had no clue."

She cleared her throat. "Have you seen Everleigh yet?"

My pulse quickened. "I'm on my way to see her now. Why?"

"Well," she began, her voice sounding slightly amused, "I don't know if this is true or not, but I believe she thinks that you and I are married. When she saw that I was pregnant, I noticed the look on her face. She was jealous. I highly doubt she would've reacted that way if she knew I married someone else."

That was an interesting scenario, but it made sense. During one of our conversations, Rachel told me that Everleigh never wanted to talk about me; she avoided the topic at all costs. If that was the case, then it could be possible she thought Michelle and I had gone through with our wedding.

We were engaged six years ago, but it didn't work out. I cared about her, but something was missing. She felt the same way and met her now husband a year after our breakup. They've been happily married for three years now, and we were all good friends.

"Did you not mention your husband's name?"

Michelle snickered. "No, and I did it on purpose. It might not have been the best timing with Rachel's passing and all, but I had an opening to test her."

"Did you bring me up at all?" I asked.

She laughed. "I did. And that's when I could see it in her eyes."

"See what?"

"That she wants to see you." A sigh echoed through the phone. "Jensen, we both know you couldn't fall in love with me because you secretly hoped Everleigh would come back. Now she's here; this is your chance to see where you stand. If I'm right about her jealousy, it must mean she still has feelings for you."

I thought I could be happy with Michelle, and I tried very hard to convince myself of such. But Everleigh and I had too much history to simply forget it all. I hated how much control she had over my heart. I wanted to stop loving her, but I couldn't.

I was almost at Beach Drive, so I slowed down to give myself a little more time.

"What do you think I should do?" I asked.

The line went silent for a few seconds as if she had to think. "Ride it out," she suggested. "When you see her, just go with the flow. Bring me and the baby up if you want to test her feelings for you. I guarantee you'll see how much it bothers her. And if that's the case, you'll have your answer."

"If Everleigh gave a damn about me, she wouldn't have done what she did." She left as if I was nothing to her.

"If I recall correctly, you didn't exactly jump on a plane and go after her, Jensen. You told her to call you when she was ready. She was trying to become a doctor at that point in her life and now she's a big-time neurosurgeon. You also had your own responsibilities with McLean Charters. Your parents needed you to take over the business. Maybe Everleigh needed to make her own path before going down one with you."

Michelle was right. I didn't go after Everleigh, but I wanted to more than anything. She couldn't stay and I knew it, so going after her wouldn't have done a damn thing.

"I hate it when you're right," I said, huffing.

Michelle giggled. "Which is most of the time."

I finally turned onto Beach Drive and my pulse raced. "All right, I'm almost at Everleigh's."

"Are you nervous?" Michelle asked.

"A little," I confessed. "With Rachel gone, it makes things a little more complicated."

"You'll be fine. I know you and Everleigh will work through this. At least, maybe, you two can become friends again. You guys have too much of a past to throw it away for good."

We said our goodbyes just as my parents' house came into view. Right next to it was Rachel's blue cottage on stilts. But now it was Everleigh's for however long she decided to stay in Oak Island. Knowing her, it wasn't going to be long at all.

8

JENSEN

As I neared the house, my heart thumped wildly in my chest like a train barreling down the tracks. Thankfully, no other cars were around except for Everleigh's silver CRV parked near the stairs. Everything about this was so familiar that it felt like time had stopped for me.

There was still the chance that Everleigh won't even let me in the house or speak to me, for that matter.

Rachel always used the house's back door as the main entrance, so I walked over to the stairs. Gripping the railing tightly, I took each step slowly, but when Everleigh's soft cries echoed through the air, my feet froze mid-step. I could see her around the corner just a few yards away from me.

Time seemed to stand still as I stared at her. Her golden-blonde hair was pulled back, but I could tell it was longer than the last time I saw her. She wore black shorts that hugged her toned legs and a teal tank top that perfectly fit her curves. Her arms were crossed over her chest, and her head hung low as if she was deep in thought. Even without seeing her face, something inside me stirred with long-forgotten emotions. I had told myself over the years that if I saw her again, it wouldn't affect me. What a lie that was. I missed her.

One of the wooden boards creaked and Everleigh gasped, lifting her head and wiping away her tears. I figured she would turn around to see who was with her, but she didn't.

"I walked into her room today. It felt like she was right there with me."

I knew she wasn't expecting me, but I replied anyway. "She'll always be with you, Everleigh."

The second she heard my voice, her body tensed. It was as if an electric current buzzed between us, pulling me to move closer. Time moved in slow motion as she turned her head to glance at me over her shoulder. When her hazel-green eyes met mine, all I wanted to do was hold her.

"Jensen," she breathed, turning to face me.

I stepped closer, my lips pulling back into a smile. "Hello, Everleigh. It's good to see you again."

More tears flooded down her cheeks and she laughed. "Liar. I know you hate me."

I couldn't take it anymore. I had to go to her.

Closing the distance, I reached out and pulled her into my arms. She clutched me hard, her shoulders shaking as she cried against my chest.

"I could never hate you, Everleigh," I said softly. It was strange having her in my arms after all these years. But all too soon, she backed away and swiped at her face.

"I'm sorry. The last thing you probably want is me crying all over you."

I stepped closer, but she kept her head down, almost as if she was too afraid to look at me. "It's okay. Your grandmother just passed away; it's perfectly normal to cry. And trust me, I feel the pain of her loss. She was an amazing woman and I loved her dearly."

She nodded and lifted her watery gaze. "I know you did. She loved you, too."

Her shoulders rose with an intake of breath, and she turned to the sea, releasing the air slowly from her lungs.

"When did you get in?"

"A little less than an hour ago," I replied.

Her eyes widened, and she swiveled to face me. "Seriously? You docked and then came right here?"

I gave a noncommittal shrug and propped my elbows on the wooden railing beside her. A small smile curved the corner of my mouth.

"Well, I went home and took a shower first. You know how bad the guys and I smell after being at sea for weeks at a time."

She nodded with understanding, amusement sparkling in her gaze. "Oh yes, I remember all too well. I'll never forget when your dad came home from being away, and your mom made him take two showers because he stunk so bad."

My chest rumbled with laughter as the memories flooded back to me. We were eleven years old and had just finished doing our math homework together at this very spot on the back deck when my dad pulled up at our house next door. The wind had carried his fishy odor all the way to us, and Everleigh's grandmother had teased him about it for years afterward.

Once our laughter died down, Everleigh focused on me with a guarded expression. "I never thought I'd see you again."

I nodded in agreement. "I often wondered the same thing." There was more I wanted to say, but I didn't want to throw the past up in her face. "How have you been?" I asked her.

She shrugged. "As good as can be expected." There were so many emotions swirling in her eyes and I couldn't tell what she was truly feeling. Our time apart had changed her; she'd gotten better at hiding her feelings. When we were younger, I always knew how to read her. Everleigh dropped her gaze to her clasped hands. "I hear McLean Charters is doing better than ever."

"It is," I agreed. "My guys and I work our asses off."

McLean Charters had been a family business for several generations. Before taking it over, I graduated from UNC Wilmington with an Ocean Science degree. My parents wanted me to have something to fall back on if the business went under. Hopefully, one day, I'd have someone to pass the McLean legacy down to.

Everleigh snorted. "I know a thing or two about working your ass off. It's all I do these days."

It was quiet as Everleigh and I gazed out at the ocean.

"I'm sorry you didn't get to go on the trip with your grandmother," I said quietly, my arm almost touching hers. She didn't move away; it felt nice for me to be close to her again. "I know she was really looking forward to it," I added, glancing her way.

Her lips quivered. "When did you two last speak?"

There were things that Everleigh probably wasn't aware of, stuff Rachel had kept from her.

"Two weeks ago," I replied. "The day before I left."

Everleigh's head snapped toward me, surprise written on her face. "She didn't tell me that."

With a sigh, I leaned against the railing and crossed my arms over my chest. "Rachel and I talked pretty often," I admitted. "And weren't you the one not wanting to hear anything about me?"

She looked taken aback by my statement. "I . . ." she began but stopped short.

Waving off her words, I pretended not to care even though it wasn't true at all. "It doesn't matter now," I lied. "We've both moved on with our lives and are happy."

"Right. We're happy now," she said low.

She turned away from me, but a hint of doubt lingered in her voice, making me curious if Michelle was right about Everleigh being jealous. I wanted to test it out.

"Why don't we go for a walk," I suggested, hoping it would break the tension.

Everleigh sucked in a breath and stood up straighter. "Sounds good to me."

She took off first and I followed her down the stairs to the wooden walkway at the back of the house which led down to the beach. Once we got to the end, Everleigh kicked off her sandals and I took off my boots. The thick, white sand was still warm from the afternoon sun, and I welcomed it as we walked toward the water.

"Tell me about your job. You know, being a fancy surgeon and all."

A grin lit up Everleigh's face when she looked over at me. "I'm nowhere near fancy. Especially as, according to my aunt Sandy, I don't live my life like a well-off surgeon would."

Thinking of Sandy made me grimace. "Never cared for the woman," I confessed. "She was a pretentious—"

"Bitch," Everleigh said, finishing the sentence with a laugh. "I had a few choice words to share with her. It felt good to say them."

"Good for you. I wish I could've been there."

Everleigh bent down to pick up a seashell. "She gave me grief about my car. I couldn't care less about driving an expensive vehicle or living in a mansion."

My lips curved into a smile when she said that. I had been worried about how much medical school would change her, but it seemed like Everleigh was still the same person underneath it all.

"I'm guessing Sandy headed out of town?" I asked.

She looked at me as if I were crazy. "Seriously? She was gone as soon as she got the chance," she replied.

"Yeah, I figured," I muttered in response.

Everleigh placed the seashell back in the sand and stood up. "What makes it even sadder is that my cousins didn't attend the funeral. My grandmother tried so hard to get them to stay with her for summer vacations. Every time they'd decline, I could hear the pain in her voice."

Tears welled up in her eyes and she shifted her gaze to the pier in the distance. There weren't many people on the beach, just a few scattered around and some children building sandcastles. One of the things I loved most about Oak Island was that there were hardly any crowds.

"They'll regret it later," I said confidently.

Everleigh shook her head and kept walking again. "No, they won't. I don't think I'll ever see them again."

Suddenly, she stumbled into a hole, and I instinctively grabbed her arm to steady her. She laughed and clutched at her chest with relief. "Thanks. It's been a while since I've walked on the beach."

"Same," I confessed. I peered at the ocean and breathed in the salty sea air. The water was rough with the winds. "It's been months since I've walked out here."

Everleigh's arm brushed against mine, but she moved away when my eyes locked onto hers. She cleared her throat and averted her gaze to the pier.

"How long are you inland for?"

I loved hearing the sound of her voice. There were so many times I wanted to call her over the years, but I couldn't do it. My pride wouldn't let me.

"A few weeks, maybe more," I answered.

Her eyes widened. "Wow. Is that a first for McLean Charters? Your dad used to stay gone all the time."

I nodded. "Yeah, he did. This'll probably be the only time my guys will get this much time off. I needed to get Seth back."

Everleigh gasped. "Oh my God, Seth. I haven't seen him in forever. How is he?"

"He's doing great," I replied. "He's also married. Her name is Trisha. We met her in Wilmington at the St. Patrick's Day festival about ten years ago, and they've been together ever since." This was my chance to test her. "And now they're expecting a baby girl," I added. "That's why I wanted to make sure we were back before she gave birth."

Everleigh kept a smile on her face, but she turned away from me. "That's awesome. It seems like everyone's having babies right now."

Michelle was right . . . there was a hint of jealousy in her tone. It took all I had to keep from grinning smugly. Everleigh brightened her smile and focused back on me.

"Congratulations, by the way. I guess I should've told you that I ran into Michelle while I was in town." She bit her lip and glanced down at the sand. "How does it feel to know you're about to be a father?"

I had a choice to make. Either go along with the charade or tell her the truth. I wanted to know if she'd missed me just as much as I missed her over the years. Maybe even a part of me wanted to see a fraction of regret on her face. I tried to move on, but something stopped me every time. Rachel always told me it was *hope*. The hope was that Everleigh would come to her senses one day and find her way back home. Now she was back, and it wasn't because of me. I didn't want that realization to fuel my resentment, but it did. It would make things much better if I knew our separation hurt her just as much as it did me.

My silence caught Everleigh's attention and she lifted her head, her hazel-green eyes regarding me curiously. "Are you okay?" she asked.

I nodded. "I just needed to think about your question."

Her brows furrowed. "You are happy with becoming a father, aren't you?"

She was going to kill me when she found out I was lying to her, but I needed to see her reaction.

"I am," I replied, searching her face. "Michelle and I are ecstatic."

Longing flashed in her eyes, but it disappeared quickly; it wasn't enough of an answer for me.

"I'm happy for you," she said, taking a step away which

put more distance between us. Then, she turned around and pointed in the direction we'd just came from. "We should probably head back. I'm sure your wife is ready to spend time with you since you've been gone for so long."

I felt terrible for lying to her, especially after everything that had happened with her grandmother. But if Rachel were here, I knew she'd coax me to keep it up. She never wanted me to give up on Everleigh.

Everleigh picked up her pace, almost as if she was trying to run away.

"What about you?" I asked, catching up to her. "Anyone special in Boston?"

I hated the thought of her with other men, and Rachel knew that, but it didn't stop her from telling me when Everleigh was seeing someone. It just so happened that a couple of weeks ago she told me that Everleigh was still single. I was curious to see how Everleigh responded, but she kept her focus straight ahead, her expression blank.

"There's been a few," was all she said.

I waited for her to elaborate, but I could tell she didn't want to speak any more about it. The last thing I wanted to do was push things when here I was, the one lying about everything.

We arrived back at the walkway, and I grabbed my boots while she picked up her sandals. Everleigh's gaze lingered on her grandmother's blue house, her eyes full of sadness.

"My dad told me the house is yours," I said, my voice low.

She nodded and slipped on her sandals before we walked up the path to the back deck. "I still can't believe she left it to me," Everleigh replied, her words full of disbelief. "I thought for sure she'd leave it to my mother."

When we reached the deck, I looked down at her, a small smile playing on my lips. "I'm not surprised," I said as I stood before her. "This house reminds me of you just as much as it does your grandmother. I guess the question is . . . are you going to keep it?"

Her jaw clenched and she lowered her head. "I don't know. I wasn't expecting any of this," she said softly. "I love this house, but my life is in Boston right now, and I don't have time to take care of everything here. It's not fair to my grandmother's memory." She sighed heavily and met my gaze with a determined one of her own. "She'd come down from heaven and kill me if I neglected her house."

"That is for damn sure," I agreed, picturing Rachel in my mind.

She was a spitfire, even if she was only five feet tall. If a bird took a shit on her railing, she'd go outside and curse at it. The woman had no filter. It was what made things interesting as a kid.

Reaching out, I placed my hands on her shoulders, wanting more than anything to pull her into me. "If you decide to sell, sell it to me," I said, the words leaving my lips without a second thought.

Her mouth dropped and she gasped. "Really? You would buy this place?"

I nodded. "In a heartbeat. I know how much Rachel loved it here. I can take care of it."

She stared at me as if trying to decipher if I was being serious, but there was also happiness mixed with relief in her gaze.

A laugh escaped her lips and she smiled. "I'll let you know what I decide. I'm still going to think about it."

I moved my hands off her shoulders. "Take all the time you need. I'm not going anywhere. Well, except for home. You've probably had enough visitors this past week to last a lifetime."

She snorted out a laugh. "Just a little. I'm not complaining, though. It's been nice seeing everyone."

There was an awkward silence between us. I wanted to ask when I could see her again, but before I could speak, she beat me to it.

"Do you still live off Yacht Drive?" she asked.

I nodded. "I do. So, if you ever need me, you know where to find me. My phone number is still the same."

She smiled. "I'll keep that in mind."

I took a step back toward the stairs. "Take care of yourself, Everleigh."

Turning on my heel, I started for the stairs. I was just about to get into my 1974 blue convertible Bronco when Everleigh's mother pulled into the driveway beside me. Becky got out of her car and waved, her blonde hair billowing in the wind.

"Hey, Jensen," she said warmly.

She jogged over and hugged me, her petite frame fitting snugly against mine. When she pulled away, I spotted tears welling in her hazel-green eyes; they were the same as Everleigh's.

"Glad to see you made it back on shore. I bet Everleigh was beside herself at the sight of you."

She let me go and I smiled sadly. "It *was* a shock to her, but I could say the same for myself. It's been a long time. I just hate the circumstances."

Her voice broke when she spoke. "Me too."

"I'm sorry about your mother," I said sincerely. "I'm going to miss her."

Becky nodded. "So am I. I know she was really fond of you. She always said you reminded her of your grandfather. They used to be good friends." Rachel used to tell me stories about my grandfather. He had died before I was born, so I never met him. From what I was told, he was an adventurous man. Becky glanced up at the house. "I take it you and Everleigh are on speaking terms now?"

I shrugged. "It appears so. I told her I would buy the house if she wanted to sell."

Becky's eyes watered even more. "Oh, Jensen," she said, placing a hand over her heart. "I'm at a loss for words. My mother would be happy to have her home belong to you."

I held up my hands. "That's if Everleigh will sell it to me. It's up to her."

Becky squeezed my arm. "I wouldn't worry about that."

We said our goodbyes and I got in my car, uncertainty settling in my gut. With Everleigh back in town, I didn't know what was going to happen. One thing was for sure, she probably wasn't going to be happy the next time she saw me, or at least that was what I was hoping. The truth about me and Michelle wasn't going to stay hidden long. If she got mad, I had to believe she still cared about me. But if she brushed it off, then I could only assume it didn't bother her. Either way, I had to be prepared.

9

EVERLEIGH

Through a small slit in the blinds, I watched as Jensen and my mother talked. Spending time with him was not a good idea. The past couple of hours had been a whirlwind of emotions. I honestly didn't know if I could handle it all.

My hands trembled the second I heard his voice when he came up on the back deck, and excitement coursed through my veins. I'd waited so long to see him but feared it at the same time. A part of me was afraid to turn around and look at him, but I had no choice. I'd hoped it was my imagination running wild on me, but I knew I was in trouble when I saw him. There he was, all tall, rugged, and handsome in a pair of jeans and a plaid flannel shirt that hugged his muscular arms. His dark brown hair was a little longer on top in that messy hair sort of way, and his grayish-blue eyes made my heart flutter like it did that Christmas night so long ago. My heart raced in my chest, yet guilt filled me for even feeling that way; Jensen was married, and he was not mine. He never would be. It was so easy to forget when I was with him.

I got caught up in the moment, at least until the mention of children came up. He was about to be a father. At that moment, everything came crashing down and reality set in. Jensen would never be mine and I had to live with that. It obviously wasn't meant to be.

Jensen hopped in his Bronco, and I watched him disappear down the street. I used to love riding around town with him with the top down. He had just turned sixteen when his father took him to Wilmington to surprise him with it. At that point, it was a piece of junk, but they spent countless hours fixing it up; it still looked pristine.

My mother made her way up the steps and around to the back door. There was still a sadness in her eyes, and I knew it'd be like that for a long time. We just had to get through each day at a time. However, there was more color to her cheeks, and she looked exquisite in her light blue maxi dress with her blonde hair in curls down her back. In her hand was a small, golden clutch that matched her sandals. When she walked in the door, I was standing there waiting for her.

"Hey," she called out, a smile lighting up her face. "I see you had some company."

"And I see you're looking hot tonight," I countered, not really wanting to talk about Jensen.

My mother pursed her lips. "You're deflecting. Did things not go well with you and Jensen?"

I waved her off. "It's fine. We talked and caught up, that's it." My grin widened at the sight of her outfit. "What about you? Is there something special going on tonight?"

She twirled around in her dress. "Your father is taking me out on a date. He thought it might cheer me up to get out of the house for a while." Her smile faded slightly. "I know he's trying to help get my mind off things." She dropped her clutch onto the coffee table and walked over to me. "I wanted to see if you'd like to join us."

I snorted. "It's your date night, so no." Then I waved a hand down at my clothes and sandy legs from mine and Jensen's walk on the beach. Also, I knew my hair was a tangled mess. "I'm not dressed to go out to eat."

My mother laughed. "You look amazing." Her eyes twinkled. "And speaking of amazing, Jensen told me he offered to buy the house. That takes a lot of stress off you." She flourished a hand around the room. "Plus, we know he'll take care of it."

That was true, he would. However, a small part of me didn't want him to buy the house, not when he was going to live happily ever after in it with someone who wasn't me.

With a groan, I ran a hand over my face, hating myself for even thinking that way. My mother cocked her head to the side, regarding me curiously.

"What was that about?"

I shook my head. "Nothing. Just thinking."

A sly smile spread across her face. "About Jensen? I bet it was nice seeing him again."

"It was," I admitted truthfully. "I had forgotten how easy it was to talk to him."

Her smile turned sad. "You two were always so in tune with each other; it used to scare your father. He feared you'd end up together and you would give up your dreams of being a doctor to stay here with Jensen."

I snorted. "Well, that definitely didn't happen."

She walked up to me and looked into my eyes. "Sometimes I wonder if you'd be happier if you did." My heart caught in my chest. I wasn't expecting those words to come out of her mouth.

"It's too late for that, Mom."

"Nothing is ever too late. Aren't you going to see him again?"

My mouth dropped and I stared at her as if she'd lost her mind. How could she even suggest I see Jensen again and insinuate a future with him? He was a married man with a baby on the way. There was no way in hell I would ever try to break him and Michelle up. Yet, my mother's hopeful look made me question her sanity.

"Really, Mom?" I fired back. "What exactly do you think is going to happen if I see him again?"

She shrugged. "I don't know. Maybe you two will finally realize you're meant to be together." How could she be saying this to me? Before I could respond, she held up a hand, cutting me off. "Look, I know something happened between you and Jensen that one Christmas night. After you left, he was never the same. And frankly, neither were you. I just want to see you happy."

I scoffed. "Well, it won't happen with a married man, Mom! For Christ's sake, Jensen and Michelle are about to have a baby!"

She guffawed unexpectedly, but then confusion quickly replaced the amusement on her face. "Wait, what? What are you—" She stopped abruptly, and her eyes widened with what appeared to be understanding. It was like I'd entered a twilight zone; nothing made sense.

"We are talking about the same Jensen, right?" I asked, wondering what was going on.

She opened her mouth, closed it, and then bit her lip sheepishly like she'd said too much. There was something she wasn't telling me.

"Why did you burst out laughing? What I said wasn't funny. You basically want me to be a home-wrecker."

Laughing, she held up her hands in defeat. "Definitely not, Everleigh. I would never condone that kind of behavior." More laughter ensued and she grabbed her chest. "But I think there's been a misunderstanding. And I have a strange feeling I'm about to throw someone under the bus."

I had never been so lost. "What are you talking about?" I demanded.

She motioned toward the couch. "You might want to sit. There are some things I think you need to know."

10

JENSEN

On the way home, I couldn't stop thinking about Everleigh. She knew where I lived and that my phone number was the same, so she could contact me if she wanted to. The question was . . . would she? I'd have to tell her the truth about me and Michelle at some point.

My phone started ringing, so I grabbed it from the center console and saw Trisha's name on the screen. It had to be Seth since his phone was at the bottom of the ocean.

"Hey," I answered, holding the phone to my ear.

Seth cleared his throat. "Thought I'd call and see what you're doing. Trisha made a lot of chili over here, and we wondered if you wanted to come eat."

I had just pulled into my driveway and was about to shut off the ignition, but going over to Seth's was just what I needed. So, I put my Bronco in reverse and backed out onto the street.

"I'll be right there. There's something I want to talk to you about anyway."

Seth lived further down the island near the pier, which was a little more populated. He chuckled into the phone. "Oh yeah? You giving me a raise?"

I snorted. "You just got one, greedy ass. Did you not notice it on your paycheck?"

With Seth being my first mate, I paid him very well. I knew it wasn't easy for him to leave Trisha for long periods, especially now that they were about to have a baby. That was the way of life for a fisherman, though. My guys knew the risks and sacrifices they had to make before taking their jobs.

Most of my crew used to work for my father and they were loyal. But luckily, I had men calling almost every day looking for jobs. I don't think I'll ever have a problem filling positions which was a good problem to have.

Seth burst out laughing. "Okay, fine, I noticed the pay increase. That's another reason I called; I wanted to thank you."

That made me smile. "You're welcome. You deserve it."

"Got that right," Seth agreed. "I know how to bring in the business."

Seth was a guru at marketing. Because of him, McLean Charters started bringing in extra income by offering deep-sea fishing excursions on top of our regular work. There were a lot of extra hours involved, but my crew was ready for it.

We've taken people out to sea from all over the world who wanted to try catching some of North Carolina's top saltwater fish. Then afterward, we'd direct those who caught fish to head to The Beachcomber restaurant, which Seth's aunt, Debbie Carroll, owned. There they could get their freshly caught fish cooked to order.

Once I was on the main road, the smell of rain became apparent. I looked toward the ocean and could see dark clouds on the horizon.

"Looks like we have a storm coming in," I told Seth.

"Well, hopefully, you got that top up on the Bronco. Don't want you having to redo the interior because you let it get flooded."

Luckily, the top was up and secured. "It's up," I assured him. "I don't want a repeat of the past."

A big storm had rolled in once, and I'd left the top down. As a result, the wind ripped it apart, and all the rain flooded the inside. It took a lot of work to fix the water damage.

"So, what did you want to talk to me about?" Seth asked.

A smile spread across my face. "Guess who I just saw?"

"Holy shit," he gasped. "It was Everleigh, wasn't it?" I turned off the main road toward the pier. Seth's house was only a couple of blocks from it.

"Yep. I might've done something I shouldn't have."

"Oh, hell, I can't wait to hear. I got us some beers ready."

"Good. I'll be there in a minute," I said, chuckling.

A few minutes later, I pulled into Seth's driveway, and he was already outside with two beers in his hands. He looked different from earlier this morning. He'd shaved off the long stubble on his face, and his blond hair had been freshly cut. His wife was a hairdresser and always took the clippers to him when he came home from long trips.

Shaking my head, I smiled as I exited my vehicle,

slipping my phone into my back pocket. Seth brought over the beers and handed me one.

"Nice haircut," I teased.

Seth ran a hand over his hair and smooth face. "You know how Trisha is. She hates all the hair when I come home."

After taking a swig of the beer, I placed a hand on Seth's shoulder, not even attempting to hide my grin. "You mean the *patches* of hair?"

I loved teasing Seth about his facial hair. He could never grow much in high school; when he did, it was in sporadic patches on his face. That was why everyone on the boat called him Patchy. It had been his nickname for the past fifteen years.

Seth flipped me off and took a sip of his beer. "One of these days, I'm going to come up with a good nickname for you."

I shook my head. "I'm your captain. Better watch it."

Trisha appeared in the front doorway of the house and waved. Her long, dark hair was braided to the side and her belly looked twice as big as it did when Seth and I left a couple of weeks ago.

"Hey, Jensen!" she hollered. "Dinner will be ready in fifteen minutes. I'm just waiting on the cornbread."

I waved back and could smell the food wafting from the kitchen. "Perfect! I'm starved!"

It'd been over two weeks since I'd had a home-cooked meal and was one of the things I missed being away at sea. My stomach growled just smelling the chili.

Trisha looked up at the darkening sky and shook her head. "You boys might want to come in soon; this storm looks like it's gonna be a doozy."

She frowned, tucked a strand of hair behind her ear, and headed back inside. I let my gaze drift upward and felt a wave of contentment wash over me as I watched the clouds swirl together. Thunder rumbled in the distance, and a streak of lightning forked through the air. I loved storms but didn't like being out at sea when they came. My concern was always for my crew and their well-being. I had to make sure they were always safe.

Seth cleared his throat to get my attention. "Tell me about Everleigh. How was it seeing her again?"

As I turned my attention to him, I felt an anxious knot form in my chest. Taking a deep breath, I leaned against my Bronco and glanced down at my beer bottle.

"Well . . . she's still as beautiful as ever," I said with a smile, even though dread flooded my senses.

Seth's eyes lit up with curiosity, and he pressed his lips together mischievously. "Any chance for you two? You should invite her over. I'd love to see her and have her meet Trisha."

Letting out a humorless laugh, I eyed him warily. "That's where I have a problem," I began gruffly. "It turns out that Everleigh thinks Michelle and I are married and expecting a baby."

Seth's mouth dropped open in shock, and he threw his head back in laughter. "What the hell? How is that even possible?"

Sighing heavily, I ran a hand over my face. "You know how I still kept in touch with Everleigh's grandmother and we saw each other all the time?"

Seth nodded knowingly while wiping tears of laughter from his eyes. "Of course. You always visited her. I know it was so you could get the scoop on Everleigh."

"Well," I continued, a sigh escaping my lips, "it turns out that Everleigh strictly forbade Rachel and her parents to speak about me."

Seth shook his head incredulously. "Wow. Why do you think that is?"

I shrugged. "I'm not sure of the exact reasoning, but I always hoped it was because Everleigh regretted leaving. However, Rachel did break that code and let Everleigh know when I got engaged."

I kept waiting for the day when Rachel would tell me that Everleigh had met someone and was going to get married. It was always a relief when that was never the case.

Seth chuckled. "Rachel was always on your side, wasn't she?"

I nodded. "She was. I could really use her wisdom right about now."

Seth waved his hands impatiently. "So, I'm assuming you didn't correct Everleigh about the you and Michelle debacle?"

My hesitation was answer enough and Seth laughed even more. "You are in a world of trouble, brother. If I were you, I'd tell Everleigh the truth as soon as possible before she finds out from someone else. We both know how hardheaded she can be. When she gets pissed at someone, it takes a long time for her to get over it."

Groaning, I grabbed my beer and finished it off. "Yeah, I know. It was just a test to see if I could pick up any lingering feelings she might have."

"And did you?" Seth wondered.

I shrugged. "There was something, but she's gotten good at building walls. Maybe that's what happens when you become a surgeon. You have to shut off the emotions when you're trying to save lives." More thunder rumbled overhead, and I looked up at the thickening gray clouds. "I just hope she doesn't stay mad at me for long." I met Seth's gaze again. "Now that she's here and I've seen her again, I don't want her to leave without knowing how I feel."

Seth stood in front of me and slapped his hands on my shoulders. "Here's what you need to do. Eat dinner here and then go right back over to Everleigh's either tonight or tomorrow morning and tell her the truth. Lay it all out. This is the chance you've been waiting on."

There was still a connection between me and Everleigh; I could feel it. Even if she didn't forgive me for lying, I wasn't going to let her go without hearing me out.

11

EVERLEIGH

I have never felt more like an idiot than I do now. My heart raced as the heat of fury surged through me like lava. Out of everything my mother could've told me, this was not what I expected to hear.

Jensen was *not* married.

How had she kept this from me? My mouth dropped as I glared at her. I pointed an accusing finger, trying to keep my voice steady.

"Did you know what Jensen was planning?"

My mother shook her head, but there was a playful glint in her eyes that made me even angrier. She reached down and grabbed her golden clutch off the coffee table.

"No, sweetheart," she said airily. "But whatever the reason, it seems to me that he wanted to see how you would react."

I scoffed, crossing my arms over my chest in defiance. "Really? And why would he want that?"

My mother smiled and stepped closer, a knowing look in her eye. "Because if you didn't care about him, none of this would make you so angry. You wouldn't be reacting like this if you didn't still have feelings for him."

"Or he just wanted me to look like an idiot," I fired back.

My mother laughed softly and cupped my cheek. "Everleigh, you're the one who refused to talk about him the past several years. Jensen and Michelle broke off the engagement six years ago. It worked out for the best because she's happily married with a baby on the way." She paused for a second and sighed. "If you looked like a fool with Jensen, you can only blame yourself. I would've told you, but I distinctly remember there was a Jensen-related ban placed on all of us. You were obviously scared to hear anything about him. You might want to ask yourself why that is."

I already knew the answer to that, and maybe she was right, I was scared to hear about him.

My mom patted my cheek before walking to the door. She opened it but then stopped and faced me, her hands clutching her purse. "Now that you're home, maybe it's time to settle things with Jensen, once and for all. Especially with the circumstances. I know you got tired of hearing your grandmother talk about fate and whatnot, but you need to take a good look at what's going on." Her expression softened. "You're thirty-four years old and single. So is Jensen. You haven't found happiness and neither has he. Think about it."

All I could think about was how embarrassed and angry I felt. I still couldn't believe he outright lied to me.

She walked out of the glass patio door and gently shut it behind her. I grabbed my phone and wanted to call Nyla and tell her everything, but my gut wanted me to do something else.

Once my mother backed out of the driveway, I waited for her to disappear down the road before grabbing my keys. Was I about to make a mistake? People always said your first instinct was usually the right one. I could pretend I didn't know the truth and then keep the charade going until it blew up in Jensen's face. But there was only one problem with that—I didn't like playing games. I wanted to go to his house and let everything out.

For the first time in years, things became clearer. Feelings I kept hidden deep within me had finally surfaced, feelings I didn't even know I harbored. I grabbed my purse off the kitchen counter and hurried to my car. A storm was coming in from the sea, and it reminded me of the storm brewing inside me.

Jensen lived about ten minutes away, but I made it there in seven. His Bronco wasn't there when I arrived, but I hoped he'd be back at some point. I hopped out of my car and sat on his front porch as the rain poured in. The thunder crashed and the lightning lit up the sky.

I placed a hand over my heart, feeling it race with each passing second. I was furious with Jensen, and once I said what needed to be said to him, things were going to change.

THE RUMBLE of Jensen's old blue Bronco echoed off the trees as it came down Yacht Drive. I was still on his porch, my anger simmering like a pot waiting to boil over.

When he pulled into the driveway and stepped out of

his car, there was an expression of regret and shame written across his face. His grayish-blue gaze only seemed to sharpen with each moment that passed.

I stood up and marched down the steps, my heart racing in anticipation. "Why did you lie, Jensen?" I snapped. "Do you know how stupid that made me look?"

He leaned back against his car door, defiantly crossing his arms over his chest. All traces of regret had been replaced by pain and anger.

"That was never my intention, Everleigh. I can't help that you never cared about what was happening in my life." He flung his arms out wide. "Do you want to know why Michelle and I aren't married?"

My heart lurched in my chest at the sound of all the emotions in his voice. I could hear the pain, frustration, and even passion in his words. Before I could even say anything, he pushed off his car and walked toward me. His body was so close to mine as he looked down at me. The energy around us crackled like fire, burning my skin.

His heated stare was enough to take my breath away. There was a wildness in his eyes I'd never seen before.

"You know," he said, running a hand through his hair, "I've been waiting to say all this to you for so long that I don't even know where to begin." He turned away from me and sighed. "Michelle and I are not married because I never loved her the way I loved you; it wasn't fair to her." His head hung low, and he shook it. "She deserved someone who could be what she wanted."

The breath hitched in my lungs as those three words left his lips. He said it in the past tense, but it made me wonder if he *still* loved me. If he had said he did on that Christmas night, I don't know if I would've had the strength to leave him. I had a feeling it was going to be impossible to leave him now. I thought I would have the upper hand when I confronted him, but that steadily seemed to dissolve away.

"If you loved me, you definitely didn't show it," I grumbled low, my heart throbbing in my chest.

Jensen spun around and scoffed at me, his eyes piercing through mine. "Neither did you, Everleigh!" he spat back. "Tell me, did that night mean anything to you?" My regret cut like a knife as Jensen moved closer to me, his gaze raw and determined. "The truth, Everleigh," he demanded. "I think we both deserve it. Was I just a one-night stand to you?"

Tears streamed down my face as I tried to compose myself.

"No," I whispered, my voice barely audible. "I loved you too, but you knew it wouldn't work between us, not with me being in Boston and you here." Jensen's expression softened a bit as he took another step toward me. "And now," I growled, moving away from him, "you intentionally lied about Michelle and becoming a father. Why would you even do that?"

He let out a harsh laugh devoid of any humor or joy. "Seriously, Everleigh? It was a test! I wanted to see if you still had feelings for me like Michelle seems to think you have. I thought she was crazy, but I had to see for myself."

"And what did you see?" I asked coldly, crossing my arms over my chest.

He shrugged helplessly. "I don't know," he admitted. "There were moments where I could feel the connection, but then you'd shut yourself off."

We locked eyes with each other for what felt like an eternity as time slowed down around us. As much as it pained me to admit it, building walls around my heart was the only way to protect myself from the hurt I unintentionally caused myself when I cut off all communication with him. I thought I'd be able to move on, build a life for myself, both professionally and romantically, and this his absence wouldn't affect me. How wrong I was.

On the way over, I told myself I wouldn't hold back. *Speaking the truth will set you free*. That was a saying my grandmother always told me. Of course, I knew she was referring to Jensen, but I never entertained the thought. Now was my chance to get it all out in the open. Maybe speaking the truth *would* set me free.

I swiped at my eyes and let out an angry breath. "I put the walls up to help with the pain," I confessed. Jensen's expression shifted and the tension left his shoulders. He started to move closer, but I held up a hand. "No, let me get this out. I didn't want to leave, but there was no other way. It never would've worked. And if I'm being honest . . ." I let the sentence trail off as I let him see the vulnerability behind my eyes. "I was angry that you didn't come after me. Yes, you told me to call when I was ready, but a part of me wanted you to fight for me." More tears welled in my eyes. "And you didn't."

Jensen swallowed hard and lowered his gaze. "You're right, I didn't. I wish you knew how much I'll regret that for the rest of my life."

"We can only blame ourselves," I said, wiping my tears away.

Jensen lifted his head, his gaze penetrating mine.

"You're right, but now we have the chance to do something about it."

I shook my head. "No. Too much has happened. I don't have the energy to deal with whatever is going on between us."

Jensen sighed heavily but kept his eyes on me. "I understand. You're going through a lot right now. But you need to know I'm not going anywhere. I've spent years waiting to see you again. If you love me like you say you do—or did—then we deserve this chance."

Pulse racing, I stepped away from him before he could touch me. I didn't trust myself.

"I have to go."

I hurried to my car, ignoring as he called out my name. Instead, I got in and sped away from his house. Tonight did *not* go as planned. I thought my anger would help me get over him, but all it did was light a fire of longing within me. *What am I going to do?*

12

JENSEN

The second I saw Everleigh waiting on my porch last night, I could see it on her face . . . she knew. We were both to blame for our downfall and maybe I had a bigger hand in it. I should've fought for her. I should've flown up to Boston and let her know I'd do anything to keep her in my life. I knew she would've said no, but I could've given her no other option. I would've rather spent the distance apart knowing she was mine, than go through all these past years without her. Her schooling was important, and I understood that. If only I had let her know I was happy to wait for her, things would be different now.

One thing was for sure, I wasn't about to let her return to Boston, to let her leave again without knowing that.

As soon as the sun rose, I dressed and headed over to Everleigh's. She was only going to be in town for less than two months now, so I didn't have much time to take her on dates, to show her what life with me could be like. After last night, I had no clue if she wanted to see me ever again, but I had to try. Fighting for her was what I've wanted to do for so long. My opening had finally come, and I wasn't going to waste it.

When I pulled up at Everleigh's, her car was in the driveway. It was early, but I knew she'd be awake. I looked over at my parents' house and my mother was by the window, drinking her coffee. She smiled and waved but then pointed at the back deck of Everleigh's house. I had no doubt she was there, drinking a cup of coffee while taking in the view of the sea. It was what her grandmother did every morning; sometimes, I even joined her.

I started up the stairs, but then I heard her footsteps shuffling toward the door and the sound of it slamming.

Seriously, Everleigh?

Of course, when I turned the corner to the back deck, Everleigh was nowhere in sight. I knocked on the glass door and peered inside, but she wasn't there.

"Everleigh," I called out, waiting for her to appear around the hallway corner. "Everleigh, we need to talk. I came here to apologize. I never actually did that last night."

With her arms crossed over her chest, she walked out of the hallway and into the living room, dressed in short pink pajama shorts and a tank top; she was so damn beautiful. Her long, caramel-blonde hair hung loose down her back, but some strands were tangled around her face like vines.

"You said it!" she shouted, waving me off. "Now, will you please go? I have plans today, and they don't involve you."

That made me smile. I held up my hands in defeat. "All

I want is to talk to you. If you come outside, it'll only take a minute."

She shook her head, her lips pursed in defiance. "Not going to happen."

I shrugged, an easy smile on my face. "No worries. I'll just sit out here all day if I have to."

Everleigh disappeared back down the hall, and I sat in Rachel's red rocking chair, already regretting my decision. Everleigh was the most stubborn woman I knew—no matter how long I sat on the deck, she wasn't going to give in. I propped my feet up on the deck railing and gazed out at the ocean-blue horizon.

"When are you going to sell me this place?" I shouted, knowing Everleigh could hear me.

I was surprised when she responded with a sharp retort, her voice muffled by the walls between us.

"Not going to happen now! You don't deserve it!"

A laugh escaped my lips and sure enough, I heard her thunderous footsteps coming closer. Then, through the glass door, I saw her appear, hands on her hips, and with a fiery expression that I'd always found endearing about her.

"I mean it!" she challenged. "You are the last person I'd ever sell this house to!"

I smiled wider, undeterred by her words. "Whatever you say, Everleigh."

She rolled her eyes and gestured for me to leave with a wave of her hand before disappearing again into the hallway.

Chuckling softly, I focused back on the sea. It may not be today, but I was going to wear Everleigh down.

A FEW HOURS PASSED, and Everleigh still hadn't made an appearance. Suddenly, a light tapping sound came from the stairs, and I looked to see my mother emerge around the corner of the house. She had a white plate in her hands with a neatly cut ham sandwich, chips, and a water bottle. She smiled softly as she handed it to me, and I could see the amusement sparkling in her eyes. Her dark brown curls blew in her face from the wind, so she shook her head until they moved out of the way.

"I thought you might be hungry," she said casually. "I take it you two haven't talked since spilling your guts last night?"

I laughed, taking a bite out of the sandwich. "Nope. And now I told her I'm not leaving until she talks to me. I didn't exactly think this through, did I?"

She sat down on the other rocking chair with a chuckle. "I would say not." She pointed to the inside of the house. "It doesn't look like Everleigh's going to come out anytime soon."

I shrugged before taking another bite of the sandwich. "And I knew she wouldn't. It's just hard to give in."

My mother patted my arm gently. "You two were always so competitive. It used to make me and your dad laugh." A giggle escaped her lips. "I'll never forget the time you face-planted in the sand after she tripped you during the Fourth of July race."

I rubbed my jaw, remembering how it hurt like hell. "That was no fun."

She giggled again before standing up and brushing off her skirt. "Well, I hate to tell you this, but you'll have to let

Everleigh win this one. Your dad and I need your help moving some things around in the house."

I looked up at her. "I'll be right there."

She waved me off. "Take your time. We'll see you in a few."

My mom turned on her heel and disappeared around the corner, and I listened to her walk down the stairs. After a few minutes, I finished my lunch and stood. "All right, Everleigh, I'm leaving!" I shouted. "My parents need help over at their house."

Everleigh's laugh echoed through the walls. "Excuses! Excuses! I knew you wouldn't last."

It felt good to banter with her again, but I wanted more than that. I wanted to be close to her, to have her in my life again the way we used to be.

"This isn't over!" I called out.

There was no response, but I knew she'd heard me.

13

EVERLEIGH

"This isn't over!" Jensen shouted.

Chills of excitement ran through my body at the sound of his words. Last night made me realize how much I wanted Jensen back in my life. The problem was that I didn't know what to do. I had less than two months now to spend in Oak Island before I needed to return to Boston. The problem was that I still had no clue what to do with my grandmother's house. Adding Jensen into the mix only confused me more.

I slowly exhaled the deep breath I was holding and listened to everything around me. Jensen still hadn't left yet because I could hear him moving around the deck. I'd spent all morning in my grandmother's room, going through her closet, hoping it would get my mind off him. However, one thing that did make me happy was being able to find joy in being surrounded by my grandmother's things. Since the first time I entered, it's gotten easier being in there. The smell of her room was comforting, and I felt as if she was right there with me; I even found myself talking to her. It was moments like which told me it would be hard to sell the house. The house was my connection to her.

The thump of Jensen's retreating steps made my heart stop. I rushed out of the closet and over to the window to see if I could see him, but I couldn't. The last thing I wanted was for him to trick me into thinking he was leaving when he wasn't.

I hurried across my grandmother's room as quietly and quickly as possible, only to snag my toe on one of the wooden floorboards and trip. The pain shot up my leg, and I hissed as I slammed against the floor.

"Son of a—"

The thud of my body hitting the floor echoed through the house, and I held my breath to make sure I didn't hear Jensen coming back. When I didn't, I got to my feet and hobbled into the living room to peek out the windows overlooking the driveway. Jensen was already at his parents' house and walking through the door.

Relief washed through me, but there was still a stinging pain throbbing in my toe. I glanced down and there was blood around my nail from where my skin ripped. I had no clue what I'd even tripped over.

After grabbing a wet paper towel from the kitchen, I wiped off my toe and returned to my grandmother's room. However, when I stopped at the door, I noticed one of the floorboards had lifted on one of the corners; my toe must've hit it.

I trudged over and slowly bent down to see if I could slide the wooden board back into place. When I tried to push it down, it wouldn't move. So, instead, I pulled it away and froze when I caught a glimpse of something hiding underneath the floor. I couldn't see clearly what it was, so I grabbed my cell off the bed and turned on the flashlight. I was scared of what I'd find. In the movies, something terrifying was always lurking in the darkened corners. Luckily, that wasn't the case this time.

My light shined on a dust-covered light blue box with flowers carved into the wood. There was no room to get it out, so I pried away two more floorboards. Once that was done, I reached in and grabbed the box, swiping away all the dust. It didn't look as if anyone had touched it in many years. The box was heavy, and things shuffled around inside when I shook it. I was curious to see what was in it, and when I went to open it, I found that it was locked.

The box was handmade and beautifully so. The keyhole was something you'd see on an antique door in a castle; it was very magical and medieval looking.

A gasp escaped my lips as a memory from my past rushed to the surface. There was a time, many years before, when I'd seen a key that would fit the lock. I was in this very room, snooping through my grandmother's jewelry box. And inside, underneath her necklaces and bracelets was a small, golden key. But, of course, I never asked what it was for.

Heart racing, I looked over at the dresser where my grandmother's white porcelain jewelry box sat. It was one of the things I had yet to look at since she passed away. Holding the light blue box in my arms, I stood and set it on the bed so I could open the jewelry box. The second I opened it, the music started to play the "Rippling Waves Waltz." My grandmother used to let it play while she got dressed, and I would always be out in the hallway dancing to it.

Carefully, I sifted through my grandmother's necklaces until I found the key. It had tarnished over the years but was just the right size to unlock the box. In a way, it felt wrong to open something that was a secret my grandmother so obviously wanted to keep hidden. But my curiosity was going to get the best of me; I *had* to know what was in it.

With the key in my hand, I sat on the bed and brought the box to my lap. I slid the key in and was both relieved and intrigued when it went smoothly. When I turned it, I could hear the latch release the lid and it popped open just a little. My fingers trembled with excitement as I pushed it open the rest of the way, revealing the contents inside.

There were letters . . . tons of them, all discolored with age.

I grabbed one and gently opened it, afraid the paper would rip. The cursive handwriting inside was graceful and neat, something you didn't see much of these days. It was a love letter to my grandmother.

My dearest Rachel,

My love for you continues to grow with each passing day. You have captivated my heart and my soul since the day I first laid eyes on you. I can feel your presence with me even when you are miles away. Everywhere

I go, I see your beauty in the vast ocean and the rolling waves.

I am so thankful for the moments we have shared together and the memories that will stay with me for an eternity. You have been an incredible light in my life, my love! Your laughter calms me and your bright eyes bring a peace I cannot find anywhere else.

I know that my travels take me away from you often, but I want you to know that you will always be in my heart and my thoughts. The bond we share is something I will never take for granted.

Yours always,

T

WHO WAS T? It was obviously the first letter of the man's name, but that could be anything. Timothy. Tom. Ted. Toby. My grandfather's name was Arthur. I was both mesmerized and intrigued and couldn't help but reach inside the box for another letter. The date in the top corner of the note was almost sixty-five years ago. My grandmother didn't marry my grandfather until a few years after that. This next letter was a little different.

My dearest Rachel,

As I sit here on my boat, surrounded by the vast and unpredictable sea, my thoughts keep returning to you. Your radiant smile, your sparkling eyes, the way your hair catches the sun's rays—all of it is etched in my mind. I can think of nothing else but you.

But our love, my darling, is like the sea itself—wild, powerful, and often unforgiving. Your parents have made their disapproval of me clear, and we both know that we cannot openly declare our love for one another. Our relationship must remain a secret, hidden away like a precious pearl within its shell.

Yet even in the face of such adversity, I cannot help but feel an overwhelming sense of hope. The sea teaches us to be resilient, to weather any storm that comes our way. Just as I have learned to navigate the tumultuous waters, so too will we find a way to be together, come what may.

I dream of the day and pray for it to come swiftly.

Yours always,

T

. . .

My HEART HURT at the thought of my grandmother being in love with a man she couldn't have. But if she had stayed with T, then she wouldn't have met my grandfather and had my mother. Things tended to work out the way they were supposed to, but I couldn't help but wonder what my grandmother went through when she was younger. She never spoke a word about another man to me other than my grandfather.

Why didn't she tell me?

I rummaged through the box, all the letters holding secrets that had stayed buried for decades. I read them until the room dimmed with the setting sun. The last letter I read was the one that shattered me. I could only imagine what it did to my grandmother.

My dearest Rachel,

I write to you with a heavy heart, knowing that this letter may be the last time we communicate. I cannot stop thinking about you and the life we could have had together if only things were different.

I still remember the day we met by the sea, the sun shining down on us and the sound of the waves crashing against the shore. You were so beautiful, standing there with your hair blowing in the wind. I knew from that moment that I wanted to spend the rest of my life with you.

But now, your parents have put a stop to our love. They do not understand the connection we share, the bond that draws us to each other. I wish I could make them see we are meant to be together.

I am writing this letter to ask for one last meeting with you. I know it may be dangerous for us to see each other again, but I cannot let you go without saying goodbye.

Meet me by the sea, where we first met.

Yours always,

T

TEARS STREAMED DOWN my face as I folded the paper and gently set it back into the box with the others. I wanted to know what happened. Why did my great-grandparents not approve of this man?

Releasing a shaky breath, I closed the box and placed it beside my grandmother's jewelry box on her dresser.

"Is that why you always pushed me not to let Jensen go?" I whispered, wishing my grandmother could answer me.

The room was silent, but I could hear the waves crashing just off the shore. I wanted to believe my grandfather was her one true love, but what if he wasn't? What if T was?

I walked over to the window and peered out at the darkening sky.

"So many secrets," I said, my voice low.

I glanced over my shoulder at the hole in the floor. I had a strange feeling that the box of letters was just the beginning.

14

JENSEN

"Would you like another beer?" the waitress asked, knowing very well I always drank three when it was Tuesday night at The Beachcomber restaurant.

Her name was Evie, and she was Seth's cousin and the daughter of his aunt Debbie.

I nodded at Evie. "Just one more, please."

Seth held up a hand. "I'd like another one, too."

Evie walked by him and slapped his head playfully in passing. "Coming right up."

Trisha shook her head and laughed. "I think she missed you."

Every Tuesday, if we weren't at sea, we'd eat at The Beachcomber; it was tradition. Everleigh used to join us when we were younger, and a part of me hoped she'd rejoin the tradition today, but she'd been ignoring my calls and texts for the past two days. I kept waiting for her to walk through the door, but the night was almost over.

Trisha clasped her hands underneath her chin and

smiled at me. "If annoying Everleigh into submission isn't working, what's your next game plan?"

Seth chuckled and tossed a french fry into his mouth. "I'm going to call her ass up and tell her how disappointed I am in her. She might not want to be around you," he said, pointing at me, "but I was her friend, too. I didn't do anything to her."

Trisha agreed with a nod. "That's true, but she did just lose her grandmother on top of everything going on with Jensen. There has to be a lot going on in her mind." She rubbed a hand down his back. "Maybe we should stop by her house and see her. I'd love to meet her."

Evie came over with our beers, and Seth smirked at me over the rim of his glass. "We might just do that." He winked at me. "How pissed are you going to be if she sees me and not you?"

I waved him off. "I have no doubt she'll be happy to see you. All I know is I'm not giving up."

The door to the restaurant opened and Seth's eyes widened. "Well, well, look who just walked in."

My pulse skyrocketed and I jerked my head around, thinking it would be Everleigh, but it wasn't her; it was Michelle and her husband, Grady. Even though Michelle and I didn't work out, I was happy we were able to stay friends. Her husband was a good guy. They spent many Tuesday nights with us here at The Beachcomber, but I didn't think they were going to show up tonight.

Michelle waved and grabbed Grady's arm as they walked over. Seth and I stood and shook Grady's hand when they reached the table.

"Good evening, fellas," Grady said. "Sorry, we're late."

Seth slapped a hand on his shoulder. "No worries, man. We were just talking about Jensen's failed love life."

"Thanks," I grumbled, gulping down my beer. "You don't have to remind me that I'm the fifth wheel here."

Michelle sat down beside me and frowned. "What's going on? Did you play along with the ruse?"

Seth burst out laughing. "He did and it backfired in his face."

Michelle slapped a hand over her mouth. "Oh, Jensen, I'm so sorry. Did you get what you wanted, though? Do you think she still has feelings for you?"

I nodded. "She does, but she's still keeping her distance. I've been trying to get close to her."

Michelle's smile widened. "How? By being annoying?"

Trisha snickered across the table. "That's what I'm saying. You're not going to get the girl like that."

"Then what do you suggest?" I asked.

Trisha leaned closer, her gaze lit with mischief. "Show her what she's missing." She glanced down at my arms and smiled. "I mean, come on, Jensen, I've seen how women look at you."

Seth jerked his head toward her. "What are you saying, love? Do you think my best friend is sexy?"

Trisha laughed and kissed his cheek. "I'm just trying to tell Jensen that he needs to use what God gave him. He has a smokin' body and women love that. If Everleigh has been single for as long as I've heard she has, then she won't be able to resist."

Michelle nudged me with her elbow, and I looked over at her. "Trisha's right," she agreed. "But don't make it obvious that you're trying to get under her skin." She set her hand on my wrist. "Everleigh will come around. Just be patient."

Sighing, I finished off my beer. Patience was something I didn't have. I knew there was a time limit on Everleigh being here which meant I had to move quickly if I wanted to make her realize we were meant to be together. I didn't have much time.

15

EVERLEIGH

Jensen hadn't shown up, which was surprising since it was late morning. He had been hanging out on the back deck for the past two days, trying to draw me out. I had to admit, I've wanted to go out there and be with him, but I couldn't bring myself to give in; at least, not yet.

Turning away from the window, I focused on my grandmother's box of love letters on her dresser. They sparked something inside of me. A part of me felt guilty for being so intrigued, especially since the letters were not from my grandfather. I loved my Poppy, but I wanted to know who T was. I've always heard that most people fall in love three times in their life. You have the first love, which usually happens in high school. It's all-consuming and most people think it'll last forever. But, of course, it doesn't. The love isn't as deep and raw as the other relationships you experience later. Then, you have the intense love that feels like a rollercoaster. The relationship comes with massive highs and dramatic lows, a love that will turn your world upside down. The heartbreak from that one can be indescribably painful, but it also helps you grow and find the inner strength to move on to the final love. It's the one where you find unconditional love. The one that comes out of nowhere and feels completely right; it is the beginning of forever.

All I've ever known was Jensen. He was my first love, and I knew without a doubt that was my intense as well. However, I had yet to find out if he was my unconditional, but a part of me hoped it to be true.

I walked back to the window and peered out, not seeing him anywhere. I decided to change into my teal bikini and sunglasses and once I'd done so, grabbed my grandmother's favorite pirate romance and my phone, and headed outside to the garden where I already had a lounge chair by the koi pond; I didn't want to sit out on the beach today.

The sun was hot overhead, but the intermittent clouds floating by gave me some short moments of relief. I opened the book and was just about to start on page one when a familiar sound echoed down the road. It was Jensen's Bronco. He could easily be going over to his parents' house, but I doubted it.

Instead of running inside and avoiding him, I planned on doing the opposite today. If he wanted to annoy me, I had ways to torment him. But who was I kidding? I wanted to be around him, and staying away only made me want him more.

Resting a hand behind my head, I held the book in my other, stretching my body out on the lounge chair. His car door slammed and a few seconds later, I heard him marching up the stairs to my deck. He wouldn't be able to see me unless he looked down. But unfortunately, I couldn't see him in the position I was in.

I waited for him to call me, but all I heard was his footsteps as he descended the stairs to the walkway. He wandered over to the other side of the pond, shirtless with his shorts hung low on his hips. My heart started to race, and I was glad he couldn't hear it. He set down the bucket he'd been carrying and peered deep into the pond.

"No snarky comments today?" I said.

He knelt beside the pond and shook his head. "No time for that. I have work to do."

"What kind of work?" I asked, setting my book aside.

He looked me up and down, his predatory gaze sending shivers throughout my body. No one had looked at me like that in a long time—and I didn't realize how much I needed it until now.

Jensen turned away and gestured to the pond. "I don't know if you knew this, but every month, I come here to clean your grandmother's pond—it's way past due for its monthly cleaning." He was right, I didn't know that.

"It seems you and my grandmother spent a lot of time together."

Jensen reached into the pond and tossed a handful of slimy muck in the bucket. "She was all I had as far as a grandparent is concerned," he replied, his voice deep and smooth as he continued to clean out the pond. "You already know all my others passed away years ago."

So had mine. My grandmother was all I had left.

"What else do I not know?" I questioned. "It seems like my grammy kept lots of secrets from me."

Jensen's brows furrowed when he looked over at me. "Me visiting her wasn't a secret, Everleigh. You just didn't want to hear about it." He reached into the water and pulled out more debris. "Is there something else on your mind? I can hear it in your voice."

He stopped what he was doing and rested on his knees, his full attention on me. The only thing on my mind was my grandmother's mysterious love letters, but I wasn't about to talk to him about them.

"I'm fine," I said, waving my hand dismissively. Then, sighing, I looked up at the house. "I'm still trying to decide what I'm going to do with this place."

Jensen stood and grabbed the bucket of muck. "The offer still stands; I'll buy it."

Grinning, I cocked my head to the side. "Didn't I tell you the other night that I'm not selling to you?"

A smirk spread across his lips; it was very sexy and devilish. The sight made my body heat up like fire. "Maybe. But I can always persuade you to change your mind."

"And how do you plan on doing that?"

His smile widened and he stepped closer, his gaze raking over my body. I shivered in anticipation of what he might say next, but my phone trilled from beside me before he could answer. I grabbed it off the cushion, noting Nyla's name flashing across the screen.

"It's my friend from Boston," I said, sliding my legs off the lounge chair. "She'll be here in a few days for the rest of the summer."

A hint of disappointment passed over Jensen's face before he nodded and backed away. "I see. Are you going to take her around to all the favorite spots?"

I gave him a smile as I got to my feet, my heart

pounding hard in my chest. "Of course. I'll make sure you meet her."

Spinning around on my heel, I sprinted up the stairs two at a time, knowing I couldn't answer the call with him around. He would definitely hear her talking about him. When I reached the top step and opened the glass patio door, I had very little time to accept the call before it went to voice mail.

"Hey!" I said breathlessly as the air conditioning blasted against my skin, sending chills all over my body.

"Good morning!" Nyla replied happily. "I have a quick break, so I thought I'd catch up with you. I'm excited about coming down there—it's all I can think about!"

Laughing, I peered out the door at Jensen below me, admiring how his muscles flexed as he moved around, mending the pond liner with new stones and plants.

"It's all I can think about, too. It'll be nice having you here."

She giggled. "I'm sure it hasn't been too lonely with Jensen around all the time. Is he there now?"

I glanced out the door and smiled. "Yes. He's cleaning the pond; it looks a million times better."

"I can't wait to meet him," she gushed.

"You don't have to worry about that," I said, laughing. "He's here every single day."

If he cleaned the pond today, I wondered what his excuse would be tomorrow. It didn't matter either way; I wanted to be around him.

"You know he's just doing that to spend time with you, right?" Nyla mused.

I focused on Jensen, watching as droplets of sweat

rolled down his bronzed skin as he swung the rake back and forth across the water's surface.

"Yeah, I know. He's kind of wearing me down."

Nyla laughed so loud I had to hold the phone away from my ear and take a few steps back.

"I don't know why you're fighting it. You want him, end of story. Might as well enjoy this time before you come back to Boston. If he was mine, I know I definitely would be."

"He's not *mine*," I corrected her, trying but failing to push away the warmth in my chest at the thought of Jensen belonging to me. "Besides, I can't go down the same path I did before."

Nyla scoffed. "You don't have to. Figure out a new path where you can both be happy."

I moved away from the door and sat on the couch. "I don't even know what that is."

"You'll figure it out," she said softly. "I have faith in you."

"Thanks. I needed to hear that."

Her break ended and we said our goodbyes. As soon as we hung up, I went back to the door to peer out at Jensen. Was it possible for us to find a way we could both be happy? At work, I always had the answers. I knew exactly what needed to be done and how to do it. Why was I having so much trouble now? Love should be easy to navigate but it was, by far, the hardest.

I took one last look at Jensen before turning for the hallway to my grandmother's room. Grabbing the box of letters off her dresser, I sat down on the bed and opened it. There were over a hundred love letters. I shuffled through them and grabbed one at random, wondering what it was going to say. Would it be one with T professing his love or one full of heartache and longing for what he and my grandmother couldn't have? Carefully, I unfolded the paper and held my breath as I read the words.

My dearest Rachel,

As the waves crash against the shore and the seagulls call out above me, my thoughts drift to the day we snuck onto the pier and shared that special moment. The way the moonlight danced on the waves and the smell of salt in the air made it feel like it was just the two of us against the world.

I remember the way your hand felt in mine as we walked along the pier, stealing kisses in the shadows. And I recall the exact moment I said the words I had been holding back for so long - "I love you." The way your face lit up with joy and love made my heart swell.

That moment will forever be etched in my mind and heart. It's a memory that I have held onto during my long days at sea, and it's what brings me home to you each and every time.

My life is unpredictable and dangerous, but I find solace in the fact that I have you waiting for me. When I return, I plan to speak to your father, to ask for your hand in marriage. Calling you my wife would be the greatest honor.

Yours always,

T

IF ONLY THERE were letters from my grandmother to T. I would love to know her replies and what truly happened between them. I could only guess that it had to have ended in tragedy. I folded the letter and put it back in the box with the others.

Setting the box on the bed, I stood and returned to the window. It looked as if Jensen was almost done cleaning the pond. My heart swelled at the sight of him, and I knew deep down that I'd never stopped loving him. I loved him so much and regretted leaving him so much that I drowned myself in school and work to get him out of my mind. None of it worked, though. All it did was make my misery and loneliness worse.

A few minutes later, Jensen finished with the pond, and I moved into the living room so I could watch him get into his Bronco. A part of me wanted to go down there and tell him not to leave, but I was afraid. I hated the fact I was terrified of the unknown.

Why did I put up so many walls to protect myself?

Doing so only resulted in me being scared that I might not find my way out from behind them. Groaning, I closed my eyes and rested my forehead on the cool windowpane.

What am I going to do?

16

EVERLEIGH

When I went to bed last night, I knew I wanted to do something different today. Both my parents had made comments about me visiting my father's medical practice, and that was exactly what I was going to do. I needed to get away from the house for a while, even though I was tempted to search every nook and cranny for more secret compartments. I haven't told my mother about the love letters, but I planned on doing it today and had placed the wooden box in the passenger seat of my car.

In a way, I was nervous to show them to her. Her loyalty was to her father, who clearly didn't write the letters.

It only took a few minutes to get to my father's office, and when I pulled into downtown Southport, I couldn't help but smile. It was different from the massive hospital I worked at. The buildings and shops were all different colors, like a street of rainbows. My father's clinic, Seaside Family Practice, was bright green with white trim and shutters. It was cheery and inviting, which helped a lot when scared sick kids would visit.

I pulled in behind the building and walked around to the front with the box of letters resting against my chest. Before going inside, I looked up and down the tourist-filled street. The last time I ventured into the bustling, cozy beach town, I ran into Michelle. So much has happened since then.

When I entered the office, I found my mother at the front desk. In one corner of the room, a woman and a young boy with tousled hair sat slumped in the chair, his hand clutching his abdomen as he leaned forward and rested his head against a trash can. A sense of protectiveness swarmed through me at the sight of him; I wanted to make him feel better.

"Everleigh," my mother gasped, catching my attention.

I turned to see her eyes lit with excitement, but she was on the phone. She beckoned me over with a wave of her hand, her smile just like my grandmother's.

Still holding the box in my arms, I walked through the door that led around to the office. My mother hung up the phone and stood, spreading her arms wide. I set the box down on the desk and hugged her hard.

"You finally made it by. Your father and I were wondering if you'd ever show up." I let her go and she smiled wider. "Must be kind of hard to get away with Jensen being over at the house."

"That is not what's going on, Mom," I said, laughing. "He's been more of a pain than anything. At least until yesterday; he came over to clean the pond."

She nodded. "Oh yeah, he used to do that every month.

There was a long list of things your grandmother wanted done at that house."

"Where is that list?" I asked. She bit her lip sheepishly, and it wasn't hard to guess who had it. "Jensen has it. I should've known."

My mother shrugged. "Hey, he was happy to take on the load. A lot of it was stuff your father doesn't have the strength for." She shook her head and snickered. "He's not as young as he used to be."

"I heard that," he called out from behind us.

He walked into the office while a lady holding a little girl in her arms walked out the door so they could come around to the front of the desk to check out. My father gave my mother the little girl's chart so she could send them on their way.

"It's good to see you, pumpkin," he said, kissing the top of my head. "You doing okay?"

One of his nurses called back the little boy from the waiting room, so I knew he didn't have much time to socialize.

"I'm fine," I said, hugging him tight. "I've missed coming in here."

He laughed. "Well, I've missed you being here." He patted my back and smiled. "I have to go, but I'll see you later."

Once he was gone and the waiting room was empty, I picked up the box and leaned against the desk, facing my mother. When she looked at it, she smiled.

"That's really lovely. Where did you get it?"

Her comment answered the question in my mind . . . she must not have known about the letters, either.

I snorted. "I found it. Do you want to know where?"

Her head cocked to the side, her eyes bright with anticipation. "Where?"

I grinned. "Under the floor in Grammy's room. My toe snagged on the edge of a floorboard, and it lifted up. When I tried to put it back in place, I couldn't do so without shifting some of the others. That's when I saw this," I said, holding the box out to her, "covered in three inches of dust."

She took the box, her gaze alight with wonder as she ran her fingertips over the ornately carved exterior.

"I have never seen this before."

I was curious to see her reaction and hear her thoughts when she read some of the letters. She opened the lid and then looked up at me, lifting her brows.

"Letters?"

I nodded. "Love letters. To Grammy from someone whose name starts with the letter T. Do you know who that could be?"

"No," she whispered, turning her attention back to the box as she picked up a letter and unfolded it gently, examining the perfectly elegant penmanship within. I'd never seen a man write so neatly.

My mother's face was unreadable, her eyes wide as she scanned the page.

"I have no clue who this guy is," she said. "It's obvious my grandparents didn't approve of him, but I wonder what happened to break them up."

She rummaged through the letters until she found the one from T saying he was going to ask for my grandmother's hand in marriage. She ran her thumb over the creases, her lips pressed together into a tight line.

"My mother sure did have some secrets, didn't she?"

She looked at me for confirmation and I nodded. "I thought she shared everything with me, but it looks like I was wrong. I wonder if Georgia knows anything; she was Grammy's best friend."

Carefully folding the letter, she tucked it away in the box and sighed before turning her gaze back to me. "Maybe. You could always ask her. I'm sure your grandmother had reasons for keeping the relationship a secret. I just wish we could find out more."

I gestured to the box, shaking my head. "I've read every single one of these letters, and there are no clues whatsoever as to what happened between them."

The door opened, and a petite woman entered the room with a little girl in tow. The mother had bright red hair that cascaded down her back in wavy tendrils, while the little girl's was tightly coiled into Shirley Temple curls. Both had matching freckles sprinkled across their fair skin.

As they approached the desk, the mother's gaze was desperate. "Hi. I'm so sorry just to walk in, but my little girl is sick. Her throat hurts and she's not eating or drinking anything. I think she has strep. Is there any way you can squeeze us in to see the doctor?"

My mother smiled sweetly at the little girl and then focused back on the mother. "It's no problem at all. The doctor is with a patient right now, but it shouldn't be too long."

I placed a hand on my mom's shoulder. "No, let me take it. I'm here, so I might as well help out, right?" Without waiting for her reply, I turned to the mother and held out my hand. "I'm Dr. Everleigh Abbott."

She shook my hand and smiled. "Rosalee Whitaker."

There was a picture of my father on the wall, along with his credentials and I pointed at it. "This is my father's office, but I would love to see what's going on with . . ." I let the words trail off and shifted my attention to the little girl, lifting my brows in question.

Rosalee leaned down toward her daughter. "Tell her your name, honey."

The little girl swallowed and winced; I could tell she was in pain. "Emory," she whispered hoarsely.

"All right, Emory," I said softly, "I'll bring you back in a minute. Your mommy has to fill out some paperwork first, okay?"

Once my mom handed Rosalee the paperwork, she grabbed her daughter's hand, and they sat down.

"Thank you," my mom said to me. "I used to love it when you'd help us out. You fit in so well here."

There had been hints thrown at me for years from both my mom and dad. I knew they'd give anything to have me working with them and take over the practice.

"Don't get any ideas," I teased, smiling at her.

She held up her hands in defeat. "Okay, okay. Janie is in the back somewhere if you want her to help you."

I shook my head. "I got this. Do you still have a pair of extra scrubs in Dad's office?"

Her grin widened. "I do."

Rosalee was still filling out the paperwork, so I hurried down the hallway past the exam rooms to my father's office. The extra scrubs were in his closet, and I changed into them quickly. When I returned to the front, the paperwork had been completed.

"Emory," I called, beckoning her and her mother to follow me down the hall.

I led them to one of the exam rooms and shut the door behind us. Emory looked pale and tired when she climbed up onto the exam table. After going over Emory's medical history with her mother, I checked the little girl's vitals, and everything was normal except for a fever. Her throat, however, was bright red and her tonsils were swollen.

"I think you might be right," I said to Rosalee. "I'll swab little Emory's throat to make sure, but I believe she has strep."

Taking a sterile swab from the tray on the counter, I slowly tickled Emory's throat with it, trying my best not to trigger her gag reflex as her mother held her tiny hand in a comforting grip. When I was finished, Janie must have been waiting by the door because she almost instantly appeared with a pair of tongs and carefully placed the sample in a plastic container before rushing off to the lab.

"It won't take long for the results," I assured Rosalee.

Emory slid off the table and climbed into her mother's lap, instantly closing her eyes.

"Are you from around here?" I asked, even though I was almost positive they were tourists; it was easy to tell from the accents.

Rosalee shook her head. "We're from Boston. Oak Island is where we like to vacation."

My eyes widened. "Really? I live in Boston. I work at Massachusetts General Hospital."

Rosalee smiled. "Small world. I take it you're here visiting your family?"

I nodded. "For the summer."

It sounded so simple, but it was anything but that. I wasn't about to go into detail about losing my grandmother, reconnecting with a lost love, and deciding what to do with my grandmother's house.

Rosalee rubbed her hands soothingly over Emory's back as she started to doze off. "As much as I love Boston, I would choose this place over there any day. It's so beautiful here."

"Yes, it is," I agreed. "If there was a neurosurgeon job close by, I might consider moving back, but there's nothing down here. That's why I stayed in Boston after finishing college."

There were other reasons, too—Jensen being the main one—but with my skills, I needed to be in a big city.

A soft knock sounded on the door and Janie came in, holding a piece of paper with the test results. As predicted, Emory had strep. I wrote an antibiotic prescription and handed it to Rosalee so they could be on their way.

Still holding Emory in her arms, Rosalee walked with me to the front desk, and my mother checked her out. "Thank you for seeing Emory," Rosalee murmured.

I smiled. "I was happy to. Enjoy the rest of your vacation. Emory should start feeling better tomorrow once she has a full day of antibiotics in her system."

There were more people in the waiting room, and I could tell by the hopeful look on my mother's face that she wanted me to stay.

"Give me a chart," I said, holding out my hand and laughing.

My mother beamed and handed me a file. "We don't need the help, per se, but you're so good with kids. You're a natural when it comes to them. It seems to be all we have on the schedule today." Most of my surgical patients were adults, so I never saw many children.

"It's okay," I replied, "it feels good helping out. I'll be here if you need me again in the next two days. Nyla comes in after that and I plan on showing her around. But I'm sure she won't mind if I leave her to come here."

My mother waved me off. "Oh, no, sweetheart. You need to spend time with your friend since she's coming all the way down here." She moved closer, her gaze narrowed mischievously. "But . . . what I do want from you when you get the chance is to search your grandmother's room and see if you can find anything else. Maybe you could go see Georgia and talk to her. I'm curious to see if there's more."

Excitement bubbled in my chest. "I can do that." Seeing Georgia again sounded like a great idea. "It might take me some time searching through Grammy's room," I added. "The box hidden under the boards was stealthy."

My mother giggled. "That's my mom for you. She was a crafty woman."

That she was.

I'd searched through the room already, but I had a feeling I needed to go deeper. It was an adventure I looked forward to and one I knew Nyla would be ecstatic for.

17

EVERLEIGH

Three days had passed, and I'd barely seen Jensen. Most of my time was spent at the clinic with my parents. There was an influx of tourists coming in with various ailments, and I didn't want the office turning people away. However, when I got home each day, I could tell something new was done to the house. The siding had been pressure washed and a fresh coat of sealer was on the deck. Jensen had been by every day, and I was disappointed that I hadn't been able to see him. At the very least, he deserved a thank you for everything he's done for me.

I hoped I'd see him today. With Nyla coming in later this morning, I wasn't going to the clinic, and instead was staying at the house and getting it ready for her. I'd moved my clothes out of my bedroom and into my grandmother's room. It was going to be strange sleeping in her bed, but I felt comfort in having her things surrounding me. I kept wondering what secrets still lay hidden inside. Unfortunately, I hadn't had much time to search through her room with working at the clinic, but I *was* able to check all the floorboards, only to discover there was nothing else hidden underneath.

My phone beeped and I grabbed it off the bed to see a text from my mother.

Mom: Have you spoken to Georgia yet?

With being so busy, I'd totally forgotten to seek her out. I jerked my head toward my grandmother's alarm clock, and it was eighty-thirty. Georgia was an early riser, so I knew she'd be awake. I texted my mom back.

Me: Going to ride by her house now.

Jensen usually came over around nine o'clock, and I wanted to be back so I could see him. So, hurrying out of the bedroom, I grabbed my keys and got in my car. Georgia lived down Beach Drive, so it only took three minutes to get to her house.

When I arrived, she was locking up her door. I rolled my window down and hollered out to her. "Good morning, Georgia!"

She turned around and waved while slowly making her way down the stairs. "Hey, Everleigh. What are you doing here?" she asked with a bright smile that was framed by her short white hair. Her tanned skin seemed even darker in the early summer sunlight, making me suspect she spent most of her days outdoors.

"I came to see you," I told her. "Where you off to?"

She pointed toward the road. "I was going to walk to the antique store. I like looking at all the trinkets."

I beckoned her inside my car. "No need to walk. I'll take you."

Georgia beamed. "That's so sweet of you. I promise I won't be long in there."

I laughed. "I'm not worried about it. Get in."

The woman was eighty-five years old and still walking all across town. My grandmother used to be her sidekick. It broke my heart thinking of her walking by herself now. When Georgia got in, we headed on our way.

"How have you been?" I asked.

She shrugged. "As good as can be expected. I miss my partner in crime."

A burn settled behind my eyes. "I know how you feel."

She looked over at me. "What about you? You doing okay?"

"I am," I answered honestly. "I worked at the clinic for a couple of days and my best friend from Boston is set to arrive in a couple of hours."

Georgia smiled, her eyes twinkling. "And Jensen? How are things with him?"

A laugh escaped my lips. "Not bad. We're on speaking terms, at least. I'm hoping to see him today."

Georgia's grin widened. "Your grandmother always wanted you two together."

Yes, she did. I still didn't know what was going to happen between us, but after seeing all the work he'd done at the house, I couldn't push him away any longer. Truthfully, I was afraid of getting hurt, but the thought of leaving with things being resolved hurt even more. It was time I made a move; I was tired of being miserable.

"Speaking of my grandmother," I began, "do you know anything about her past relationships?"

Georgia's brows furrowed. "You mean with men?"

I nodded. "Did she ever talk to you about a guy she met before my grandfather came along?"

Georgia pursed her lips, and a look of concentration passed across her face. "The only man she ever talked of was Arthur, your grandfather."

I could see why my grandmother might not have wanted me or my mother to know of her past love, but why would she keep it from her best friend?

"Why are you asking about that?" Georgia asked.

Shaking my head, I focused back on the road. "No reason. I was just curious."

Georgia was my last hope for information. If my grandmother didn't confide in her, there definitely wasn't anyone else.

A few minutes later, we arrived at the antique store. It was an old, single-story building with a flowery sign above the door that said "The Piccolo Antique Store." Georgia and I got out of my car, and I opened the store door for her. While she looked around, picking up little trinkets and marveling over them, I followed along behind her.

"Hey, Everleigh," a voice called out.

I turned around to see Brenda Rothberg, the owner of the store. She was about seventy years old with long, white hair that was smoother than silk and a face that could pass for someone much younger. My grandmother was confident she'd had some plastic surgery done, but

Brenda always denied it. The last time I saw her was at the funeral.

"Hi, Brenda," I said, smiling at her.

She came up and hugged me, her grip firm. "How are you?"

I let her go and smiled. "Good. I brought Georgia so she could look around."

Brenda found Georgia across the way and sighed. "She used to come in here with your grandmother."

I nodded. "I know."

Her eyes brightened. "Have you decided what you're going to do with your grandmother's house? Last I heard, you still didn't know."

I shrugged. "I'm still thinking about it."

She squeezed my arm. "Okay. Let me know if you want to sell. People all over this town would jump at the chance to buy it. I wouldn't be surprised if it went into a bidding war."

I had no doubt. People had been trying to buy my grandmother's house for many years.

"I'll keep that in mind," I promised.

Sadly, I wasn't going to sell to the highest bidder; it wasn't about the money for me. Brenda started to walk away but then gasped and turned around.

"Oh, and another thing, and I hope this isn't insensitive, but if you decide to pass along your grandmother's bedroom set, I would love to buy it back. She purchased it from me thirty-five years ago, and I've had many people asking for furniture like that."

"Wow," I replied in disbelief. "I didn't realize it was in such high demand."

Brenda snorted. "Oh, yes, my dear. I think it's the hidden compartments that people find so intriguing."

My heart stopped and I stared at her, my mouth dropping in shock. "What? What do you mean, hidden compartments?"

Brenda's grin spread across her face. "Your grandmother loved that about it. I think it was the selling point for her. But also, the furniture is quite lovely."

It was another secret my grandmother had kept from me. Pulse racing, I was ready to get home.

"Do you remember where the secret compartments are on the furniture?" I asked. Even if she didn't, I was going to search around until I found them.

Brenda nodded excitedly. "Of course. They're in the big armoire, the one with the middle door and the line of drawers on either side. All you have to do is open that middle door and feel around toward the back." She moved her hands in the air as if she was doing it. "There are two secret compartments in that piece, one on both sides. You'll find a hole on either side; you only have to push a finger into them, and the hidden drawers will pop out."

My whole body thrummed with excitement. I was ready to see if something was hidden in those secret drawers.

"Thanks, Brenda. That's very interesting. I'll have to go home and check them out."

Brenda smiled again and said goodbye before walking over to a group of women who had just entered the store. Luckily, I didn't have to go searching for Georgia. She walked up with a sad expression on her face.

"I couldn't find anything I wanted to buy today."

"Are you ready for me to take you home?" I asked.

She nodded. "Please. Martin's probably ready for a walk now."

That was perfectly fine with me. We went out to my car, and I was thankful there weren't any police officers around when I pulled out onto the road. My foot hit the accelerator a little harder than necessary, anticipation surging through my veins like adrenaline.

18

EVERLEIGH

By the time I dropped Georgia off and returned home, Jensen had yet to show up. It was a little disappointing, but in a way, it was perfect. I didn't want anything keeping me from rushing into the house.

Racing up the stairs, I unlocked the back door and ran inside. Of course, it felt as if I was moving in slow motion. When I entered my grandmother's room, I stopped in front of the armoire, holding my breath. It had a unique design; vines were carved in such a way that I could see how they might be hiding some secret compartments.

I reached out and opened the middle door, which had two shelves inside where my grandmother kept her nightgowns. Brenda said there were two holes—one on each side—but I couldn't see them. My hands trembled with anticipation as I slid my arm inside and felt around for the hole on the left side. I held my breath and pushed my finger into it when I found it. The second I heard the drawer pop out, my heart skipped a beat. I was excited to see what was in it, but I also wanted the moment to last. It had been a long time since I'd felt such intrigue and curiousness.

I inhaled a big breath in anticipation and after letting it out, peeked into the drawer. There I found an unmarked brown envelope. I reached in and pulled it out, but it was sealed. It wasn't a thick envelope, but I could tell something was inside.

Gently, I slid my finger under the flap to break the seal. There were three sheets of paper inside, and I carefully slid them out, my pulse thumping in my ears when I noticed it was my grandmother's stationery.

A gasp escaped my lips when I read the contents on the rose-covered paper; it was my grandmother's perfume recipes. I was so afraid they were lost for good, but I had them right in my hands.

Tears filled my eyes. There were three recipes, the rose-scented one my grandmother always wore, the raspberry for my mother, and the honeysuckle for me. They were sacred . . . and something I would cherish for the rest of my life. I carefully put the recipes back in the envelope and into the hidden drawer. If that was where my grandmother wanted them, I was going to keep them there.

"What other secrets am I going to find, Grammy?" I called out, wishing she could answer me.

If Brenda never told me about the secret compartments, my grandmother's perfume recipes would never have been found. Disappointment flooded through me. It was unlike my grandmother to keep something like that hidden without telling *someone*. She never would've wanted a stranger to come across her perfume recipes. So there had to be something I was missing. But what?

Reaching into the armoire again, I felt around on the right side until I found the hole for the other hidden compartment. I pushed my finger into it and the drawer popped out. My curiosity was piqued, especially after finding the perfume recipes in the left-hand compartment. When I looked inside, I didn't see anything at first, and just as I went to close the compartment, I noticed something pushed into the corner; it was a silver-toned heart-shaped locket tarnished from age. I pulled it out and ran my finger over the design; it was similar to the locket my grandmother gave me for my sixteenth birthday. The silver heart was adorned with a black enamel background and silver floral scrollwork around a gold braid and hammered heart in the center. There was a clasp on the side that allowed you to open it.

What was I going to find inside? Was the locket from my grandfather, or was it from my grandmother's mysterious love?

I unsnapped the clasp and looked inside, only there was no picture. But there was an inscription . . . *Yours always.* T put that at the end of all his letters; it had to be from him. It was fascinating finding my grandmother's hidden gems, but what if I never found them all?

The locket needed to be polished, so I put it in my grandmother's jewelry box for later. Once it was put away, I grabbed my phone out of my back pocket and was about to call my mom to tell her what I'd found, but the sound of a hammer pounding on wood outside caught my attention.

When I looked out the window, Jensen was there replacing wooden boards on the walkway. My heart started to race as I rushed out to the back door, way past ready to talk to him. Of course, he was shirtless and showing off his tanned muscles while he worked.

I opened the door and a warm smile spread across his face when he looked up at me. I felt my stomach flip with excitement. It had been too long since we last talked; three days felt like an eternity.

"Hey," he called out, setting his hammer down. "I haven't seen you in a while."

Laughing, I walked down the stairs. "That's because my parents put me to work at the clinic." When I reached him, I smiled and leaned against the railing. "Actually, that's a lie. I wanted to work. It felt good to be there."

Jensen ran a hand through his disheveled hair and grinned. "Yeah, I heard you were there." He nodded toward the walkway. "Did you see what I've done?"

I looked at all the new wooden boards he'd replaced. "That's why I wanted to come out here," I said, turning back to him. "I wanted to say thank you."

His lips spread into a devilish smirk. "Is that all? There's not something else you want to say or do?"

There were plenty of things I wanted to do more than say. With not seeing him the past few days, I had to admit I missed him. Things were getting better between us, and I yearned for more. Although, I didn't want to admit that to him . . . at least, not yet. So many things were still up in the air. If only I could decide what to do with the house. My heart knew what it wanted, but I didn't know if it would be feasible.

Before I could say anything, a car door slammed out front. Jensen's gaze shifted to the driveway, and I let out a shrill of delight as I turned to look. I couldn't see Nyla, but I was expecting her.

"It's Nyla," I exclaimed happily, even though I was a little disappointed we got interrupted. "I'll be right back," I said to him.

He nodded and picked up his hammer. As I walked away, I could feel his eyes on me, and I loved it. When I turned the corner of the house, I saw Nyla standing by a blue sedan, fumbling with the handle of her suitcase. The wind blew her auburn hair all over her face and watching her try to move it away was way too much fun.

"Hey!" I shouted, making her jump. Her crystal blue eyes lit up when she saw me, and she pushed her suitcase to the side so she could run to me.

"I made it!" she exclaimed, throwing her arms around me. We both laughed and it felt amazing to have her here. Nyla let me go and when she gazed up at the house, her mouth dropped in awe. "This place is fantastic. Why would you ever leave it?"

I kept my voice low. "It wasn't easy."

And it sure wasn't going to be when I had to leave in August to go back to Boston.

The sound of a hammer hitting nails echoed through the air and Nyla gasped, her eyes transfixed toward the back of the house.

"Is that *him*?"

Rolling my eyes, I couldn't help but laugh. "Yes. Let's get your stuff inside, and then you can talk to him all you want."

I grabbed her suitcase while she picked up her flowery Vera Bradley bag. The second Jensen saw us walking up the stairs, he put the hammer down and started toward us.

"I'll get those," he offered.

I held up a hand as Nyla and I trudged up the stairs. "It's okay, I got it. We'll be out in a minute."

He went back to working on the walkway, and I could hear Nyla snickering behind me. Finally, we made it up to the back deck and I opened the door.

"What are you laughing at?"

Nyla walked past me into the house. She set her bag on the floor and peered out the door at Jensen, playfully fanning her face. "He is so hot. How are things between you two?"

I rolled her suitcase down the hall and into my bedroom and she followed me. "No progress, really. Every time we start to talk, or things get a little flirty, something interrupts us."

Nyla laughed. "And I bet that happened when I arrived, didn't it?"

Grinning, I turned to face her. "I love you and all, and seeing you is the best thing ever, but you honestly had bad timing today."

She held up her hands. "Hey, don't worry. I plan on giving you plenty of space. I'm rooting for you and Jensen. The last thing I want to do is come between your time with him." Her smile faded slightly. "I know you only have a few weeks."

I didn't want to think about that. I wanted to concentrate on the here and now. Once all her things were in the bedroom, I waved for her to come with me to my grandmother's room. I grabbed the box of letters and motioned for her to sit on the bed. She sat down and I handed it to her, her face filled with curiosity.

"I might need your help while you're here," I said as she opened the lid.

Nyla pulled out one of the letters and read it. "What is all of this?" she asked, brows furrowed with confusion.

"These," I stated, pointing toward the box, "are letters from my grandmother's secret lover. I found those underneath the floorboards here."

I tapped my foot on the floor in the exact spot I had discovered and watched Nyla's mouth drop open in shock.

"Seriously?"

"And that's not all," I said excitedly, walking over to the old jewelry box on the nightstand. I fetched the delicate heart-shaped locket from inside and let it dangle from my fingers in front of her. "I came across this just a few minutes ago, hidden in a secret compartment on the armoire."

I moved to the antique dresser and showed her how I got into the secret drawers, revealing my grandmother's perfume recipes. I knew Nyla would find it fascinating; she loved a good mystery.

She carefully took the locket from me and opened it. "'Yours always.'" She read the inscription and a laugh escaped her lips. "This is interesting." She gave me the locket and I put it back in the jewelry box. "Was your grandmother cheating?"

"No," I answered quickly, turning to face her. "The dates on the letters were all before she met my grandfather."

Nyla cocked her head to the side. "So, it's a mystery? Are you going to see if you can find out who this T guy is?"

I snorted. "I would love to, but I'm not having any luck. My mom wants me to keep searching the room.

She'll be surprised when I tell her I found the perfume recipes and the locket."

Nyla peered around the room, intrigue clear on her face. "I will be happy to help you search this place. I'm good at finding things."

Taking the box from her, I closed it and set it on the nightstand. "Perfect. Hopefully, we'll get to the bottom of it before returning to Boston." I held out my hands and when she took them, I pulled her off the bed. "Let me introduce you to Jensen, and then we can take a quick walk on the beach. Sound good?"

She beamed. "I'm ready."

JENSEN WAS HAMMERING AWAY on the walkway but stopped when we made it down to him. "Jensen, I'd like you to meet Nyla Clark. She's a good friend of mine and an ER doctor at my hospital."

He smiled and held out his hand. "It's nice to meet you, Nyla. Welcome to Oak Island."

Nyla shook his hand, grinning back at him. "Thanks. It's great meeting you, too. I like having a face to go with the name. I've heard so much about you."

Jensen smirked and cut his grayish-blue eyes at me. "Oh yeah? What did you hear?" he asked her, but still kept his focus on me.

Jokingly, I waved him off. "Just that you're annoying, as usual."

I smiled and he laughed, the sound warming my heart. "I'm working on that," he replied, giving me a wink.

Butterflies danced in my stomach, so I nudged Nyla

forward, hoping Jensen couldn't see how flustered he made me. "Nyla and I are walking to the pier. We'll be back in a few."

His eyes never left mine; there was so much intensity in them. "Have fun. I'll be right here."

A sense of comfort warmed my soul at hearing him say that. I liked knowing he was close by; it reminded me of old times when we were growing up. Luckily, Nyla didn't say anything until we got far enough down the walkway from Jensen to where he couldn't hear.

"You two grew up together, right?" she questioned.

My feet sunk into the sand, and I walked toward the water. "We were always together," I replied, looking over at her. "When I reflect on those times, it's almost like it was all a dream. We were so different back then."

Nyla smiled. "That's because you've grown up. Things happen and people change." Then, a hint of sadness took over her face. "I wish I kept in touch with some of my childhood friends. We all went our separate ways after high school. I was literally friendless until I met you."

I snorted. "That's because you work twenty-four seven."

She shrugged. "I had to do something to get over my divorce."

"And now?" I wondered. "With being here and taking a break, do you think you'll slow down?"

Her grin came back. "I think I should be asking *you* that question. You look absolutely radiant out here. It's like a light's flipped on inside of you." She hooked her arm with mine. "I really like it. It makes me want to find that kind of happiness. Whether it's being here in this place or finally being around Jensen, I think you need to hold onto whatever's making this change in you."

That was easier said than done. Being here in Oak Island made me happy, but my livelihood and career were in Boston. I couldn't just leave it. I kept my focus on the pier; we were almost there. The water lapped at my feet and sloshed up, soaking my legs.

"So, are you saying I should leave Boston?"

I could see Nyla glance over at me from the corner of my eye. "That is a question only you can answer, Everleigh. However, I will say that you don't even look like the same woman I last saw a few weeks ago." I turned to her, and she smiled. "I'm envious of you," she confessed in all seriousness. "I'm honestly thinking of changing things in *my* life. The first step was taking a vacation and coming down here. It's the best decision I've made in a long time." Her eyes watered. "I have you to thank for that. You're the one who lit the fire under my ass. I just know this summer is going to fly by, and then it's back to the craziness."

"When you say 'changing things'," I asked, "What exactly do you mean?"

Nyla averted her gaze and focused straight ahead. "I think I *do* want a slower pace of life, Everleigh. I've worked sixty-hour weeks ever since I became a doctor. I feel like I've missed out on so much. I mean, hell, I lost my husband over it." She sighed sadly. "I still love him and there are days I want to rip out my heart because I feel miserable. I know we can't leave everything to fate, but I do wonder if Miles *was* the true love of my life, and I was too busy to see what was right in front of me."

It sounded exactly like Jensen and me. Did fate bring

him back into my life? The world worked in mysterious ways, and I knew I would never fully understand it. Living life one day at a time was all I could do. I squeezed Nyla's arm, and she looked over at me.

"If Miles is the one you're supposed to be with, you'll find your way back to each other. If not, you'll find happiness again. Now that you're *here*," I said, flourishing my arm toward the ocean, "maybe things will be different. You can go out and meet people, actually have time to see what's around you."

Nyla beamed with excitement. "You know what, you're right. And who knows . . . I might just meet that special someone down here." The closer we got to the pier, the more people were around. Her gaze roamed over several men and she smiled. "Well, if I don't meet Mr. Right, it'd be nice to meet a Mr. Right Now. It's been a very long time, if you know what I mean."

She winked at me, and I snorted with amusement; it had been a couple of years since I'd been intimate with a man.

"Yes, I do."

We finally made it to the pier and were almost at the end, watching everyone fishing from the sides. One person caught a small shark and tossed it back, while others had coolers full of king mackerels, red drums, and many others.

As we got closer to the end of the pier, I noticed someone I recognized. She was sitting in a blue portable rocking chair and eating a chocolate cake pop. A man was close by her, casting a line into the water; it had to be her husband.

"Do you see someone you know?" Nyla asked.

I nodded toward Michelle. "That's Jensen's ex-fiancé, the one I thought was pregnant with his baby and married to him."

Nyla snickered. "Hey, I don't blame the guy for tricking you. It got you to admit your feelings."

I rolled my eyes. "But it also made me look stupid."

Nyla waved me off. "That's water under the bridge now."

Michelle turned her head toward us and was about to take a bite of her cake pop, but then her eyes widened at the sight of us. She waved and put her cake pop away before standing, her light purple sundress billowing in the wind.

Nyla and I walked over to her, and I smiled warmly. "Hey, Michelle," I greeted her.

She looked delighted to see us. "Hi, Everleigh."

I introduced her to Nyla and she, in turn, introduced us to her husband, Grady, who only nodded before returning his attention back to fishing. Michelle reached out and placed a hand on my arm.

"I'm sorry for the ruse Jensen played on you. It was my fault."

I narrowed my gaze as I tilted my head to the side. "*Your* fault? How's that?"

Michelle chewed her lip. "Well, after seeing you downtown, I called Jensen, but he was still at sea. When he returned my call, we got to talking and I kind of got the feeling that you believed me and him were still together." She glanced sheepishly at me. "I could be wrong, but I did sense a little jealousy when you noticed I was pregnant."

Nyla's head jerked my way, and I looked over at her.

"Okay, it's true," I admitted shamefully. "I was jealous." Then I turned back to Michelle. "I'm not proud of it."

Michelle giggled. "It's okay. Jensen's an amazing guy. It didn't work out because I knew he was still in love with you, and he knew it, too." Her friendly smile was genuine. "I just don't want any hard feelings between us."

I shook my head. "Never. I do hope to see you around more. I've been tempted to try those famous cake pops you raved about."

Michelle laughed and winked. "You and Nyla can always meet me at the bakery one day. We can have a girl's date."

Nyla nodded happily and I smiled. "We would love that."

She started to go back to her seat but then turned around. "I hope it works out between you and Jensen, Everleigh. It's not every day you find your soulmate." She smiled lovingly over at her husband. "I was lucky enough to find mine."

We said our goodbyes and Nyla and I headed back to the house. Jensen was still there, sweaty and working hard. Before we could get too close to him, Nyla leaned in close.

"Don't you think it's time you two stop the foolishness? Why don't you go out on a date already?" Of course, I wanted to, but I also didn't want to leave her when she just got into town.

"You just got here," I replied.

Nyla scoffed and shook her head. "Please. I have a whole summer of vacation time, Everleigh. I didn't come here to be up your butt twenty-four seven. I don't mind having some quiet time to myself."

Jensen spotted us and leaned against the railing, his grin growing wider the closer we got to him. My whole body trembled as nervousness set in. Goose bumps fanned out over my skin and my stomach fluttered.

"You ladies going back out, or are you done for the day?" he called out, setting his hammer down.

Nyla and I stopped in front of him, and she put her arm around my shoulders. "No, I'm going to relax with a strawberry mojito." She looked over at me. "Isn't there something you wanted to say to Jensen?" she added.

My heart thudded in my chest. Then, pursing my lips, I stared at her, knowing full well she was about to embarrass the hell out of me.

Nyla laughed and focused back on Jensen. "Are you busy tonight?"

He smirked at me and then shifted his attention to her. "No."

Nyla patted my shoulder. "Good. Neither is Everleigh. I think a date night would be perfect for you two."

Jensen chuckled and I huffed in mock annoyance, even though I was glad the ice had been broken. He moved closer to me and grinned.

"How about I pick you up at six?"

"Great," I answered casually. "But I'm picking what we do. And it's *not* going to involve drinking eggnog. There are going to be no repeats of the past."

Jensen's gaze flashed with remembrance, and I could feel the heat rise to my cheeks. As much as I *wanted* a repeat of that Christmas night, it was not what we needed. At least, not at this moment.

Jensen nodded, his lips pulling back devilishly. "That works for me. I'm almost done here, but I'll see you later."

Without another word, I turned on my heel and headed up the stairs to the back deck. I knew Nyla would have something to say the second we walked inside.

"No repeats of the past, huh? Are you talking about night of the infamous one-night stand?"

Groaning, I walked over to the bar stools by the kitchen counter and sat down. "We don't need to get drunk and stumble into bed together. That's not how this needs to start."

Nyla came up beside me. "By the way you were both staring at him at each other, the tension was about to choke me. If you two find yourselves alone, there's no doubt you won't be able to resist."

Sighing, I hung my head. "That's what I'm afraid of."

More hammering ensued outside, so I went to the glass door. Jensen finished with the last board and tossed his hammer into his tool bag.

"This week has been insane," I confessed. "I can't get him out of my mind."

Nyla giggled and joined me by the door. "Do what feels right, Everleigh. We only live once. I'd give anything to find someone who looks at me the way Jensen looks at you." She bumped me with her shoulder and nodded toward the kitchen. "Come on. You need to drink a mojito with me so it can loosen you up. Then, we're going to get you ready for this date."

She walked away and I followed her to the kitchen, sitting back down on the bar stool while she gathered all the ingredients for the strawberry mojitos. Was I ready for my date with Jensen? In a few short hours, I was about to find out.

19

JENSEN

After leaving Everleigh's, I returned home and showered before heading back to her house. I was dressed in a pair of khakis, a mint green polo shirt, and boots. When I arrived, Everleigh was standing on the stairs, her golden hair in a low ponytail with wisps blowing around her face. In her arms was a picnic basket, and she wore a light blue dress with a thin white sweater. She looked like an elegant summer breeze, and my heart raced in anticipation. I wanted her to be mine, but I told myself to be patient. What I hated was that time was not on our side. It was already mid-June, and she was planning to leave for Boston at the beginning of August. We needed to do things right this time, and I hoped and prayed I could do just that.

Grinning, I exited my car and nodded at the wicker basket. "A picnic, huh?"

Everleigh smiled at me and nodded. "Well, I thought about messing with you and asking you to take me to Boca in Sunset Harbor, but . . ."

Her smile widened and I chuckled. "I would've gladly taken you there," I said genuinely.

She shrugged casually. "I know, but eating a three-hundred-dollar meal isn't my style."

Boca was an expensive restaurant not far from Oak Island that specialized in Spanish, Mediterranean, and Moroccan-style tapas. It wasn't the type of food I preferred, but I would've taken her anywhere.

I opened the passenger side door for her and she hopped in. "Did you not have any of those arrogant doctor types up in Boston taking you out for pricey meals?" I joked.

Everleigh smirked with mischievousness in her eyes. "Lots of times," she said sarcastically before rolling her eyes and exhaling loudly. "I'm kidding, it wasn't a lot. But yeah, I went on several dates to high-profile restaurants, and it turned out it wasn't my thing. I like simple . . . I always have. So that's why you and I are going to have a picnic in the park. Then, after that, we'll get ice cream and walk around downtown Southport."

That brought a smile to my face. "Just like old times?"

She nodded. "Exactly. I was feeling nostalgic."

After shutting her door, I went to my side and set the basket in the back seat before getting behind the wheel. The evening air was a little humid, but riding around with the top off on the Bronco felt good.

"So, what are we eating?" I asked, glancing over at Everleigh.

She grinned and kept her gaze on the road. "You'll see. Nyla helped me get it all together."

We pulled up to the park a few minutes later and found the perfect spot near the water to have our picnic. I set the basket down on the ground and Everleigh opened it, shielding the contents from me. She reached in and pulled out a red and black plaid blanket, then spread it out on the ground.

"Sit," she commanded, giving me a smirk. "I hope you're hungry."

I did as she said and watched as she set everything out. There were two ham sandwiches, pasta salad, a cucumber salad with tomatoes and avocado, and freshly baked chocolate chip cookies.

"I'm impressed," I said, my stomach growling as I scanned the feast before me. I pointed at the pasta salad. "Is that your grandmother's recipe?"

Everleigh beamed. "Of course. She was the best."

That she was.

Everleigh handed me a plate from the basket, and I loaded it up with the pasta salad once she'd gotten her food. We ate in silence for a few moments, both of us lost in thought as we looked out to the deep blue expanse of the sea. The seagulls called out and the waves lapped gently against the shoreline. The tension between us was palpable—nearly electric—but it was a good feeling. We'd grown accustomed to picking on each other playfully, but now that playful banter was replaced with something deeper.

Everleigh turned her attention away from the ocean and studied my face intently. "Have you ever considered doing anything with your Ocean Science degree?" she asked, raising an eyebrow.

I swallowed the last bit of my ham sandwich and laughed softly. "Believe it or not, no one has actually asked me that before. People assume my family's boat chartering business is my life purpose." I pushed a hand through my hair and stared back at the water momentarily before continuing. "In reality, I use what I learned from college every time I'm out there. It helps me understand the sea better than most people would," I said, turning to meet her gaze again. "Some people might think all the money my family spent on college was pointless, but I don't regret it for a second. If McLean Charters goes under, I'll always have something to fall back on." My lips spread into a genuine, easy smile. "I could always get a job at one of the aquariums."

Everleigh clutched at her chest, her eyes gleaming with admiration. "Ah, I'd be so jealous. That would be such a fun job."

I chuckled and shook my head. "Are you saying my current job isn't fun?"

She rolled her eyes in mock exasperation, her gaze intent on mine. "No, of course not. I just know that what you do is tough work and takes a lot of effort to do well." Then, reaching over, she gripped my bicep affectionately, her touch gentle yet determined. "You have the muscles to prove it, too," she added playfully, referring to the tautness of my arm from hours spent reeling in fish each day.

I winked at her in response before taking another bite of my pasta salad. "Working at McLean Charters has its perks, but I'm finally taking a break from taking on so many jobs this summer. It feels like everyone else is taking some time off, too."

Everleigh nodded in agreement, her grin widening as she spoke. "I know, right? I'm still shocked Nyla has taken off so much time from work and that the hospital let her."

Taking the last spoonful of pasta salad, I set my plate down on the blanket beside us before looking up at her carefully.

"And she'll be staying with you for the entire time?" I asked cautiously, trying not to sound disappointed and failing miserably if the mischievous glint in Everleigh's eye was anything to go by.

She tried to hide her smile but couldn't help herself as she replied teasingly, "Are you worried that you won't see me?"

Shrugging nonchalantly, yet completely serious in my intent, I stared back into her emerald eyes. "Can you blame me?"

"You have nothing to worry about," she said, a broad smile on her face. "Nyla made it perfectly clear that she doesn't want to be 'up my butt twenty-four seven'. Those were her exact words."

A wave of relief surged through me, and I smiled in response. "Good to know."

She opened the plastic container of chocolate chip cookies and offered them to me. I took two, and Everleigh did the same. "Were you being serious when you said you wouldn't sell Hide Away by the Sea to me?"

She raised her eyebrows at me and grunted before shoving a cookie into her mouth, her eyes twinkling with amusement. "At the time, yes," she finally spoke around a mouthful. "You really pissed me off. But if I decide to sell, you'll be first in line."

The decision was still up in the air, so I couldn't tell yet whether this was good news or not. After finishing my cookies, I reached for a third one. Everleigh followed suit and we both laughed.

"After all these cookies, do you still want ice cream?"

She clutched her stomach as she swallowed her last bite. "No way," she groaned. "I think we need to walk around downtown a few times to burn off all these calories."

Once we were completely done eating, we quickly packed up the picnic basket and I carried it back to my Bronco. We slowly strolled down the busy downtown Southport streets, side by side. With it being summer, the area was alive with tourists; their laughter echoing off the brick buildings as they enjoyed their time in town. I couldn't imagine Boston having the same charm.

Lost in thought, I didn't notice Everleigh had stopped walking and was staring at me. "What are you thinking about?" she asked with a raised eyebrow.

As if on cue, a family walked past us with two young boys holding their melting ice cream cones tight in their little hands.

"Why do you stay in Boston? You could have gone anywhere after med school. Do you just like it up there?" I asked as we resumed our slow gait.

Growing up here on the Carolina coast, I couldn't fathom living away from home. Everleigh had this place in her blood. Even if I didn't have an ulterior motive, I knew she belonged here.

Everleigh released a heavy sigh but kept her attention straight ahead. "I do like Boston, but I'm not going to lie, it's nothing like home."

"If you were offered a job close by, would you take it?" My stomach clenched as I waited for her to answer.

She stopped mid-step and faced me, her expression sad. "A month ago, I would've said no. But after being here these past couple of weeks, I've realized how much I miss home."

"So, your answer is yes?" I asked.

She smiled. "Yes, I would accept a job around here if one was available." Her smile faded. "But that's the problem. Most of the jobs are in big cities. The closest large hospital around here is in Wilmington. They haven't had a position for someone like me in a long time."

That caught my interest. "Does that mean you've tried to look for one?"

She shrugged. "Not seriously. I think it was more curiosity than anything. I never liked being away from my family, especially my grandmother." Tears filled her eyes. "If I could go back and change things, I would've gotten a job closer to home. Thinking about it now, I should've just worked with my dad." She averted her gaze and started walking again, so I kept in step beside her. "There are so many what-ifs that I don't even know what I would've done if I had a chance to change things. We've made our choices, and this is where we ended up. I'm trying not to dwell on those what-ifs."

"I understand," I said softly. "I'm trying not to do the same."

Our walk took us to her father's medical practice and Everleigh's face brightened. It was a Sunday night, so no one was there. Her father was my doctor and still is to this day. However, the man was getting older and had to be close to retirement.

Everleigh sat down on the stairs right by the door and I did the same. "Has your dad mentioned when he's going to retire?" I questioned.

A single laugh escaped her lips before her expression

became somber. "I have no clue, but it's probably soon," she replied sadly.

"Will he sell it to someone?" I wondered.

She hung her head. "I keep hoping he'll work and live forever so I wouldn't have to see him sell. It breaks my heart to see it go to someone else."

Growing up, I always knew she wanted to be a doctor. Everyone thought she'd end up working with her father and one day, take over. So, it was a shock when she decided to go further into her medical career and become a neurosurgeon.

Everleigh's sadness was almost tangible in the air.

I held out my hand and smiled warmly. "Come on. It looks like it might rain soon, and I should probably get you home before it starts."

Her expression gradually brightened, and she chuckled. "Jensen, it's only nine o'clock!"

I quirked an eyebrow in surprise. "Are you saying you can still stay out until two in the morning like when we were carefree twenty-one-year-olds?"

She took my hand, sending a jolt of electricity up my arm from her touch. We walked hand in hand until we reached my Ford Bronco, where I opened the door for her.

"Have I really turned into this old woman who needs to be tucked in bed so early?" Everleigh asked me with a mischievous quirk of her mouth.

A wisp of her hair floated across her face, and I softly brushed it away and tucked it behind her ear; my heart hammered against my chest as I willed myself not to kiss her right then and there.

Taking a deep breath, I slowly smirked at her before

answering. "Yes, Everleigh—you are definitely an old lady now."

The corner of her mouth twitched upward as she playfully smacked my arm and laughed. "You're such an—"

With a chuckle, I shut the car door just as she finished the sentence. We listened to our favorite Jack Johnson songs on the way back to her house. It brought back so many memories of our past.

When we arrived, I grabbed the picnic basket from my back seat and followed Everleigh up the stairs to her back deck. Nyla was just inside, sitting on the couch, but when she saw us, she waved and disappeared down the hallway; I assumed it was to give us privacy.

Everleigh took the basket from me and set it down on the porch. "Thank you for tonight. I had a good time," she stated happily.

I nodded. "So did I."

I looked down at the walkway. "Your grandmother's to-do list is almost done," I said, focusing back on her. "Which means it doesn't give me an excuse to come back here."

Everleigh giggled and shook her head. "Are you saying I need to give you more things to do?"

I shrugged. "That or you can just say you'll see me again tomorrow."

She bit her lip and smiled. "I'm sure we can make that happen," she murmured, stepping closer to me. "I plan on taking Nyla around town tomorrow, but after that . . ." She let her words trail off as if giving me an open invitation.

"After that," I suggested, "would you be willing to let me choose what we do on the date?"

Her grin widened. "Sure. What do you have in mind?"

It was so easy to get lost in her hazel-green eyes. All I could think about was kissing her.

"It's a surprise. Can you be at my house around two?"

Moving closer to her, I brought my hands up to her face, gently holding her within my grasp. Her breath hitched and she lifted her chin, her lips only a breath away.

"Yes," she whispered. "I'll be there."

Without thinking, I pressed my lips to hers, her body melting into mine. Her lips were soft and warm, and I couldn't help but lose myself in the moment. Kissing her felt like I was home, that a life without her in it was no life at all. When we parted, I looked deep into her eyes, knowing she could see the longing in mine.

"I've missed you," I said, my voice filled with emotion.

She smiled, her eyes sparkling with a mix of happiness and desire. "I've missed you, too. I'm curious to see where this goes."

I kissed her again. "Me too. Goodnight, Everleigh."

She murmured goodnight to me and I left, feeling more determined than before. I hopped in my Bronco and looked up at the house; Everleigh was still on the back deck, watching me. She waved and I smiled.

One way or another, I wanted her to be mine. I didn't care how long it took or how hard it would be. I was up for the challenge. All I had to do was make her see that no distance between us could break apart what we had.

20

EVERLEIGH

I spent the morning showing Nyla my most beloved spots in Oak Island: the pier, the lighthouse, and downtown Southport where we visited my parents at their clinic. Then, to wrap up our day, we got manicures.

It was almost two o'clock now, and I was heading to Jensen's house. I had a feeling I knew what we were going to do; I'd wanted to go to this specific place for years but never took the time due to the memories it evoked.

When I parked, Jensen emerged from his house dressed in jeans and a form-fitting dark gray T-shirt. He walked over to me, gently placed his hand on my hip, and kissed me without a thought—it felt so natural.

"Did you have a good day with Nyla?" he asked, smelling like he'd just showered.

"I did," I answered before he took my hand and lead me to his Bronco where he opened the passenger's door for me. "Where are we going?" I inquired.

A knowing smirk spread across his face. "I think you

already know. If not, you'll figure it out in just a few minutes."

He got in the driver's seat, and we headed down the road. A few minutes later, we arrived at the ferry entrance where the boat was about to depart for Ft. Fisher.

"Any guesses?" Jensen asked, grinning mischievously.

Excitement rushed through me and I laughed. "We're going to the aquarium."

He reached over and grabbed my hand. "I know you love it there. Then, when we get back, I'm cooking you dinner."

I squeezed his hand and smiled, feeling my cheeks flush with desire and anticipation. As we boarded the ferry, I couldn't help but feel relieved that I let go of the past. So much time had been wasted, but now, Jensen was here . . . with me. We could do things differently this time. All I knew was I was happy and didn't want to let it go.

The ride to Ft. Fisher was short, and soon we were walking through the aquarium's cool and dimly lit halls. I could feel Jensen's eyes on me as I marveled at the colorful sea creatures swimming around us.

We made our way through the different exhibits, holding hands and taking our time to admire the beauty of the ocean. The aquarium had expanded over the years, and seeing all the new additions was nice.

Finally, we reached the main attraction, a massive tank filled with sharks of all sizes. I stood in awe as I watched them glide through the water, their powerful bodies moving with grace and ease.

Jensen stepped up behind me and wrapped his arms around my waist, resting his chin on my shoulder. "Beautiful, isn't it?" he whispered in my ear.

I nodded, feeling a shiver run down my spine as his warm breath tickled my neck. "Yes, it is," I replied, my voice barely above a whisper.

His touch was gentle, his body warm against mine. I turned in his arms and looked up at him, the desire in his eyes making my heart skip a beat. There was no one else around . . . it was just us. Without saying a word, he leaned down and pressed his lips to mine. We were lost in each other, and I melted into his kiss. But the spell was broken when his cell started to ring.

Groaning, Jensen broke away and reached into his back pocket for his phone. It was probably for the best, considering we weren't alone anymore. A young couple with three small kids ventured into the shark exhibit, their gazes lit with wonder at all the sharks. Jensen and I moved over to a corner so we wouldn't be in the way of the family.

"It's Seth," Jensen said, accepting the call. He put the phone to his ear and smiled. "Hey, brother. What's up?"

Seth was Jensen's best friend growing up besides me; we always hung out together. I had yet to see him since I've been back. I moved closer to Jensen and leaned against him while he talked to Seth. It just so happened that I could hear him through the phone.

"Trisha just had our little girl!" he shouted excitedly.

Gasping, I moved in front of Jensen, my body thrumming with delight. I was happy for Seth.

Jensen's face brightened and he chuckled. "Congratulations, Seth! I'm so happy for you and Trisha. What'd you name your daughter?"

I listened in and heard Seth tell Jensen they'd named her Amelia Marie Hampton; it was a beautiful name.

Still talking to Seth, Jensen reached for my hand and pulled me to his side. "Everleigh and I are at the aquarium, but we'll stop by the hospital and see you guys."

He lifted his brows at me and I nodded; I was perfectly fine with that. They said their goodbyes, and Jensen pocketed his phone.

"I'm so glad he didn't miss his baby being born."

I cupped his cheeks. "Me too. But I can't wait to see Seth. We have a lot of catching up to do. Plus, I'm excited to meet his wife."

Jensen grinned. "She's ecstatic about meeting you, too. She's heard a lot about you."

We started on our way toward the exit. "Uh-oh, is that good or bad?" I questioned.

Jensen's eyes twinkled playfully. "It's all good, I promise. But you should probably know it was Trisha's idea for me to strut around you with my shirt off."

I tilted my head back with a laugh, and it echoed throughout the exhibit. "That's too funny."

Jensen leaned in close, his voice by my ear. "It worked, didn't it?"

We made it to the exit and walked out into the blazing sun. "Yes, it did," I confessed, winking at him. But then I added sarcastically, "I couldn't help myself."

Once at his Bronco, he opened the door and caged me in. "You say that like you're playing, but I think you're being serious. You couldn't resist me, could you?"

I wrapped my arms around his neck and shrugged noncommittally. "You'll never know." I quickly kissed him on the cheek. "Now let's go. I'm ready to see the baby."

He made no attempt to move. Instead, he stared at me, his grayish-blue eyes regarding me seriously.

"Do you want kids, Everleigh?"

That was something I've wanted for a long time.

"I do," I admitted, feeling that desire grow within my chest. "I always have." Jensen's gaze bore into mine, and I could've sworn I saw a hint of relief flashing through his eyes. "What about you?" I asked. "Do you want a family of your own?"

A slow smile spread across his lips and he nodded. "I do. I'm just happy to know we're on the same page."

We got in his car and headed back to the ferry so it could take us back to Southport. Revealing my innermost desires to Jensen scared me, but I told myself I needed to be open; it was the only way to see if things could work between us. I wanted a family more than anything. But what was crazy was that in all the years I'd been in Boston and dated other men, I couldn't see myself starting a family with any of them. The only one was Jensen . . . it had always been him.

SEEING Seth and meeting his wife and baby girl warmed my heart. I held Amelia in my arms for over an hour as Seth and I caught up on everything that had happened in our lives over the past decade. My life wasn't as exciting as his with all his adventures out at sea with Jensen.

Trisha was a beautiful woman and sweet as could be. In a way, she reminded me of Nyla. If I stayed in Oak Island, I could see Trisha and me becoming good friends.

It was almost seven o'clock when we made it back to Jensen's house. My stomach had been growling nonstop for the past thirty minutes.

"Are you sure you don't want to just pick up something to eat?" I asked as we walked to his door.

Jensen smirked over at me. "We could, but I don't think you'll want to miss out on what I made."

My curiosity was piqued. "Oh yeah? What is it?"

He slid his key into the lock and opened the door. "It's one of your favorites. I prepped it this morning, and all I have to do is put it in the oven."

My stomach growled even more. "It's lasagna, isn't it?"

His grin widened. "Your grandmother's recipe. She gave me a whole box of handwritten ones."

Tears burned my eyes, but they were happy tears. "I have a box of them, too."

Jensen ushered me inside and I was hit with a wave of nostalgia at how familiar the house was. Everything was just as I remembered it from all those years ago when Jensen first bought it. The kitchen was small, but Jensen had it all updated with new stainless-steel appliances and granite countertops before he moved in. What I loved most about his house was the living room.

I moved past the kitchen to the wall of windows overlooking the sound. There was a giant oak tree in the middle of his backyard that was taller than any of the others around. And just past that was a long dock that went a little way out into the water, where a small white boat was tied up to the side.

"I love the sound of the waves crashing, but there's something so serene about being on this side of the island. The water almost looks like glass out there."

Jensen came up beside me. "I like it. You won't believe this, but I saw four manatees by my dock about two years ago. I haven't seen them since, though."

"Oh, wow," I gasped. Manatees have been known to travel in North Carolina, but seeing them was rare. "I wish I could've seen them."

Jensen smiled over at me. "Maybe you will one day." He left me to go into the kitchen, and I heard the oven beep as he turned it on. "We have about forty-five minutes until the lasagna's done. Do you want me to open a bottle of wine? I promise I'm not trying to get you drunk."

Laughing, I glanced at him over my shoulder and then turned to face him. "Wine sounds great."

I joined him in the kitchen and leaned against the counter while watching him open a bottle of Pinot Noir. He poured us both a glass and I took a sip, loving the hint of cherries, raspberries, and strawberries on my tongue. The oven beeped once it got to temperature, so Jensen grabbed the lasagna from the refrigerator and put it in to cook. When he faced me, his gaze shifted to something on the counter.

"I have something that needs to go home with you." I followed his line of sight to the glass dish sitting to the side. "That was your grandmother's."

Brows lifted, I turned my attention back to him. "And why do you have it?" I asked curiously.

He came over to me and set his wine glass down. "I doubt you know this, but she used to bake me her famous dark chocolate brownies every time I went out to sea." He moved his focus to the glass dish. "They would always be waiting for me along with a welcome home note."

Of course, my grandmother kept that a secret from me. But it didn't surprise me one bit; she loved Jensen. A giggle escaped my lips, and I wiped the tear away that started to fall down my cheek. I hadn't told Jensen about all the love letters I'd found.

Before I could mention it, he pulled out the drawer to his right and grabbed a folded piece of white paper. There was a sadness on his face when he handed it to me.

"This is the last one she wrote. It was written right before you and your grandmother were supposed to leave on your trip."

My stomach clenched and I forced myself to hold back the swarm of tears I knew wanted to fall. Taking in a deep calming breath, I took the note from him and opened it up. I was no longer holding back the tears when I read my grandmother's words.

Jensen,

Welcome home! I had to make your brownies a little early this time since I'll be gone on vacation when you get back. Hopefully, they'll still be good. If not, I'll make you more when Everleigh and I get home. Maybe it'll give you both a chance to talk? Eleven years of silence is just about ridiculous. I'm just sad you and Everleigh both inherited my stubbornness. Through hell or high water, I'm going to get you two in the same room again.

Love always,

Rachel

Closing my eyes, I held the note to my chest. "I can only imagine what she would've done to get us talking again."

I turned to Jensen and he wiped away my tears with his thumbs. "Knowing her, she would've locked us in a room together and thrown away the key."

That made me laugh. "I wouldn't put it past her." I handed him back the letter and he tucked it safely away in the drawer. "Speaking of keys, letters, and locks," I said, moving into the living room with my glass of wine.

I sat on the brown leather couch and Jensen watched me curiously. "What are you talking about?" he asked, coming to sit next to me.

I drank the rest of my wine and set my glass on the coffee table. "Hide Away by the Sea has many secrets within its walls," I stated plainly.

Jensen's eyes widened. "How so?"

"Well," I began, remembering how it hurt when my toe clipped the edge of the floorboard in my grandmother's room. "I found a box of old love letters from a man who wasn't my grandfather; they were dated a little while before she met him."

Jensen's mouth dropped. "Interesting. Do you know who that guy is?"

I shook my head. "All of his letters are marked with just the letter T. And that's not all," I said, moving closer to him. "There are secret compartments in the armoire in my grandmother's bedroom. I found her perfume recipes in one of the hidden drawers and a locket in the other. I think the necklace was from T. All that was engraved inside were the words 'yours always'. He signed off all his letters with those words."

Jensen shook his head and smiled, his eyes crinkling at

the corners. "Looks like we have a mystery on our hands. Do you think there's more in the house?"

I shrugged, rubbing my forehead in frustration. "No clue. I've been through every closet and drawer in the place. I even asked Georgia if she knew anything since she was close to my grandmother, but she had nothing to offer."

A gust of air escaped Jensen's lips as he ran a hand over his hair. "I don't know where else you could look for clues other than your house. At this point, it seems like a dead end."

I nodded slowly, sinking back into the couch with a sigh. "Sadly, we'll probably never know who her secret love was."

It was a secret my grandmother took to the grave, and the thought made me ache with sadness. She must have cared for T deeply if she had kept his letters safe for all these years.

JENSEN and I talked until the digital timer on the oven dinged. The intense aroma of garlic, oregano, and freshly grated cheese greeted us as we opened the oven. We carried our steaming plates outside to the patio, where we sat at a round glass table covered in a red checkered tablecloth. The chilled night air was surprisingly refreshing after the heat of the day, and while we ate, the crickets serenaded us.

Jensen gave me ideas on places to look in my grandmother's house for more clues. It was kind of a stretch to think she would hide something with the canned goods in the pantry, but there was no telling. This was my grandmother we were talking about. Anything was possible with her.

Once we had finished dinner, I helped Jensen clean up the kitchen. When I looked over at the microwave clock, I noticed it was nine o'clock.

"Uh-oh, it's getting close to my bedtime. I should probably go," I joked, placing my wine glass in the dishwasher.

Jensen chuckled and placed the last dirty plate inside. "You're not staying for dessert?" he said, turning to face me.

There was a desire-filled longing in his eyes that made my heart flutter. I didn't want to leave. Yesterday, I told him there wouldn't be a repeat of that Christmas night all those years ago, but who was I kidding? I wanted that connection with him, to feel his touch and allow myself to get close to someone. And it wasn't just anyone I wanted to be close to . . . it was him. It had always been him.

"What do you have for dessert?" I asked, my voice breathless.

Jensen stepped closer and his gaze seemed to search my face as he spoke. "Actually," he said, the warmth in his grayish-blue eyes growing brighter as he closed the distance between us. "I didn't make anything. I was just hoping you'd stay."

His lips were mere inches away now, and my chest felt heavy with anticipation. "For how long? An hour? Two?" I wondered nervously, not daring to look away from the mesmerizing depths of his gaze.

He shook his head, a subtle smirk appearing on his lips

as his breath brushed against my skin. "I was thinking all night."

My heart pounded in my chest and so many emotions swirled within me. Were we ready to take that step so soon? Jensen brought his hands up to my face, caressing both cheeks tenderly until our noses were nearly touching.

"Please, Everleigh," he pleaded softly, brushing his lips against mine in a gentle kiss. "I want you, and I know you want me, too. Haven't we waited long enough?"

I felt my resolve weaken as I placed my hands over his, our fingers locking together like two pieces of a puzzle. Yes, we had waited long enough—there was no doubt about that in my mind.

"Yes," I answered quietly. "We have."

With that, he deepened the kiss, his tongue exploring every corner of my mouth as his hands roamed over my body, igniting a fire within me that I hadn't felt since our first night together all those years ago. I moaned softly as he swept me up in his arms and carried me to the bedroom, never once breaking the kiss.

As he laid me down on the bed, I couldn't help but feel a mix of excitement and nervousness. He leaned over me, his lips brushing against my ear.

"Are you sure this is what you want? There's no going back."

"I don't want to go back," I whispered. "All I want is you."

21

EVERLEIGH

The thunderous sound of rain pelting against the roof jolted me awake from a dream so vivid I thought it was real. I didn't realize I had been crying until I felt the wetness on my pillow. It was the first time I'd dreamed of my grandmother since she passed. We were on the beach in Aruba, and she was dressed in the skimpy red bikini she had bought to embarrass me. Not a moment went by where there was silence between us. There was so much I had to tell her, and she was right there with me, happy and so full of life. We floated on rafts in the ocean and drank strawberry daiquiris adorned with little umbrellas. I wanted to believe it was her visiting me; that was how real it felt.

I sat up and noticed Jensen's side of the bed was cold. Luckily, I could hear him moving around the kitchen. I got out of bed and dressed quickly. When I reached for my phone on the nightstand, there was a text from Nyla.

Nyla: Good morning! I hope you had a great time with Hottie McHotpants. Not to rush you or anything, but I found something you're going to want to see.

My heart flip-flopped in my chest with excitement. Did she find something else my grandmother had hidden in the house?

Grinning to myself, I fired off a quick reply.

Me: Be there shortly!

Since I didn't have any toiletries other than a small floss container in my purse, I hurried into Jensen's bathroom and ran my fingers through my hair to get out all the knots. It still looked like a rat's nest when I finished.

Jensen was in the kitchen making breakfast, his was shirtless, and had on a pair of gray sweatpants that hung low on his hips. He glanced at me over his shoulder and smiled.

"The bacon is done, and I'm almost finished with the eggs."

There were two empty plates on the kitchen table and in the center of the table was a plate filled with bacon and another stacked high with pancakes. He even had two glasses of orange juice already poured.

I stared at it all in awe, my mouth gaping. "This is perfect."

Jensen smirked and turned back to the stove. "I know

it's early, but I figured you'd want to get back home to spend some time with Nyla."

He walked over to the table with the pan of scrambled eggs and spooned some into our plates. I sat down and grabbed a few pieces of bacon and two pancakes, soaking the pancakes in syrup.

Jensen chuckled and shook his head when he noticed my drenched plate. "Do you want some pancakes to go with your syrup?"

Rolling my eyes, I smiled and dug into my food. "What can I say? I love it. It's been a long time since I've had pancakes. Usually, I grab a protein bar and eat it on my way to work."

Jensen's smile faded. "Breakfast was always your favorite meal."

"I know," I replied sadly. "It's been nice being back here and finding joy in the things I used to love."

And still love, I wanted to say, but I kept that to myself.

"What are yours and Nyla's plans for the day?" he asked, stuffing a bite of eggs into his mouth. I didn't want to leave so early, but I was dying to see what she had found.

"I'm not sure, but she texted me and said she found something at the house. I assume it's another hidden gem my grandmother had stashed somewhere."

Jensen chuckled. "Rachel was a sneaky woman. This doesn't surprise me one bit."

"Me either," I agreed. "Honestly, I find it fascinating. It's like a treasure hunt, only there's mystery with a bit of intrigue involved."

His smile widened and he gave me a flirtatious wink.

"Maybe tonight you can tell me all about what you found?"

Electric excitement surged through my body at his invitation, and I cocked my head to the side with a smirk.

"Is that your way of saying you want to see me again?"

"Maybe," he replied, brightening even further. "Is that okay?"

My heart swelled and I smiled softly back at him. "Yes. I'm sure we can figure out something to do."

After we finished breakfast, I grabbed my purse and Jensen walked me to my car. He took both of my hands and stepped closer, his breath tickling my skin. I could smell the sweet scent of maple syrup on his lips.

I looked up at him with a raised eyebrow. "What are *you* going to do today?"

The corners of his mouth tugged up in a slow, teasing smile. "I was thinking of seeing Seth and Trisha at the hospital. There's something I want to talk to him about."

My brow furrowed as I tried to decipher the twinkle in his eye. "And what would that be?" I asked.

He chuckled softly and pressed a gentle kiss to my lips. "I might tell you later," he whispered against them before pulling away. "Right now, your friend is waiting for you. I'll see you later."

Taking a deep breath, I nodded and opened my car door. As I drove down the street, my heart beat faster and my foot grew heavier on the gas pedal. I was ready to see what Nyla had found.

When I pulled into the driveway and raced up the stairs to the back deck, Nyla was sitting in my grandmother's red rocking chair, her auburn hair piled on top of her head in a messy bun, and she was wearing a bathing suit underneath a white lacy cover-up.

She jumped up and grinned excitedly. "Good. You're here," she said, hurrying to the door. She opened it and waved for me to come with her. I shut the door behind me and followed her down the hall to the library.

"I don't know how or why, but I got curious and wanted to look at your grandmother's books."

Nyla and I stepped into the library, and my eyes darted to a book sitting on the desk—a beach romance novel titled *One Day* by Ellen Thomas. Its cover boasted bright colors with a couple standing on the shoreline. I set my purse down on the desk and Nyla gestured for me to open the book. Tucked between the pages was an old photo—slightly faded with bent edges. The quality wasn't perfect, but there was no mistaking the young blonde-haired woman in the picture. She beamed joyfully, her cheeks flushed, and soft laughter danced in her eyes. Beside her, a man with dark hair had his arm around her shoulders, and they were sitting on a bench surrounded by bushes and flowers with a canopy of Spanish moss above them. Unfortunately, the guy's face was blurry; I couldn't make out who he was.

Nyla glanced at me questioningly. "Is that your grandfather?"

I shook my head sadly, feeling a pang of grief for my granddad. "No, he had dirty blond hair. This has to be T."

Nyla reached for the photo, and I let her take it. "Do you think we should look through *all* of the books? If she hid a picture in one, there are hundreds of others she could've done the same with."

Taking a deep breath, I let it out slowly, raking my

gaze along the shelves. "Yes," I answered. "Let's do it today."

I hadn't thought to look through them all, but it was probably for the best. I was determined to find everything I could. The picture wasn't enough to identify who T was. Maybe he was still alive? If I could identify him, then I could find him. He was the only one with the answers to my grandmother's mysterious past.

Nyla started on one end of the bookshelves and I went to the other, grabbing one book at a time and flipping through it. I'd only gotten through three novels when my phone beeped with an incoming text. I went back to the desk and rummaged through my purse until I found it.

Jensen: Think you can meet me on the pier tonight at 7?

NYLA GLANCED over at me and smiled, clearly knowing it was Jensen. "Do you mind if I meet Jensen tonight?" I asked her.

Nyla snorted and continued to look through the books. "I already told you, I don't plan on being up your ass. I wish you knew how relaxing it was just to listen to the waves today." When she turned to me, there was nothing but a genuine look on her face. "Seriously, Everleigh. If you and Jensen can see each other every day, then do it. It's clear you two had an amazing night from all the glowing you're doing right now," she said, waving a hand at my body. "You better believe if I found someone like him, I wouldn't be letting go." She pointed at my phone. "Now text him back. One day, though, I'd love to hang out with him."

I nodded. "You got it."

Grinning, I texted him back.

Me: I'll be there.

22

JENSEN

As soon as Everleigh left, I stripped off my clothes and jumped into the shower. The hot water soothed me, and I lingered until it ran cold. Then, I dried off and pulled on a pair of shorts and an old T-shirt before heading to the hospital.

When I arrived, Trisha was asleep in the bed and Seth was slumped down in a chair beside her. Little Amelia was being monitored in the nursery so Trisha could rest. Once Seth found the energy to get up, we went down to the elevators and outside the building into the brisk air. His usually spiky hair lay flat against his head, and he stifled some yawns.

"It won't take long," I promised him with a smile. "I know you're exhausted."

We crossed a grassy courtyard with benches surrounding a bubbling fountain. Seth tiredly took a seat and gestured for me to join him, but I didn't want to sit.

He grinned up at me. "Now, what do you want to talk about?"

After last night with Everleigh, I felt a new rush of emotions within me. At first, I had wanted to take things slow, but each passing day reminded me just how much time we had wasted already. She needed to know everything, that I was all in, no matter what it cost me.

Taking a deep breath, I looked into Seth's eyes and sighed. "I want to tell Everleigh how I feel—no more hiding or holding back anything. But what if it scares her away?"

Seth waved away my doubts with a chuckle. "You're past all of that now, buddy. Just say what you mean and get it out there. You're not getting any younger; you need to make your move."

"Thanks," I laughed. "Great way to make me feel ancient."

Seth chuckled. "We're thirty-four, man. I'm right there with you. Most people we graduated with have been married for years with two or more kids already."

That was the truth. We both got started a little later in life, me more than anyone. It was hard to take that next step when the woman you wanted to be with lived almost a thousand miles away.

Smiling, I held out my hand to help Seth up. "Thanks for the advice. Everleigh's meeting me on the pier tonight. I'll tell her everything there."

Seth grasped my hand and groaned when I lifted him up. "You and Everleigh will make it work."

"Even with her living in Boston?" I replied.

Seth sighed as we started back toward the hospital entrance. "It won't be easy, but I have faith in you two."

"Thanks," I said, walking with him inside.

I made sure he made it back up to the room without

falling asleep somewhere. Once he was safely tucked back in his chair beside Trisha's bed, I closed the door and stopped by the nursery to see Amelia. I'd always wanted a family of my own; it was a future I feared would never happen for me—until now.

Since I still had several hours before meeting Everleigh at the pier, I decided to stop by the marina to check on my boat. The marina was busy with all sorts of activities going on. Groups of men were leaving on other vessels to take deep-sea fishing trips while others were heading out to enjoy a date out at sea. McLean Charters wasn't the only charter business in Oak Island; there were many others. What I truly appreciated about my seaside town was that all the men I worked around were genuine people. All of us stayed busy. There was no competition or people struggling for work; it was balanced.

My father used to tell me that all the time and said when I took over the business, I needed to look out for everyone. It had been that way for as long as I could remember.

I talked to other fishermen in passing and was about to get to my boat when someone called out my name.

"McLean!" I turned around to see Daniel Powell making his way toward me. We grew up together, but he was two years older than me. He owned Badfish Fishing Charters, which he started just three years ago.

"Hey, man," I said, holding out my hand.

Daniel shook it and smiled. "I haven't seen you around here the past few days," he said.

I chuckled. "Yeah, I know. I'm taking some time off. In a way, I don't know what to do with myself. I'm so used to being on the go all the time."

Daniel blew out a sigh. "Tell me about it. Business has been crazy here recently."

I slapped a hand on his shoulder, noticing he had more tattoos on his arm since the last time I saw him. "That's good. It makes me happy to see everyone thriving." His smile faded slightly, and it had me concerned. "Your business *is* doing okay, isn't it?" I asked.

Daniel's eyes widened. "Oh, yeah, definitely. I have more jobs booked than I could ever dream of."

"Then what's going on?" I questioned curiously.

Daniel sighed again. "My mother has to have surgery, and I want to be there for her. I was hoping you could take one of my jobs for me in the next few weeks. It'll be the first week of August."

That was also the week Everleigh was supposed to head back to Boston. "Is everything okay?" I asked him.

Daniel shrugged. "They found some cancerous spots on her lymph nodes, and they want to go in and take out as much as possible. With my dad being gone, I'm all she has."

I grabbed his shoulder reassuringly. There was a time when he'd helped me out when my dad went in for his first chemo treatment; I owed him.

I wanted to spend as much time with Everleigh during her last moments here, but I also couldn't let Dan down, not when he needed me.

"I'll do it," I promised. "Just send me all the details and we'll get it sorted."

I could feel the tension leave his shoulders. "Thank

you, Jensen. I appreciate you doing this for me." This time, he held out his hand and I shook it.

"We take care of each other out here."

Daniel smiled. "Yes, we do."

He turned on his heel and I climbed up on my boat. It was an 85' Gulf Craft with upper deck access that could hold up to seventy people throughout the vessel. I went below deck and grabbed a beer out of the refrigerator before heading back up top.

The marina was alive with movement—boats coming in and out at various speeds, tourists renting vessels despite having no experience maneuvering them. I sensed disaster lurking in the warm sea air, waiting to strike before the day's end. It just so happened that I had a front-row seat.

23

EVERLEIGH

The sand was still warm beneath my bare feet as I made my way down the beach toward the pier, and the sky was ablaze with orange and pink hues. A sliver of purple mingled in with the blue, enough to make me stop for a moment to take it all in. Mothers and fathers dotted the shoreline watching their kids play in the ocean, while sandcastles stood proudly here and there. It was like the beach was a work of art crafted by an unseen hand.

When I finally reached the pier, Jensen was there waiting for me at our favorite bench, gazing out at the horizon. His dark hair was perfectly coifed, and he had on a pair of khaki shorts and a Carolina blue button-down shirt that I knew would bring out the color in his eyes.

We'd spent countless hours on that bench over the years, ever since we were old enough to walk to it on our own. Memories flooded back, making me smile. Jensen turned around when he heard my footsteps approaching and grinned when he saw me.

"You look beautiful," he said, grabbing my hands.

I glanced down at my long, red and white floral maxi dress. "Thank you. I bought this dress to wear on vacation with Grammy."

"Maybe one day soon we can take a trip together," he said, his voice low. The thought sent a wave of excitement through my body.

"I think that would be great." And with that, we settled onto our bench to watch the sunset together.

"So, what did Nyla want you to see?" he asked. "I've been curious about it all day."

The picture was still fresh in my mind. "It was a photo of my grandmother and who I assume is T," I informed him. His eyes widened curiously. "Sadly, I couldn't make out his face; it was blurry," I added.

Jensen huffed and focused back on the sea. "That's unfortunate. Where did Nyla find the picture?"

I laughed. "Hidden inside one of the books in Grammy's library. Nyla and I went through every single one to see if we could find more, but there was nothing."

Jensen shook his head, his grin widening. "That doesn't surprise me. But why all the secrecy?"

I shrugged. "Well, obviously, her parents disapproved of the guy. It was clear they thought he was beneath her. Maybe her heart was just too broken to talk about him. I was the same way with you," I confessed. "I had so much regret leaving you that I didn't want anyone speaking about you in my presence; it just hurt to hear."

Jensen moved closer, his gaze flashing with sadness. "We're past that now."

"Thank goodness," I whispered softly. A slow breath escaped my lips as I focused on the darkening sky. "I'm surprised you didn't want to come to the house and walk with me over here," I began.

Jensen chuckled. "Believe me, I wanted to, but we have so many good memories here. I wanted to make some more in this exact spot and knew that if I had seen you earlier, I wouldn't have been able to wait." He turned his body to face me. "But first," he said, sighing heavily, "there's something I need to tell you."

My stomach clenched. "Uh-oh, is it bad?"

Jensen glanced down at our clasped hands. "You leave for Boston the first week of August, right?"

"Yes," I said, brows furrowed.

He sighed again and looked into my eyes. "Do you remember Daniel Powell? He was two years ahead of us in high school."

I nodded. "Of course. He played football."

Jensen nodded. "That's right. Well, he started up his own fishing charter business three years ago. He helped me out when my dad started chemo treatments. Now, he needs help so he can be with his mother while she has surgery. There's a job he needs me to do during that specific week."

A pang of disappointment settled in my gut, but I understood. I squeezed his hand reassuringly.

"It's okay," I said, hoping he could see the genuineness in my eyes. "We'll get our goodbyes out before you go."

Jensen cupped my cheek and leaned in to kiss me, his lips soft yet firm. "Speaking of goodbyes. I don't want there to be one."

I pulled away from him and smiled, knowing exactly what he meant. "Neither do I," I replied, smirking.

Relief passed across his face and he smiled, bringing

his other hand to my face. "I love you, Everleigh. I know you're going back to Boston, but I'm willing to do anything to make this work." His eyes searched mine. "Please tell me that's how you feel."

My eyes burned with unshed tears. "Everything you just said is pretty much what I was going to say as well." I placed my hands over his. "I love you, too, Jensen. And I don't want to ever stop loving you. Making this work is all I want."

Jensen pulled me into his arms, and it felt like all the weight of regret I'd harbored throughout the years had finally drifted away.

"What does all of this mean? Where do we go from here?" he asked, running his hands tenderly up and down my back.

Closing my eyes, I leaned into the crook of his neck and breathed him in. "I don't know. I say we take it one step at a time, day by day. All I know is that I want to be with you."

"Does this mean you're keeping your grandmother's house?" he asked, his voice sounding more hopeful than unsure.

I leaned back and turned my head so I could see his expression. His eyes were so full of emotion that it made my heart swell with a mix of excitement and calming contentment. Thankfully, I didn't need to make any immediate decisions about Hide Away by the Sea; I wanted to keep it for now.

A tear escaped down my cheek, and I wiped it away with a trembling hand. "I'm going to keep the house for now." Jensen's face lit up and it made me chuckle. "But it would be great if you could check on it every once in a while. I'm sure my parents will do the same. Until we figure out our future, I don't want to make any decisions on the house."

Jensen released a relieved sigh, his face lighting up with sheer joy. "I'll be happy to watch over it, Everleigh."

For the first time in my life, everything felt so right, like all the pieces of life were finally fitting together perfectly. Jensen and I were on the same path. He stood and helped me to my feet, his body so close to mine that his warmth surrounded me.

"We're going to make this work," he promised.

I nodded. "Yes, we will."

His lips closed over mine. "You're finally mine, and I'm going to hold on with everything I got."

"That's good," I whispered, "because I don't want you ever to let go."

24

JENSEN

SIX WEEKS LATER

"Thank you for having us over for dinner," Everleigh called out, waving at Seth and Trisha, who were standing by their front door. Amelia was swaddled in a blanket in Trisha's arms.

"Anytime," Trisha said, grinning wide. "We'll do it again when you come back into town. We might even have to let the guys watch the baby so we can have a girl's night with Nyla."

Over the past few weeks, Everleigh, Trisha, and Nyla had all gotten close. Seth focused on me and waved. "See ya bright and early, Captain!" he shouted.

It was already the first week of August; the summer had passed by way too fast. My crew and I were leaving first thing in the morning to take over Daniel's job. It was going to take us about five days to procure all the fish we needed. Sadly, Everleigh was scheduled to leave the day before I was supposed to get back.

Tonight was our last night together and I was determined to make the most of it. Everleigh and I hopped in my Bronco and headed back to my house. She reached into her purse and pulled out her phone, her brows furrowed with worry.

"What's wrong?" I asked, glancing back and forth from her to the road.

She kept her focus on her phone. "I'm just looking up this hurricane coming up through the Dominican."

I'd already been on top of that. The projected path was expected to veer off to the right, not even coming close to the coast. Reaching over, I took her phone and set it in the center console.

"Stop stressing. My guys and I will be fine, I promise. We might get a little bit of rough seas, but it's nothing I can't handle."

When we arrived at the house, we went inside and she followed me to the bedroom so I could pack some clothes. Everleigh sat on the bed and watched me, and I could see a bit of sadness in her eyes even though she tried to hide it. We'd spent the last six weeks together, and now we had to go to seeing each other every two weekends.

"How long do you think it'll take to find a job out this way?" I asked, stuffing a few T-shirts and shorts into my bag.

She'd been looking for weeks now, and the closest position was at UNC-Chapel Hill. But, unfortunately, that was almost three hours away, which wouldn't work for us; we needed something closer. But then again, three hours was better than thirteen, which was what it took to drive from Boston to here.

Everleigh sighed and laid back on the bed. "I don't know. I'm being patient, though. The job at Chapel Hill would be amazing, but I don't want to accept it and then something else opens up closer to home."

"But what if you miss the chance at Chapel Hill?" I replied.

With a heavy sigh, she lifted on her elbows to look at me. "That's the problem. I'm going to hold out just a little bit longer."

Once I was done packing, I laid down beside her and pulled her into my arms. "It's going to be rough until we get used to everything," I murmured, kissing the top of her head. "We'll just do what we've been planning on. You'll come visit me in two weeks, and then I'll head up to Boston two weeks after that."

Everleigh turned around in my arms, her eyes searching mine. "I've gotten so used to being with you every day. I'm not ready for tomorrow morning."

I shook my head. "Me either."

She trailed a finger down my neck to my chest. "I don't think I'll be able to sleep."

Curving one side of my mouth into a smirk, I teasingly looked down at her lips. "I know of ways to keep us awake."

The sound of her soft laughter filled the room as she leaned in closer to me. "Oh, is that so?"

Her eyes sparkled mischievously as she moved her hand to my thigh, her fingers trailing up and down, tormenting me. I shivered at her touch, and my mind began to race with all the possibilities that lay before us.

I leaned in closer, my lips grazing her ear. "Do you want me to show you?"

Her breath hitched in her throat, and I knew I had her. With a low growl, I kissed her lips passionately, my hands running through her hair. We broke apart and she looked up at me, her eyes smoldering with desire.

"Yes," she answered. "I want this night to last."

It wasn't long before our clothes were discarded on the floor, and we were lost in each other completely.

EVERLEIGH FELL asleep about an hour ago, and I didn't want to wake her to say goodbye. So instead, I kissed her gently and grabbed my bag off the floor. In a couple of weeks, I would see her again.

25

EVERLEIGH

The sky was an overcast sheet of steel gray, and the wind blew in salty gusts from the sea. Every day, Nyla and I sat on the back deck of my grandmother's beach house, watching distant whitecaps form as we talked about life and tried to soak up every second together. Our lives were different in Boston, always so busy and rushed. We never had much time to relax and spend time as just friends away from the hospital. I hadn't realized how much I needed someone like her—a best friend who kept no secrets from me, much like my grandmother had done before she passed away. Nyla seemed to fill that void. Well, I guess I couldn't really say my grandmother kept no secrets from me anymore, not with finding her hidden love letters that I had no clue about. Still, my grandmother had been my best friend for many years and knew me better than anyone.

"I'm going to miss our time out here," Nyla said softly, her gaze following the horizon.

Her red hair shone in the sunlight, her skin having taken on a sun-kissed glow since she arrived; it suited her perfectly and enhanced her freckles.

"Same," I replied with a smile. "This place sure is magical."

She laughed lightly in agreement. "That's for damn sure. I was hoping we'd find more hidden treasures of your grandmother's forbidden love."

I chuckled. "Me too. We searched high and low, but I have a feeling we haven't found everything. I'm sure I'll come across it at some point."

Nyla gave me a meaningful look. "And when you do, you better tell me. I've been so invested in that love story. I think I've read all the letters from T a gazillion times."

I huffed out a sigh. "I just wish I knew who he was. Guess I'll never know."

Silence filled the air as we watched the waves roll in. We leave for Boston tomorrow. Nyla was going to return her rental car and ride back with me in my car. Our summer was over, and it was time to go back to the real world. What was crazy was that my life was about to change significantly. It'd been three days since Jensen left for the sea and I missed him, but I had a few surprises up my sleeve. And it wasn't just him that would be impacted by my choices. Nyla had no clue, and neither did my parents, who I knew would be ecstatic.

Biting my lip, I peered over at Nyla, my stomach flip-flopping inside me. "Nyla, there's something I have to tell you."

Brows furrowed, she tore her gaze away from the sea to focus on me. Then, when all I did was smile, she gasped. "Oh my God, are you pregnant?"

Tilting my head back, I burst out laughing. "Seriously? It's a little too soon for that."

Nyla shrugged playfully. "Hey, I had to ask. I know you two have had a lot of fun the past few weeks."

My cheeks burned and I couldn't help but smile. Jensen and I have had the best time together. I never thought I could feel so connected and loved by someone. It made me sad to think I could've felt this way long ago if I hadn't run away from him. Then again, maybe we needed all this time apart to grow.

"Well," Nyla said, waving her hand impatiently, "what do you have to tell me?"

I took a deep breath before exhaling quickly, as my admission left my mouth. "I'm leaving Boston," I blurted out.

Nyla's mouth dropped and she chuckled. "I should've known. I could see it on your face when I arrived." She nodded out toward the ocean. "This place totally got to you."

Being in Oak Island and in my grandmother's home, which was now mine, had awoken something inside me. It was where I belonged.

"Does Jensen know?" Nyla asked excitedly.

I shook my head. "Not yet. My parents don't know either. So, it's going to be a surprise."

Nyla stood and leaned against the railing so she could face me. "So, you're moving back here? When?"

A chuckle escaped my lips. "When I come back in two weeks, I'll be here permanently." I spread my arms out wide. "I'm keeping the house." I stood and joined her, loving the feel of the wind whipping around me. "I don't have a job lined up yet, but I'm not stressing about it. I know I'll find one eventually. I'm still scheduled to do some surgeries up in Boston, so I'll just travel back and forth to those. And I plan on taking surgeries on a case-by-case basis until I find a job down here." I breathed in the salty sea air. "It won't be so bad leaving when I know I'm coming right back."

Nyla beamed with genuine happiness. "That's great, Everleigh. I think that's the second-best decision you've ever made."

"And what's the first?" I asked, laughing.

Her eyes twinkled. "Getting back with Jensen. You're a completely different person now." She gasped and held up her hands. "Don't get me wrong, I loved how you were in Boston, but here you're so full of life."

Tears burned my eyes. "I could say the same for you."

She nodded in agreement. "I think so, too." Her lips pulled up in a mischievous smirk, almost as if she was keeping something from me.

"Why do you look like that?" I questioned.

Nyla giggled and sighed wistfully. "Oh, you know, I just feel amazing right now. Since turning in my notice at the hospital, I've had a lot of time to think about my future."

"What?" I squealed, feeling a wave of excitement surge through me.

I flung my arms around her neck, and she laughed as we bounced around. If anyone needed a change of pace, it was her. I'd never seen her look as healthy as she did now. I let her go and grabbed her hands.

"What are you going to do? Are you going to stay in Boston?"

She shrugged. "Not sure. I just know I want a change."

We both had apartments in Boston, and her lease was about to come up for renewal, like mine. I knew exactly what she needed; I could feel the certainty of it in my blood.

Squeezing Nyla's hands, I looked right into her sea-blue eyes. "You're going to live here, Nyla. It's the right time and place; I can feel it." Nyla started to shake her head, but I clutched her hands harder. "Don't you say no to me," I snapped playfully. "You belong here just as much as I do. In just the span of six weeks, you've changed so much. I like what I see, and I know you have to be a million times happier."

Nyla smiled, her eyes misting with unshed tears. "I am. There is so much I love about this place."

"So, it's settled?" I asked, lifting my brows. "You're going to stay?"

Nyla's lips trembled with happiness. "Are you sure you wouldn't mind?"

Letting her hands go, I embraced her hard. "I would love nothing more."

My phone started to ring, so Nyla dropped her arms, and I grabbed my phone off the distressed wood coffee table Jensen had made for my grandmother; it was my mother calling.

"Hey, mom," I answered.

There was no good morning or greeting.

"Have you seen the news?" she asked, her voice hesitant.

Fear began to grip my chest, and I felt my heart stop beating for a split second. "No, why?"

She sighed heavily. "The hurricane took a sharp turn

to the west. It happened out of nowhere. It looks like it will hit in less than two days."

My only thought was of Jensen. He was out there at sea with a storm coming right at him.

"Oh my God, Mom,' I exclaimed in horror. "What about Jensen?"

"I'm sure his father is contacting him now through the radio. I highly doubt Jensen has cell reception," she said, trying to reassure me.

Nothing was going to assure me of Jensen's safety until I saw him safely on land. There was a look of terror on Nyla's face. I had no doubt she'd heard everything my mother said. Also, Nyla wasn't accustomed to hurricanes and was probably scared out of her mind.

"Do you need me and Nyla to help you and Dad prep the house?"

My mother sighed again. "No. You two stay there and make sure everything is good to go. I'm hoping the hurricane veers back off to the east like it was supposed to. There's still a chance it could do that."

That was good for us, but Jensen was already in the danger zone.

"You might want to check on your flight soon," she suggested. "It might get canceled if the storm hits."

I gazed out at the puffy, gray clouds coming in from the horizon. "I'm not going anywhere until Jensen gets back."

A small laugh echoed through the phone, but it sounded sad. "I figured you'd say that."

We hung up and I focused on Nyla, who had a determined look on her face.

"What do we need to do?" she asked, sounding as if she was ready for battle.

"You're not scared that a hurricane could be ripping through here in the next day or two?"

Nyla pursed her lips. "Everleigh, I'm an ER doctor. The kind of stuff I've seen would put a hurricane to shame. I'm ready for this." She rubbed her hands together. "Now, tell me what I need to do."

My grandmother had continuously updated her home to be hurricane-proof. So there wasn't much to do besides wait it out and pray that the surge didn't come up so far and wash everything away. I pointed at all the windows where all we had to do was secure the storm shutters.

"Start down on that end," I said, nodding toward the far windows. "Just lock the shutters in place and that's it."

Nyla nodded and hurried off while I tried calling Jensen's cell. It rang and rang and rang with no answer. Clutching my phone to my chest, I looked out at the darkening horizon. *Please let him be okay.*

26

JENSEN

I got the call, but it was too late; we couldn't outrun the storm. The hurricane was coming our way, and my boat wasn't going to be fast enough to make it home. The dark clouds moved in on us like a thick blanket, obscuring the sky and casting everything in a gloomy hue. I could feel the tension in the air, and the hairs on the back of my neck rose as the first raindrops started to fall.

The rain hit us with such force it felt like needles piercing my skin. What made it even more ominous was the impending night. All I wanted was to keep my crew safe, but I was about to put them through the most dangerous task they'd ever faced.

The waves rocked us back and forth, and I held on tight as flashes of lightning scattered across the sky. I felt the pressure in the air begin to build and a chill ran up my spine as I surveyed the raging seas around us. White-capped waves crashed against the sides of the boat, threatening to crush us. The wind bellowed like a wild beast, and I could see debris being thrown about in its fierce gusts.

My heart raced as I watched my men scurrying around the deck, desperately securing everything that wasn't tied down. Seth was struggling with a rope when I spotted him, his face strained and tense with fear.

Without hesitation, I made my way over and shouted over the wind, offering him a helping hand. But before I reached his side, another wave struck our ship, causing it to lurch violently. Seth lost his balance, and I lunged forward to grab him, but as fate would have it, the motion of the ship caused me to lose mine. I fell forward, my body slamming into the wooden deck. Pain shot through my whole body, and I let out a sharp cry. My vision blurred for a moment as stars danced in my eyes. I shook my head, trying to clear the dizziness, and looked around.

The storm had grown worse, the waves now towering above us. My ship was being tossed around like a toy in the hands of a child. I struggled to my feet, ignoring the pain in my head, and scanned the deck for Seth. But unfortunately, he was nowhere to be seen.

Panic gripped me as I realized he must have been thrown overboard. I made my way to the edge of the boat, fighting against the wind and rain. The waves were massive, and I knew spotting him in the dark waters would be nearly impossible. But then, out of the corner of my eye, I saw a flash of something being pulled behind the boat by a rope. I squinted, trying to see through the rain, trying to decipher what it was. When it became clear, fear crashed through me. It was Seth, his body being dragged behind the boat like a ragdoll. He struggled to keep his head above water, and I knew I had to act fast.

With all my strength, I lunged forward and grabbed the rope, trying to pull him back to safety. But the weight was too much for me to handle alone.

"Help me!" I screamed, hoping someone would hear me over the sound of the storm.

Suddenly, a pair of strong arms wrapped around me from behind, and I felt myself being lifted off the ground. It was Jack, one of my new guys. He had come to my aid, and together, we pulled Seth back onboard.

As soon as he was safe, I collapsed onto the deck, gasping for breath. But I didn't have much time to rest; the storm was nowhere close to being over. I started to get up, but Seth grabbed my arm, his expression full of terror.

"Jensen, your head! It's bleeding!"

There was so much rain pelting down on us that I thought the liquid pouring down the side of my head was rain water. However, when I touched the spot throbbing on my head, my fingers came back streaked in red. There was no time to worry about that. I was awake and I was alive. That was all that mattered. We needed to get back on land as soon as possible.

"Don't worry about me!" I shouted. "Let's just get home!"

Seth nodded and raced off while I hurried up to the top deck. The storm raged on, the raindrops lashing against my face with brutal force. My head pounded with every step I took, but I didn't let it stop me.

As I reached the top deck, the boat lurched through

the choppy waves, the hurricane showing no signs of dying down. Navigating through the storm was no easy feat, but I was determined to see it through.

One way or another, I was going to make it home.

27

EVERLEIGH

The wind howled outside, and the rain pounded against the windows as Nyla and I anxiously waited for news of Jensen and his crew. The hurricane had veered off to the right at the last moment, leaving us with nothing but rain and gale-force winds. In the wake of the storm, there was still no word on Jensen and where he and his men were.

We had all assumed they'd be able to outpace the storm, but now it seemed their fate had been left to the mercy of the elements. Nyla and I sat in tense silence, our eyes trained on the window as the hours dragged on. My gut warned me that the outcome wouldn't be good, but I refused to give in to the dread.

"He'll be okay, Everleigh," Nyla said soothingly.

A blast of thunder rumbled all around us and it felt as if the house shook. I kept watching the horizon even though I knew Jensen's boat wouldn't be coming back to the marina that way. Still, I couldn't tear my gaze away.

"Will it?" I whispered, on the verge of tears. "The last

time David had heard from him was before the hurricane even hit close to our coast."

Jensen's father was able to warn him and give him a head start so he could hopefully get ahead of the storm.

Nyla draped her arm over my shoulder, and we sat in silence as we watched the rain beat against the glass door. A few minutes later, it sounded as if a herd of elephants was coming up the side stairs of the house. Then suddenly, a figure in a long black coat and hood appeared at the door.

"Everleigh!" David shouted, as he banged on the glass.

Gasping, I jumped up and let him in, rain pooling onto the floor. He slid his hood back, his expression frantic as he looked from Nyla to me.

"Jensen's almost here. I'm going to the marina to help the guys secure the boat."

Heart racing, I ran to the kitchen counter to grab my keys. "I'm coming, too."

David hurried outside, but with him being sick and going through chemo, he didn't have the strength to help as much as I knew he wanted. Nyla ran to my side and followed us out into the blasting rain.

"I want to help!" she called out.

Jensen and the guys probably needed all the help they could get.

David waved for us to get in his truck. "Come on! I'll drive!"

I jumped in the front seat while Nyla climbed in the back. David had always had a lead foot, so I knew he'd get us there a lot faster than I could. Once he started the car, we were on our way.

"When did you hear from him?" I asked.

My pulse raced with impatience; I was ready to see Jensen.

David blew out a sigh. "Just a few minutes ago," he replied. "All the guys are okay."

Relief washed through me, and I grabbed my chest. "Thank God."

When we arrived, the McLean Charters boat was pulling into the slip at the marina, its sleek hull cutting through choppy waves. David shut off his car, and I rushed out into the rain with Nyla following close behind me. We saw the guys on board scurrying around, hands quickly and expertly adjusting ropes and coils as if their lives depended on it. I heard Seth shouting at us and saw him throw a rope toward us. We both grabbed it firmly, clinging to it like an anchor as we waited for someone to jump off and secure the boat.

Jensen was the last to hop off, his head dripping wet and face smeared with blood. I ran up to him and threw my arms around his neck.

"I was so worried about you. What happened?"

He hugged me tightly before replying, "I'm fine, Everleigh. I just hit my head."

When he pulled away from me, I cupped his cheeks in my hands, my gaze lingering on all the cuts and bruises covering him. Yet, despite everything that had happened, he still managed to smile teasingly at me.

"You're supposed to be in Boston."

Taking a deep breath, I shook my head. "I wasn't about to leave without knowing you were safe."

His expression softened then, fatigue showing in every line of his face. "Good. That means I have a little more time with you."

With the rain still pouring heavily down on us, I leaned forward and kissed him fiercely. I wanted to tell him my secret right then and there, that after two weeks, he was going to see me every day, but I held back until the time felt right.

Pulling away from him, I whispered back. "Yes, you do."

DAVID DROPPED Nyla off at my house while I drove Jensen's Bronco to take him home.

"I want to look at that bump on your head when we get to your house," I said, pursing my lips at Jensen.

He kept saying he was fine during the entire journey to his house, but head injuries weren't something to mess around with. He seemed okay, but that didn't mean he was okay.

We arrived at his place, and he got in the shower while I sorted through his drenched clothes to put them in the washer. Once that was done, I went back to the bedroom and sat on the bed while Jensen finished his shower.

"Was it crazy out there?" I called out.

Jensen scoffed. "It was scary as hell. I've been out in rough waters before, but this was different. I don't want to do it again."

Steam billowed out of the bathroom into the bedroom, and with it, the smell of Jensen's soap. I was so glad to have him back. Nyla and I were able to get a flight out tomorrow which meant I had this one night with him. I couldn't wait to tell him the good news.

Jensen stepped out of the shower, steam billowing

around him, obscuring his features. He grabbed a towel off the rack and wrapped it tightly around his waist before turning to me with a smirk, his eyes crinkling in amusement.

"Are you hungry?" I asked, getting to my feet.

Jensen's stomach growled in answer and we both laughed. "Do you mind fixing me a sandwich?"

His favorite had always been peanut butter with strawberry jelly. I gave him a quick peck and smiled. "Sure thing. Meet me in the kitchen as soon as you get dressed. There's something I've been dying to tell you." I knew I couldn't wait two more weeks to give him the good news.

Once in the kitchen, I grabbed the bread and peanut butter from the pantry and the jelly from the refrigerator. He liked a lot of peanut butter, so I spread a bunch on.

"What do you want to drink?" I hollered, raising my voice so he could hear me. But there was no answer except for a loud thud that reverberated through my body like an earthquake. "Jensen?" I shouted, fear gripping my heart. "Are you okay?"

No response came, so I raced down the hall toward his bedroom, only to find him lying unconscious on the floor with blood trickling out of his left ear. I gasped as I knelt beside him, pressing my fingers to his neck to check for a pulse. It was faint but steady.

Relief washed over me, knowing he was still alive, but my mind raced with the fear of the extent of his injuries. He'd hit his head on the boat and with blood coming out of his ear, I knew it was serious. Out of all my years as a neurosurgeon and seeing numerous head trauma cases, it terrified me. Not everyone could be saved.

Quickly, I grabbed my phone and dialed 911, trying to

keep my voice steady as I explained the situation to the operator. Then, after giving them the address, I hung up and focused on Jensen, trying to assess what kind of head injury he'd sustained.

Tears streamed down my face as I waited for the ambulance to arrive, whispering words of love and encouragement to Jensen, hoping he could hear me. When the paramedics finally arrived, they rushed him to the hospital, and I followed close behind in the Bronco.

The next few hours were a blur of waiting rooms, doctors, and tests. David and Martha were in the waiting room with me, along with my parents, Nyla, and Seth. It killed me not knowing what was happening, especially since I was a doctor and knew what to look for. I wanted to see the scans and assess the situation for myself. But instead, I stood in agonizing silence until finally, the doctor walked in, wearing his white lab coat and green scrubs underneath. He had an unreadable expression on his face—a look I had perfected over years of delivering bad news. From what I'd heard, his name was Dr. Andres Gamboa, and he was one of the top doctors in his class.

"The good news is that Jensen is stable. The bad news is that he has a severe concussion. We also found a blood clot in his brain," Dr. Gamboa said in a monotone voice. "We need to perform surgery as soon as possible to remove the clot and relieve the pressure it's causing."

My heart ached as I listened to the words, trying to control my emotions. I was a professional, after all, and had seen countless patients in this condition. But this was different. This was Jensen, the man I loved more than anything.

The others in the room were crying now, but I couldn't. I had to stay strong for Jensen.

"We have the best neurosurgeon available to perform the surgery. She'll be here as soon as possible," the doctor continued. "We'll do everything we can to save him."

"No," David exclaimed, the whole room turning to look at him.

The doctor's mouth dropped, and he looked confused. "Mr. McLean, I don't understand."

Holding my breath, I knew what he was going to say before the words left his mouth. He nodded over at me, his eyes pleading and sad. "There's no need to wait for anyone. Everleigh is the best damn neurosurgeon I know of. If anyone can save my son, it's her."

My mother gasped and shook her head. "David, that's a lot of pressure to put on her. What if something goes wrong? She'll never forgive herself."

She turned to me, tears staining her cheeks. Martha collapsed into David's arms, sobbing as he held her tight, his desperate gaze still on mine. So many emotions were warring inside of me, but he was right. I didn't trust anyone else to perform the surgery, but I could lose the man I loved if I did something wrong. It was a lot of pressure.

The doctor walked up to me and shifted his eyes to the corner of the room. We moved away from everyone, and he lowered his voice. "I didn't want to assume you'd be up for the surgery, Dr. Abbott. I know this is personal for you. That's why I had contacted the other neurosurgeon to come in."

I glanced over at everyone else, watching us intently. "It's okay," I said in a low voice. "We don't have time to waste." I met his brown gaze and blew out a breath. "I'll do it."

Dr. Gamboa nodded and smiled sadly. "Let's get you ready."

He left the waiting room, and Martha flung her arms around my neck. "Thank you, Everleigh," she cried.

She passed me over to David, who embraced me even harder. "We trust you," he whispered.

Once he let me go, my parents were waiting for their turn. My mother cupped my cheeks, her gaze searching mine. "Are you sure you want to do this?"

I glanced back and forth from her to my dad. "Yes. I have to."

They let me go and before I could walk out the door, Nyla grabbed my hand and squeezed. "You've got this, Everleigh." Her words of encouragement warmed my heart.

Jensen needed me and I needed him. I couldn't fail.

28

EVERLEIGH

The surgery had lasted two hours, but it felt like an eternity. I had to make every move with deliberate and careful precision, ensuring that the clot had been removed and the bleeding had stopped. But now, the hard part was yet to come: the wait. In that time of uncertainty, we would learn whether Jensen had suffered any brain damage due to the operation or the trauma itself.

The sound of the heart monitor filled the room, and I watched as his chest rose and fell with each breath. It was a comforting sound, a reminder that he was still alive. But it was also a reminder of how fragile life was. One moment you could be living your life and the next, everything could change.

A soft knock sounded on the door and David and Martha walked in, carrying a large basket of goodies. Martha set it down on the rolling table and started crying as she approached me.

"You are such a blessing, sweetheart. I don't know how we'll ever be able to thank you."

I was exhausted, so I leaned into her embrace. "Don't thank me until he wakes up," I whispered sadly. "We're not in the clear yet."

She let me go and went back to the basket, pulling out various meals and snacks. "Everyone on our street made you food. There are pinwheel sandwiches, little quiches, and Georgia even made some mini pecan pies for you."

My stomach growled, but I was too tired even to eat. However, it warmed my heart to see how supportive our neighbors were.

"It all sounds amazing," I said, focusing back on Jensen.

His face was pale, and he was so still. All I wanted was for him to wake up. David clasped my shoulder, his voice soothing.

"Why don't you go home and take a break? Martha and I will be here when you get back."

I shook my head. "I want to be here when he wakes up."

Martha grabbed my hand and squeezed. "He knows you're here, Everleigh. And you know how upset he'll be when he wakes up and sees you haven't been taking care of yourself."

At this point, I didn't care if he got upset over me being by his side. I didn't want to leave, but I couldn't deny David and Martha alone time with their son. He was just as important to them as he was to me.

"Okay," I gave in, taking one last look at Jensen. "I'm going to run by my house, and then head to Jensen's to grab him some things. I'll be right back."

Martha nudged me toward the door and grabbed a

container of pinwheel sandwiches, thrusting them in my hands. "Make sure you eat. You're no good to Jensen if you're laid out on the floor from hunger and exhaustion."

I gave her a reassuring smile. "Yes, ma'am. I promise I'll eat."

It killed me to leave the hospital, but I forced myself to get into Jensen's Bronco and drive away. The sun had started to peek through the clouds; it was the calm after the storm. Nature had a way of being brutal, and I could only imagine what it was like for Jensen to experience it with the unforgiving sea.

My stomach started to growl, so I opened the container of pinwheel sandwiches; they were gone by the time I got to my house. When I walked inside, Nyla was sweeping the kitchen floor and I saw her suitcase in the corner. Her eyes lit up when she saw me, and she tossed the broom to the side.

"Hey," she shouted excitedly, rushing over. I hugged her hard and she let me go, her gaze searching mine. "How's Jensen?"

I shrugged. "I don't know. I'm hoping he'll wake up soon. I'm just here to grab some of my things and then I'll head over to his place to get him some clothes."

Nyla nodded. "I understand. I was straightening up the house before leaving to catch my flight. I have to go in a few minutes."

"I'm sorry you have to go back by yourself."

She waved me off. "Don't even worry about that. The sooner I get back and handle my affairs, the faster I can leave. I plan on being here permanently in two to three weeks."

The thought of that filled me with joy. "I can't wait to have you here."

Her brows furrowed. "What about you? When do you think you'll head back to Boston?" It all depended on Jensen; he was my main priority.

"I'm not sure," I replied truthfully. The lease on my apartment would run out in three months, so I had plenty of time to get my stuff out. The only problem was my work schedule. "I made some calls this morning so my surgeries could either get rescheduled or they can find another surgeon," I explained.

Nyla sighed. "I know that has to be hard on you. You love taking care of your patients."

I nodded. "I do, but I'm needed here. When Jensen is on the mend, I'll get back to work. I can't sacrifice my personal life anymore."

Nyla smiled sadly. "I'm just glad we both figured out our priorities before it was too late."

"Me too," I agreed.

If we'd continued to work nonstop, we would've found ourselves close to retiring without having anyone to spend the remainder of our lives with.

Nyla glanced around the house and smiled. "I know I'm coming right back, but I'm going to miss this place." She hugged me one more time and walked over to her suitcase. "I should probably get going. Don't want to miss my flight."

"Do you want me to walk you out?" I asked her.

She shook her head. "I got it. I'll see you in a couple of weeks, okay? And be sure to give Jensen a hug for me."

My eyes burned. "I will."

Once she was gone, I packed some clothes into my

small overnight bag along with my toiletries. My grandmother's favorite pirate romance book was on the nightstand, so I snatched it up along with the wooden box full of the love letters from T. With Jensen's recovery, I was going to have a lot of time on my hands. What better way than to spend the downtime immersing myself in a mysterious love story, even though it ended in heartbreak.

After packing everything, I locked the house and hurried to Jensen's. There were bundles of flowers on his porch when I arrived, and it took me a few minutes to get them all inside. I couldn't wait to see Jensen's face when he came home to see his house decorated in every color under the sun. Surprisingly, someone had come in and cleaned. I thought I'd still see the peanut butter and jelly sandwich I'd left on the counter and Jensen's dirty clothes by the laundry room. Instead, his clothes were washed and neatly folded on the kitchen table, and there were freshly made casseroles in the refrigerator.

I went back to his bedroom and found a duffel bag in his closet. If everything went according to plan, Jensen would only have to stay in the hospital for two to three days. I packed him some T-shirts, shorts and boxers, his toothbrush, and toothpaste. The only thing missing was socks. I pulled out his sock drawer and reached inside to grab a few pairs, but then I felt something odd. After pushing the socks aside, there in the back was a small black box, one that would fit a ring.

"Oh my God," I breathed, my heart racing out of control. I pulled it out and stared at it, my fingers itching to open the lid. "No," I scolded myself, putting it back.

If it was an engagement ring, I didn't want to see it without Jensen. Quickly, I grabbed some socks and shoved them into Jensen's bag. I had to get out of there before I snuck a peek.

Excitement bubbled in my chest as I went out to Jensen's car and headed back to the hospital. Over the past few weeks, Jensen and I had talked about marriage, and I knew it would happen one day.

If it was an engagement ring in his drawer, that meant the next step of my life was coming up fast. All I needed was for Jensen to be okay so we could take that path together; I was ready for it.

JENSEN STILL HADN'T awoken by the time I returned to the hospital. His vitals were excellent, which was a good sign. David and Martha stayed for a few minutes longer, and Martha told me she was the one who'd cleaned up Jensen's house. She wanted it to be perfect for him when he got home.

Once they walked out the door, the only sound came from the beeping of the machines hooked up to Jensen. The sun beamed in through the window and it made me smile; it was cheery and bright. That was the atmosphere Jensen needed.

I sat down in the recliner beside Jensen's bed and watched him sleep for a few minutes before pulling out the box of love letters from my bag. I'd read every single one.

Carefully, I stacked them into a pile and pulled them out, setting them on my lap so I could reread them. My phone started to ring and I gasped, the sound so loud it echoed through the room. It was disappointing that

Jensen didn't stir slightly, but I had to stop the ringing before it woke up every patient on the floor. Unfortunately, my phone was in my purse across the room.

I quickly jumped up and stumbled over my feet, knocking the box and the letters to the floor.

"Dammit," I hissed, seeing the carnage. The letters were scattered everywhere, and the box looked as if it'd been broken. Frustration coursed through me, and I huffed as I fished my phone out of my purse. The words that flashed across my screen said "Potential Spam". I turned off the ringer and ignored the call.

When I turned back to the floor, my heart hurt at the sight before me. Kneeling on the floor, I scooped up all the letters and set them on the bed with Jensen while I inspected the box. The hinges were still intact, and the lid opened and closed normally. However, there was something broken inside. The wood had cracked on the bottom of the box, but as I inspected it further, I found it was thinner than the outside; it was like a thin piece of plywood placed as a barrier. When I touched it, it lifted to reveal a piece of paper beneath. My heart stopped and the breath caught in my lungs. Was it seriously another secret compartment?

I lifted one side of the broken wood and pulled it out of the box. The paper underneath was brown with age, and I could see something written on the other side. I turned it around and there were three sets of numbers: 34.214924 and -77.828454, and 24 9 12. The first two were a set of coordinates, but I had no clue what the third set of numbers could be.

Curiosity got the best of me, so I looked up the

latitude and longitude on my phone, and it turned out to be a spot inside Airlie Gardens in Wilmington. There were so many questions running through my mind. Why was there a hidden note with coordinates to Airlie Gardens?

My mom and grandmother had taken me there many times when I was a little girl. Jensen and I had even gone with our friends in high school.

Looking at the map, the coordinates pinpointed a specific place in the gardens; it had to be a clue to something. It was one of the first places I wanted to go when Jensen got better.

I placed the paper back in its secret hiding spot and covered it with the broken wood before setting all the letters inside. With everything I'd found over the past few weeks, it was utterly mind-boggling.

After putting the box on the floor, I reached for Jensen's hand and held it to my cheek. His skin was warm, and I kept hoping he'd squeeze my hand, but he didn't. Instead, I stared at him for what had to be an hour, waiting to see his eyes flutter or catch a hint of movement in his body.

"I have so much to tell you when you wake up," I said, whispering the words. Sheepishly, I bit my lip. "And I also have a confession to make." I lowered his hand to the bed and kept hold of it. "I promise I wasn't snooping," I confessed, "but I found something in your sock drawer. Did I look at it? No, and it killed me not to. What woman wouldn't want to peek inside a box that was the perfect size for a ring? Not to mention, I've spent the past few years thinking it wasn't even possible that I'd ever get the chance to be married." Shaking my head, I laughed. "I'm seriously jumping to conclusions, aren't I? It's probably earrings or something like that." I moved closer to the bed, reaching out to run a hand gently through his hair. "But if it's an engagement ring waiting for me, I hope you don't wait forever and a day to ask me to marry you." I laughed again. "Not that I want to rush you, but I'm dying to take that next step." Closing my eyes, I rested my head on our clasped hands. "I don't want to waste any more time."

"Then we won't." His voice cut through the silence and I gasped, jerking my head up to look at him. Jensen was awake, his grayish-blue eyes full of love. A wave of joyous relief washed through me and my heart soared.

Letting his hand go, I brought my face to his, holding him tight as I pressed my lips to his. "You're awake," I cried.

His arms encircled me and he chuckled. "I am."

I kissed him over and over, and then I pulled back so I could look at him. "How long were you awake?" I asked, watching his grin grow wider.

He shrugged and gave me a wink. "Long enough." His gaze searched mine. "I know this isn't what I had in mind as far as a proposal goes, but you were right. We've wasted too much time." His eyes began to water and seeing that made more tears fall down my cheeks. "I was going to take you out on the boat and ask you to marry me at sunset," he admitted. "I wanted it to be perfect."

I shook my head. "Right now is perfect."

Jensen reached for my hands and brought them to his lips, kissing each one. "You said you didn't want me to wait forever and a day to ask you and believe me, I don't want to. You're not the only one ready to take that next step." He took a deep breath and let it out slowly. "Will you marry me, Everleigh? I know I don't have the ring with me, but I'll put it on you as soon as we get out of here. That way, everyone will know you're mine."

Tears welled in my eyes, and a smile spread across my face. "Everyone already knows I'm yours."

Jensen smirked. "So, is that a yes?"

I nodded so fast it made me dizzy. "Yes!" I exclaimed happily. "When do you want to do it?"

He chuckled. "As soon as you want. Although, I figured you'd want to wait until you find a job and move back here for good."

"Well," I said, climbing onto the bed beside him. "I was going to surprise you in a couple of weeks, but I'm pretty much here for good. I have a few surgeries I need to fly up to Boston for, and I just need to move my things out of the apartment, but other than that, you have me all to yourself."

Jensen wrapped an arm around my waist, pulling me in closer. "You know, I had a feeling you were keeping something from me," he said, laughing.

I rested my head on his chest, listening to the sound of his heartbeat. "I'm so glad you're okay."

He ran his fingers soothingly down my arm. "I'm alive because of you, Everleigh. I know you're the one who saved me."

"How?" I asked, whispering the words.

"Because I heard your voice," he confessed.

My heart stopped and I held my breath. "What did I say?"

The whole time during the surgery, I focused on the task at hand, but I made sure to talk to him. Jensen tugged on my arm so I'd have to sit up. When I met his gaze, he had more tears in his eyes.

"It was strange because I couldn't feel my body. But I heard your voice through the fog. You said you weren't going to let anything take me away from you and that I had to live."

I nodded; he was right, but there was more. "What else did I say?" I questioned.

He smiled and brought a hand to my face, his thumb gently caressing my lips. "You said you loved me and will always love me." A tear fell down his cheek. "You also asked me to forgive you if you couldn't save me. I could hear the pain in your voice."

My lips trembled as I rested my forehead on his. "I was so afraid."

Jensen's gaze never wavered from mine. "I never doubted you for a second. I'm here and I'm not going anywhere."

"Neither am I," I promised. "You're stuck with me."

Jensen chuckled. "I can live with that."

29

EVERLEIGH

Three days later, Jensen's discharge day finally arrived. Although he was still weak and needed to take it easy for a few more weeks, his scans had come back clear and he was ready to go home.

I pulled his Bronco up to the hospital entrance where Jensen waited for me in a wheelchair with the nurse behind him. The look on his face was priceless. He was determined to walk out on his own, but the hospital staff wouldn't let him. I got out and opened the door for him, trying my best not to laugh.

"Do you not like being looked after?" I asked, winking at the nurse before she pushed the wheelchair back inside.

Jensen scoffed as he got into the Bronco. "It makes me feel helpless. I'm always the one who takes care of things."

Grinning, I shut the door and walked around to the driver's side. "Get used to it for a few weeks," I said as I hopped in. "I'm sure your parents and everyone else in town will be trying to help out." I started the engine, and we were on our way. "You should see the refrigerator; it's filled with casseroles and dinners."

Jensen chuckled. "Good. I'm so tired of hospital food right now." He reached over and gently clasped my hand, intertwining our fingers. His calloused palm was warm against mine as he smiled down at me. "You know, having you with me twenty-four seven over the next few weeks might not be a good thing. I'll get spoiled."

Tilting my head back, I laughed, feeling a warmth in my chest spread outward. "You better not take advantage of me, Mr. McLean."

He winked mischievously. "Don't worry. I think we'll both benefit from this arrangement," he said, his voice low. "Per my neurosurgeon's request, I cannot work for twelve weeks."

Although he probably could have returned to his job sooner, I wanted to ensure full recovery time.

I quirked an eyebrow playfully at him. "Your neurosurgeon is quite clever indeed."

Jensen brought my hand up to his lips and kissed it before releasing it. "Yes, she is."

When we arrived at his house, Seth's pickup truck was already parked in the driveway, and he stood waiting on the front porch wearing a baseball cap with a wide grin on his face. I felt bad for him the past couple of days. Every time he visited Jensen at the hospital, he was asleep, so he hadn't had the chance to talk to his best friend since the day of the hurricane.

Seth approached and walked around the car to open Jensen's door with one hand while he patted him on the back with the other.

"How ya feeling, man?"

The corners of Jensen's mouth twitched up into a smirk. "Not too bad."

Seth stepped aside so that Jensen could climb out of the car and then shifted closer to him protectively as if expecting him to suddenly collapse at any moment.

Then Seth looked over at me and raised his eyebrows. "So, Everleigh, you did say there was still a brain in that skull of his, right?"

Snickering, I grabbed Jensen's duffel bag from the back seat and hurried up the porch to unlock the front door for them.

"Yep, I saw it firsthand," I said, laughing.

We walked inside and Seth stayed right beside Jensen as he walked over to the couch to sit down. With being out of work for twelve weeks, Jensen decided to pay his crew during his downtime. He didn't want them to suffer financially because of his accident. Seeing how much he cared about his guys made me love him even more.

"Since I haven't gotten to talk to you in a few days, you don't mind if I stay over a while?" Seth asked, sitting down in the recliner across from Jensen.

Jensen chuckled and shook his head. "Sorry about that, man. They had me knocked out."

I dropped off Jensen's bag into his bedroom and joined them in the living room, sitting next to Jensen on the couch.

Jensen smiled at me and nodded over at Seth. "Should we tell him the good news?"

Seth's eyes widened in anticipation as he looked back and forth between us. "What did I miss?"

Jensen clasped my hand and smiled at his friend. "Everleigh and I are getting married."

Seth slapped his knee and burst out laughing. "Well, I'll be damned," he exclaimed, coming over to us. He hugged Jensen and then leaned down to embrace me. "Congratulations." He stepped back and sat on the edge of the coffee table. "It's about time," he added happily.

Jensen nodded. "You're right, it is. And speaking of the wedding, I want to ask you something." He moved closer to him and smiled. "Will you be my best man?"

Seth hooted and hollered with excitement and jumped to his feet. "Hell yeah, I will." He rushed over to the refrigerator and pulled out two beers. "This calls for a celebration. Hope you don't mind if we use *your* beers for this special occasion."

Jensen chuckled. "Not at all. But I don't think I'm drinking tonight. Too many pain meds in my system."

Seth laughed. "Oh yeah, that's right. No alcohol for you, then." He put one of the beers back and grabbed a bottle of water in its place. He handed that one to Jensen and tapped his beer against it. Seth was nothing but smiles and I loved it.

"Have you told your parents yet?" he asked me.

Jensen looked quickly over at me. "You might want to do that soon. Now that we've told Seth, the whole world will know."

Seth snorted. "Thanks, man. I can keep a secret, you know."

Grinning, I glanced down at my phone; it was four o'clock. My parents would still be at the clinic.

"Actually, do you mind if I go see them now? There's something else I want to talk to them about." Jensen's brows furrowed and I waved him off. "I'll tell you about it later."

Seth moved over to sit beside Jensen and slapped his shoulder. "Go. We'll be fine here. We need to figure out the bachelor party anyway."

Rolling my eyes, I let go of Jensen's hand and kissed his cheek. "Don't get too carried away," I said playfully.

Jensen turned to me and pressed his lips to mine. "We won't. I promise."

"Do you mind if I take your Bronco? My car's still at my house."

With everything going on, I haven't had a chance to grab mine. Plus, it was nice driving his car; it was a part of him.

Jensen nodded toward the door. "Get out of here. You don't ever have to ask me that."

Seth chortled. "That's right. Once you're married, what's his is yours and what's yours is . . ." He took a swig of his beer and laughed again. "Well, it's yours, too."

I winked at him and stood. "Exactly." But then, I turned to Jensen, my expression serious. "I'm kidding. I don't think that way at all."

Jensen chuckled. "I know." He waved for me to leave. "I'll be fine. Go talk to your parents. I'm ready to hear what they say about the wedding."

They were going to be ecstatic about everything. I said goodbye to them and grabbed the car keys off the counter. As I got into the Bronco, I could still hear Jensen and Seth's laughter. It was just like old times.

With Jensen being fine and everything falling into place, I felt alive and so full of joy that I thought I'd explode. The wind whipped through my hair as I made the short drive to downtown Southport to my father's medical practice. There were so many things I needed to tell my parents that I didn't know where to start first.

When I arrived, I parked out front and bounded up the stairs to the door. My mother was at the desk when I walked inside, writing something down on the calendar. Her blonde hair was pulled back into a low ponytail, and she wore light pink scrubs. There was no one in the waiting room which was perfect. She looked up and her eyes widened when she saw me.

"Hey," she exclaimed, getting to her feet. "I kept waiting for you to call and tell me you got Jensen home okay."

I walked behind the desk and gave her a hug around her neck. "Jensen's home," I said, letting her go. "Seth's with him right now."

My mother turned off her computer and stood. "You could've just called, sweetheart. I know you want to be with him and make sure he's okay."

I shook my head. "He's fine. Besides, what I need to tell you isn't something that should be done over the phone. I kind of want to see your face when you hear."

She gasped. "Are you pregnant?"

I burst out laughing. "No. Why does everyone automatically ask that question?"

Her eyes lit up. "I don't know. Maybe it's because I've been dying to have grandchildren."

"What am I hearing about grandchildren?" my dad asked as he walked down the hallway toward us.

He held out his arms and I hugged him tight. "Good. You're here. That means I don't have to say all of this twice."

He let me go, his expression curious. "What's going on?"

He went to stand by my mother and I smiled. "I'm back for good now. I have to go to Boston a couple of times over the next few weeks for a few surgeries, but after that, I'll be here permanently."

My mother squealed so loud it hurt my ears. She flung her arms around my neck, squeezing me so tight I could barely breathe.

"My baby's finally coming home. This is the best news ever."

She passed me over to my dad and he hugged me again. "What are your plans for a job? Did you find a position near here?"

"Not yet," I answered, letting him go. "But I'm not worried about it. I know something will come up eventually. Which brings me to this next question," I said, directing it to my dad.

He lifted his brows. "Go on."

I bit my lip. "When are you planning on retiring?"

His smile faded and he glanced over at my mother. "Soon. Your mother and I have been trying to figure out what we're going to do with this place," he said, gazing around sadly at the office.

I grabbed his arms, drawing his attention back to me. "I have an idea and I think you're going to like it. But first, there's something else I need to tell you." Their eyes widened and I couldn't contain my excitement any longer. "Jensen and I are getting married!" I shouted.

My mom screamed again and this time I couldn't breathe when she wrapped her arms around me. With them being this ecstatic, I couldn't wait to tell them the rest.

TODAY WAS A FANTASTIC DAY. It was as if my path had aligned with not only Jensen's but my parents' as well. My future had never looked so exciting, and now I couldn't wait to let it all play out.

Closing my eyes, I moved under the hot water and let it pound against my skin. When I got back to Jensen's after visiting my parents, I heated the chicken and rice casserole that was in his refrigerator. After that, we sat on his dock until the sun went down.

Now it was getting late, and we were going to watch a movie. I figured it was only fair to let Jensen pick since he just got out of the hospital. I was pretty sure it would be action-packed and full of suspense. However, I didn't see him staying up too long tonight. Even though he'd stayed in a hospital bed the past few days, he didn't get much rest, not with the nurses coming in every hour to check his vitals.

Once I was done in the shower, I listened to see if I could hear what Jensen was doing. There was nothing but silence. My stomach dropped and I dried off quickly, throwing on my pajamas even though my skin was still wet.

"Jensen," I called out, hurrying out of his bedroom.

I've had this overwhelming sense of protectiveness over him ever since he got hurt. I didn't want to lose him, and knowing I came close to that terrified the hell out of me.

The living room was pitch black, but as I rounded the corner, the candles Jensen had scattered around filled the room with a soft glow. The light flickered across his face, emphasizing his strong jawline and mesmerizing grayish-blue eyes. He was standing in the middle of the floor with his hands behind his back as if trying to hide something. My heart was still beating hard, so I placed a hand over my chest.

"It scared me when I didn't hear anything," I said, my voice breathless.

Jensen smirked. "I wanted this to be special."

Laughing, I glanced down at my pink pajama pants and oversized T-shirt. "If I'd known you wanted to be romantic, I would've chosen some sexy lingerie."

Jensen chuckled. "I like you like that. You look amazing."

Lifting my brows, I stepped closer to him. "What are you doing anyway?"

Just as I said that, he got down on his knee and revealed what was behind his back; it was the small black box from his sock drawer.

Jensen's smile warmed my heart. "I know you already said yes," he began, "but I at least wanted to give it to you the right way." He nodded out toward the dock. "My first thought was that I'd do it out there as we watched the sunset, but I could just see the ring slipping out of my fingers and into the water."

"Yeah, that wouldn't be good," I laughed.

Jensen took a deep breath and opened the box, revealing a stunning princess-cut diamond ring. The light of the candles seemed to dance across the diamond, making it shine even brighter.

"Everleigh," he murmured, his eyes never leaving mine, "you've made me happier these past few months than I've ever been. I can't imagine what life will be like with you as my wife, but I know it will be amazing. Are you sure you want to be with me for the rest of your life?"

Tears welled in my eyes as I nodded my head, unable to speak. There was nothing I wanted more. Jensen pulled the ring out of the box and placed it on my finger; it fit perfectly. He stood up and pulled me into a tight embrace.

I buried my face in his chest, feeling the warmth of his body seep into mine.

"I love you so much," he whispered.

"I love you, too," I replied, my voice muffled.

We stayed that way for a few moments, lost in each other's embrace. I didn't want to let him go. The good thing was that I didn't have to.

30

EVERLEIGH

TWO WEEKS LATER

The sand felt warm and wet between my toes as Jensen, and I walked down to the water's edge. A thunderstorm had just passed, leaving with it the smell of rain and a beautiful rainbow arched across the sky. It was the perfect evening for a stroll on the beach. Jensen was by my side holding my right hand, and my engagement ring was on the other, reminding me that I was about to become his wife. So much had happened in the past two weeks that I couldn't believe how much time had flown by.

I had to go to Boston to perform a few surgeries, and they went well. While I was there, Nyla and I went to our favorite sushi restaurant, and I asked her to be my maid of honor. Of course, she said yes, and we celebrated by drinking apple martinis while packing up most of my things at the apartment. All I had to do now was hire a moving company to load everything up and transport it to Oak Island.

Jensen and I stood along the shoreline, our toes buried in the sand as we watched the waves crash against the shore. Reflections of the setting sun illuminated the ocean's surface with a warm orange hue.

"Have you figured out where you want to get married?" Jensen asked.

The thought made me smile. I'd be happy doing it in a parking lot somewhere if it meant I could call him my husband. However, it was going to be our wedding day and I wanted it to be special. It turned out there was a place that came to mind.

"Airlie Gardens," I replied, turning to face him.

Jensen smiled. "Is that because of the coordinates hidden in your grandmother's box?"

I shrugged. "It's not the *only* reason. I do love that place. It's beautiful and it was obviously special to my grandmother."

Sadly, Airlie Gardens was a very popular place which meant they most likely didn't have an open weekend in the next two months for us to have our wedding.

"But," I said, wrapping my arms around his neck while he encircled his around my waist, "I would be happy marrying you right here on this beach."

Jensen grinned. "I'll marry you anywhere."

A thrill of excitement raced through me. "Then it's settled," I said, pressing my lips to his. "We're going to have a small ceremony right out here, by Hide Away by the Sea."

Jensen peered over at my grandmother's blue cottage

and smiled. "I think here is perfect. It'll be like having your grandmother with us."

Tears stung my eyes and I nodded. "Exactly."

Jensen pulled me in tighter to his body. "When do you want to do this?"

I'd already had the date set in my mind. "October 27th," I answered.

Jensen let me go and laughed, clutching my hands. "It sounds like you've given this a lot of thought. Why that date?"

I breathed in the warm, salty air. In the fall, it'll be cooler, the perfect weather.

"Because I want a fall wedding," I explained. "And it gives me two months which is more than enough time to plan something beautiful."

Jensen glanced down at our clasped hands. "There *is* something we have yet to discuss, Everleigh." His gaze lifted and he turned to focus on my grandmother's home. "What do you want to do about our living situation?" Before I could answer, he shifted his attention back to me, his lips spreading into a grin. "Because I was thinking," he said, eyes twinkling, "that if you wanted to live here at Hide Away by the Sea, I would happily sell my place or rent it to Nyla."

It took all I had not to scream for joy. "You'd do that?" I exclaimed excitedly.

He pulled me into his arms, his expression genuine. "I'd do anything for you, Everleigh. You know that."

I knew we'd have to decide where we would live at some point, but I didn't want to suggest he sell his place on the sound. I knew he loved it there.

"What about your house? You love it," I stated.

Jensen shrugged. "I do, but . . ." He glanced over at my grandmother's cottage, and it was as if I could see so many memories swirling in his eyes. "I love that place more. There's only one suggestion I feel I have to make," he added.

I lifted my brows. "And that would be?"

He pointed toward the house, a wry smile curling at the corner of his lips. "We might have to turn the library back into a bedroom." Then he winked. "We'll probably need the space if we plan on having more than one kid."

The thought of that sent waves of delight rippling through me until I could hardly contain myself; I was way past ready to start trying for a family. Jumping in his arms, I kissed him hard.

"I am so good with that. If you take me inside right now, we can get started."

Jensen chuckled against my lips before lifting me into the air and twirling me around in his strong arms.

Setting me down gently, he smiled at me mischievously. "And then, after that, we should go to Airlie Gardens and check out those coordinates. I'm curious to see why your grandmother noted them down."

I was too, and I was also wondering what the other numbers on the paper were. Of course, it could be the combination of a lock somewhere, but there was no safe or anything like that in the house.

However, I did look forward to finding more clues to my grandmother's hidden secrets, but first . . . I was ready for Jensen and me to start our own new adventure.

~

It was late in the afternoon when we made it to Airlie Gardens, but it was perfect because there weren't many people there. Out of curiosity, when we paid for our tickets, I asked the event organizer if they had any availability for a wedding in the next two months. It turned out they were booked up for events for almost a year and a half. It didn't bother me, though. I was perfectly content marrying Jensen by the ocean behind the house we were going to spend the rest of our lives in.

Hand in hand, Jensen and I took our time walking through the gardens. Everywhere we looked there was something spectacular—winding paths lined with azaleas, lush lawns dotted with camellias, and majestic trees offering shade from the heat of the day. The whole place made you feel like you had stepped in another time.

Jensen held up his phone, and I squinted to make out the small map on the screen. A bright blue dot illuminated the exact coordinates we had to get to.

We followed a path with live oaks towering all around us, their branches drooping with lush Spanish moss that draped overhead like an ethereal blanket. My heart raced faster as I watched the dot on the screen getting closer.

Jensen let out a wry laugh when he noticed how energized I was becoming. "Any guesses what we're going to find?" he asked.

Puzzled, I shrugged my shoulders. "No idea," I replied, unsure of what to expect in a public area—there weren't any secret compartments or hidden floorboards here.

When we arrived at our destination, my eyes widened with surprise, and I stopped dead in my tracks. A bench was nestled among vibrant blooming bushes and flowers with Spanish moss hanging from the branches of giant live oaks above. Immediately, something about this place seemed strangely familiar.

Jensen started toward the bench but paused when he realized I wasn't following him. He glanced back over his shoulder at me and narrowed his eyes with concern.

"You okay?" he called out as I rummaged through my purse.

My heart raced as I unzipped the inside pocket where I knew I'd left the photo my grandmother had stashed in the book at home.

"What do you have there?" Jensen asked.

I pulled out the picture and held it up to see the resemblance. It was uncanny how it all looked the same.

"This was their bench," I whispered.

Jensen came back over to me and looked at the photo, his expression full of awe. "Oh, wow, this place looks exactly the same."

It was surprising since the photo was taken many decades ago. He gently took the picture from my grasp and studied it.

"Rachel was so young here."

I nodded and walked over to the bench. "Yes, she was. I just wish I could see who the man is."

Jensen narrowed his gaze at the picture. "It's so blurry that I can't make out any features. Do you think it's T?" he asked, handing it back to me.

"It has to be," I replied, carefully placing it back in my purse. "I don't know who else it could be."

We sat on the bench, and he put his arm around my shoulders, just like T did with my grandmother. The wind blew around us, rustling the bushes and blooms, sending with it a sweet fragrance that reminded me of my grandmother's rose-scented perfume.

"Maybe this place is what inspired her to make the perfume she always wore. It smells just like her here."

Jensen nodded. "It could've reminded her of T."

Closing my eyes, I took in a deep breath, and it was as if my grandmother was right there with us.

"When I have time, I'm going to break out my grandmother's perfume recipes and make them."

Jensen chuckled. "Do it. My mother loves hers. Rachel had given her some a few months ago, and I know she's almost out." He bumped me with his shoulder. "You could make it a tradition; pass the legacy down to our daughter if we have one."

Thinking of having a little girl warmed my heart. "Knowing us, we'll probably have all boys," I teased.

He squeezed my shoulder and pulled me in closer, his lips soft as he pressed them to the side of my head.

"Doubtful. We'll have us a girl and she'll be just like you."

I snorted. "Only I'm going to make sure she's not as stupid as I was all those years ago. I don't want her running away from something she really wants."

Jensen gently tugged my chin so I'd look at him. "Don't worry," he said, piercing me with his blue eyes. "We'll make sure she doesn't repeat the same mistakes we did."

"And you think we can do that?" I wondered, knowing any child of mine was going to be stubborn.

Jensen laughed and shrugged. "I don't know, but we sure as hell can try."

That's all we can do.

We stayed on the bench for a few more minutes, but it

was getting late and the garden was about to close. Jensen stood first and held out his hand to help me up.

"Do you think your grandmother documented the coordinates because this was where she and T would meet?"

We walked away from the bench, and I glanced back at it one more time. I honestly had no idea.

"Not sure," I answered. "The sad thing is that I doubt we'll ever find out."

That bothered me more than anything. I wanted answers, but my grandmother had too many secrets.

31

EVERLEIGH

THREE WEEKS LATER

The wedding date was set, the planning was all done, and all I had to do was wait another month. Jensen had officially moved into Hide Away by the Sea with me, and we'd already converted the library into a bedroom. My original room in the house was now the one we shared. When we were finally blessed with children, our firstborn would get my grandmother's room; she would've loved that.

Jensen sold his house to Nyla, and the papers were all signed. He was going to leave all the furniture inside so she could use it until she got settled in. In a few minutes, she would be arriving, and I could barely contain my excitement. Not only was she about to step foot in her new home, but I had another surprise waiting for her. It'd killed me keeping the secret from her the past few weeks.

My phone beeped with an incoming text and I smiled, knowing it would be her.

Nyla: Thought I could make it, but I had to stop and get gas. Be there in ten.

TURNING OFF MY CAR, I grabbed the keys to what was now Nyla's home and waited on the front porch. When she finally pulled up to the house precisely ten minutes later, I ran over and threw my arms around her neck the second she got out of her SUV. She had on a cerulean blue sundress that matched the exact shade of her eyes.

"Home sweet home," I exclaimed, hugging her tightly.

She squealed and let me go. "I can't believe this is all mine now," she said, looking around the house.

Her back seat was full of her things from Boston, so we grabbed all we could, and I led her inside. She dropped her stuff on the floor and went straight to the living room, where there was nothing but a wall of windows overlooking the sound. The water was calm, shimmering like glass under the sunlight. Jensen's little fishing boat was still tied to the dock, but Nyla had agreed to let us keep it there for the time being since it was too small to keep at the marina with the bigger boats. I stood beside her and smiled when I noticed her face; her eyes were full of wonder and awe.

"How does it feel to be a homeowner for the first time?" I asked, bumping her with my shoulder.

We were both new homeowners now that my

grandmother's house was mine. It was still a something I couldn't believe—my whole life, I'd only lived in apartments.

Nyla blew out a sigh and laughed, shaking her head in astonishment. "It feels amazing. I can't thank you and Jensen enough for selling this place to me."

I waved her off. "Hey, it worked out perfectly."

When her gaze met mine, I smiled. "We were meant to be here, Nyla. I feel it in my heart."

Her lips trembled and she turned her attention back to the water. "It does seem right." She clasped a hand over her mouth and giggled. "I still can't believe this place is mine."

I squeezed her shoulder to get her to look at me. "I know you have a lot of stuff to unpack, but I want to show you something. I've been keeping it a secret for weeks, and I don't think I can hold it in any longer."

Nyla's face brightened. "What is it?"

I nodded toward the door. "I need to take you somewhere."

She practically sprinted to the door with the biggest grin on her face. "I'm ready. I love surprises."

When we got in my car, I handed her a black blindfold with a smirk. "Put this on, please."

Nyla took it with raised eyebrows and an intrigued smile. "Well, this just got interesting."

Laughing, I pulled out of the driveway. "Put it on. I don't want you to know where we're going."

Nyla slid it over her head and her eyes. "Fine," she said, grinning wide, "but if you drive crazy, I can't promise I won't vomit."

"And you'll be cleaning it up if you do," I joked back.

Once I knew the blindfold was secure, I drove us toward downtown Southport. It was a Sunday, so people were everywhere, walking around and shopping. However, the place I was taking her to was closed for the day. I had everything set up for her arrival.

Seaside Family Practice came into view a few minutes later, its bright green exterior making me smile.

"Keep the blindfold on," I commanded as I pulled around back and parked.

Nyla chuckled and held up her hands. "Yes, ma'am. Are we there yet?"

"Yep," I answered, opening my door. "I'll help you out." I went around to her side and opened her door, taking her hand. "Don't worry, I won't let you run into anything," I promised.

She laughed. "Please don't. I already broke my nose one time by running into a tree. That wasn't fun at all."

"Do I even want to know that story?" I said, my shoulders shaking with laughter.

Nyla waved a hand dismissively in the air. "Oh, there was nothing to it. Just me being a clumsy nine-year-old and not watching where I was going. I did a lot of crazy stuff like that when I was a kid."

That made me smile. If Nyla had grown up in Oak Island, I knew we would've been best friends then, too.

We ambled around the side of the building until we made it to the front.

"There are five steps," I warned her. I guided her up and let her go once she was safely on the porch. "Okay, you can take the blindfold off now," I said.

Nyla carefully slid it off her forehead, her auburn hair getting caught in the knot. She released it quickly, and her eyes widened when she realized where we were.

"Why are we at your family's practice?" she asked, brows furrowed curiously.

The answer was right behind her, leaning against the building and wrapped in shiny silver paper with a red ribbon tied around it.

"You have a present to open." I nodded toward it, and she turned to see what it was.

Slowly, she walked over to it, and I knew it was going to be heavy. "Oh my God, what is it?" she asked, grunting with the weight of it.

She carried it over and when I sat down on the steps, I held my arms out for it so she could sit beside me. I placed it on her lap the second she sat, my stomach fluttering with anticipation.

"Open it," I said, nudging her with my elbow.

Nyla's trembling fingers fumbled with the corner flap of the silver wrapping paper. In one swift motion, she tore it open to reveal a wooden sign, and the gasp that escaped her lips echoed in the air. With wide eyes and a hand clamped over her mouth, she slowly turned to meet my gaze.

"Are you serious? Is this for real?"

Tears burned my eyes as I brushed my fingers over our names engraved on the bottom of the sign: *Seaside Family Practice—Dr. Everleigh Abbott and Dr. Nyla Clark*. My dad was ready to retire and when I offered to take it over, I saw such joy in his eyes that I knew it was the right choice. He wanted the practice to stay in the family, but I also knew I needed someone by my side. So, I brought up the idea of bringing Nyla on as a partner and he agreed—that way, I could still help out at the clinic when I wasn't away performing surgeries.

Nyla hung her head and sniffled, tears dropping from her cheeks onto the sign.

"So, what do you say?" I asked, my voice thick with emotion.

Nyla threw her arms around me, her body shaking as she sobbed into my shoulder. Then, after a few moments, she pulled away and looked up at me, her eyes red and puffy.

"Yes," she whispered, her voice choked with tears. "I'll be happy to be your partner. Just tell me what needs to be done on my part."

I held up a hand. "We have plenty of time for that. I'm just glad you're happy. A part of me was afraid you might not want the responsibility of owning your own practice."

Her eyes widened. "Really? This is a dream come true." More tears fell down her cheeks. "And it wouldn't have been possible without you. I owe you so much."

I shook my head. "You owe me nothing. Having you here is going to be all I need."

Sniffling, she wiped away her tears. "What about your specialty? You're not giving that up, are you?"

I snorted. "Oh heavens, no. I love what I do, so I'll still be doing surgeries. Of course, it'll require some travel, but our clinic will have you to hold down the fort while I'm gone." A smile spread across my face as I looked down at our sign. "My dad wanted Seaside to stay in the family, and I'm making his wish come true." I met her gaze. "And

I want to share it with you. Then, maybe one day, when we have kids, we can pass it to them."

Nyla laughed through her tears and placed a hand over her heart. "That would be the life, Everleigh. Do you think it'll happen that way?"

I took her hand in mine. "I have no doubt."

32

EVERLEIGH

I was getting married in a little over two weeks! It was hard to wrap my head around the thought. Nyla was all settled into her new home while Jensen and I started to make Hide Away by the Sea ours.

"Hey, babe! Do you want to go ahead and move the furniture before we head out to the water?" Jensen shouted from our bedroom. Smiling, I finished my coffee just as I heard his footsteps thumping down the hall.

"That works," I said, turning away from the window and watching him step into the kitchen, his hair disheveled and dressed in only a pair of swimming trunks that hung low on his hips.

With him still out of work for a few more weeks, he'd picked up surfing and I watched him practice every day. It was October, but we still had some hot summer temperatures. Soon, Jensen would have to return to work and the wintertime would be coming. I was glad we had this time together.

Jensen sipped his coffee and ate one of the fresh

blueberry muffins I made this morning. He nodded over at the dresser that stood out of place in the corner of our living room. It was a piece of furniture from my apartment in Boston and as our bedroom had plenty of space, we wanted to move it in there as we needed the extra storage. The rest of my things were in storage until I could find people who wanted them.

"Did you decide where you want that in our room?"

I walked over and set my empty cup on the counter. "Yep. We just need to move the bed to the opposite wall between the windows, and that'll give us more room to put the dresser on the other."

Jensen chuckled and ate another bite of his muffin. "Sounds good to me." His grin widened. "Think you might want to try getting on the board today?"

He tried to pull me into his arms, but I playfully pushed him away. "Definitely not. I looked like an idiot the last time I tried. I'm pretty sure someone took a video and it's probably all over the internet."

Jensen laughed. "Maybe you'll go viral."

He reached for me again and I wrapped my arms around his neck. "I'm perfectly content watching you do your thing," I said.

Smirking, he leaned in and pressed his lips to mine. "Come on. Let's get this done so we can head out."

He let me go and I followed him down the hall and into our bedroom. My bed was a sturdy, mahogany frame with special pads on its legs to make it easier to slide across the floor.

Jensen went to the opposite side and tilted his head. "You ready?"

Nodding, I gripped onto the bed. "Yep. You pull, I push."

We started moving it across the room when I suddenly stepped on something and my foot slipped. Luckily, I caught myself before stumbling down to the floor. When I looked at what I had stepped on, my eyes widened when I noticed my grandmother's handwriting on a small light blue envelope.

My heart stopped as I stared at it.

"What the . . .?" I whispered, reading the instructions my grandmother had written under my name: *only open if I am no longer here*.

Jensen picked it up, his brows furrowed curiously. "This is interesting. She must have hidden it under the bed somewhere."

He held it out to me, and now my heart started to race. The house had been searched from top to bottom to see if I could find more hidden things from my grandmother, but I couldn't believe I had never thought to look under my own mattress.

"What do you think it could be?" Jensen asked, his voice soft as he sat beside me on the bed.

With trembling fingers, I slid them under the flap to open the envelope. "I have no clue," I replied, my stomach fluttering with nerves.

It was obvious my grandmother wanted me to find the envelope . . . eventually.

Once the flap was open, I slid the folded letter out and tears burned my eyes as I read the last words my grandmother ever wrote me.

My dearest Everleigh,

If you are reading this letter, it means I am no longer with you. Well, either that or you didn't follow my instructions to open this when it specifically said to do so only if I was gone. If I am still alive and you're reading this, then hopefully, I'm prepared for your questions. However, if I'm not on this earth anymore, I just want to tell you how much I love you and that I never intended to keep any secrets from you. This will be very confusing, but I need to tell you some things.

I'm hoping that with me leaving you the house, you'll find your way back. Oak Island is your home, and it's where you belong. If there was one wish I could've made for myself, it wouldn't have been for more money or a longer life . . . it would've been for YOU to be happy. I know you love your job in Boston, but even I know your heart longs for something else. There was a time when my heart did, too. And it's because of that I'm going to tell you one of my innermost hidden secrets that I've kept to myself all these years. No one knows, not even your mother.

To be loved passionately and to love

passionately is one of the best and scariest feelings a person can experience in their life. That's why I pushed you to work things out with Jensen all those times. I loved your grandfather, Everleigh, I did with all my heart. But there was a time when I loved another before him. He was very special to me, and I often wondered what would've happened if things had turned out differently. But if they had, the universe wouldn't have aligned for you. I know none of this makes sense, but it's about to.

When you love someone as deeply as I have, it's hard to let them go. If you look under the fifth floorboard from the wall in my bedroom, you'll find a notch where you can lift it up. Underneath is a box full of old love letters. It was too hard to part with them, so I hid them. Also, there's a secret note hidden in the box with a set of coordinates and a lock combination. The coordinates will lead you to Airlie Gardens, and the combination is what you'll need to get inside the box hidden in the ground beneath the bench.

A GASP ESCAPED my lips and I looked at Jensen. His eyes widened and he waved his hands for me to speak.

"What did you read? I'm only at the part where she said she knows you love your job in Boston."

My heard raced as I held up a hand, indicating to Jensen that I need to read on. "This is wild. We'll talk about it in a minute. But, first, I have to finish reading the rest."

Then, afterward, we were heading straight to Airlie Gardens.

You're going to be shocked at what you find, and I pray none of it changes the way you see me. I was a different girl all those years ago, and I think you'll be surprised at what you find. What I want from you is not to run away anymore. Promise me that, Everleigh. Don't be afraid of what your heart desires.

I love you, Everleigh. I may not be with you anymore, but I'm always looking down on you. If you haven't found your way yet, I have faith that you will.

Love Always,
Grammy

PS My perfume recipes are in a secret compartment in my armoire. I'll let you figure out how to get to them. There's also a locket hidden in there. When it comes to my recipes, I trust you'll know what to do with them.

I KNEW Jensen had more to read, so I handed him the letter and stood, my pulse skyrocketing with each passing second. I paced back and forth until he was done.

His face conveyed both shock and awe, the same feelings I had swirling inside me. Jensen set the letter on the bed and met my gaze.

"That was . . . a lot," he said.

I nodded in agreement. "Yes, it was. It turns out she *wanted* me to know her secrets."

He glanced down at the letter and chuckled. "Let me guess, we're not going surfing today?"

A giggle escaped my lips, and I shook my head. "Nope. We're going to grab a garden shovel that'll fit in my purse and head to Airlie Gardens."

Buried underneath that special bench my grandmother and T used to meet at was a box full of more secrets.

I *had* to find it.

33

EVERLEIGH

I fidgeted in the passenger seat of Jensen's car as we wound our way down the highway toward Airlie Gardens. I'd grabbed one of my larger purses out of my closet and stuffed a small garden shovel inside it, my heart racing at the thought of what we were doing.

"How are we going to dig up this buried box without anyone seeing us?" I asked, biting my nails nervously.

Jensen chuckled. "Your grandmother buried it without someone seeing, didn't she?" His smirk only made me more anxious.

I rolled my eyes. "Yeah, but that was many, many years ago. I'm sure the gardens have a lot more foot traffic now."

He shrugged and kept his eyes focused on the road. "Have faith in me, Everleigh. Just think of it as an adventure."

I couldn't help but laugh despite my nerves. "An adventure that's going to get us arrested."

He looked over at me and winked. "It wouldn't be the first time we've gotten in trouble with the law."

"That was just vandalizing the road with our mascot during graduation," I replied, smacking his arm playfully. "Digging up a section of a protected park is another situation altogether."

Jensen chuckled. "We just don't need to get caught."

My stomach twisted with worry—there was no telling how deep the buried box was beneath the ground or if it had been unearthed already.

When we arrived at the gardens, Jensen parked his Bronco, and I could hear my heart pounding in my ears as we walked into the ticket office. Luckily, it was a Wednesday morning, so there weren't many people around.

Once we paid, Jensen took my hand, and we started down the path toward my grandmother and T's favorite bench. The weather was perfect and the wind had a little chill to it. The leaves on the trees had already started to change to the beautiful red, yellow, and orange colors of fall. It was my favorite time of the year and was why I wanted to get married in autumn.

"Did you bring the paper with the lock combination on it?" Jensen asked.

I patted my purse. "In here. Although, I've had it memorized for weeks."

I knew the numbers were important; I just didn't know what they were for. If Jensen and I hadn't found my grandmother's letter to me, I never would've learned about the secret box. I was curious to see what was in it. I wanted to run the mile it was going to take to get to the bench, but I kept my hand in Jensen's and enjoyed the scenery.

When we arrived at the infamous spot, I felt a wave of emotion wash over me. My grandmother's words echoed in my mind. *To be loved passionately and to love passionately is one of the best and scariest feelings a person can experience in their life.*

She had lost her passionate love, which hurt my heart because I could only imagine what that felt like. Now that I had Jensen, I couldn't fathom the thought of losing him. The closest I'd come to it was when he got injured in the storm.

Jensen glanced up and down the path, and no one was in sight. Then, with the biggest grin on his face, he held out his hand.

"Shovel, please."

My heart was thudding so hard it made me feel light-headed. "I seriously can't believe we're doing this," I said, reaching into my purse. I pulled out the shovel and handed it to him quickly. "If we don't find it in ten minutes, we're abandoning this."

Jensen smirked and hurried back behind the bench. "Oh, I'm going to find it, babe."

While he dug, I kept watch. I was serious about only giving him ten minutes to search. For all we knew, the box was already gone. Too much time had passed where someone could've possibly found it.

Five minutes went by, then six, seven, eight, and then nine. Time was almost up.

"You have one minute, Jensen," I warned, keeping my attention on the path. Still, there was no one in sight. I glanced up at the trees, trying to see if there were any cameras. "We are so going to get caught," I grumbled.

It was only a matter of time.

With today's technology, I had no doubt we were being watched and that security was on their way. I looked over at Jensen, who had a mound of dirt piled at his side. He hadn't stopped digging since he started, and sweat gleamed off his forehead, his arm muscles flexing with each thrust of the shovel.

"We have ten seconds," I said, feeling the disappointment well up in my chest. I was hoping we would've found the box by now.

In my mind, I finished the countdown.

Eight . . . seven . . . six . . . five . . . four . . . three . . .

Just as I was about to get to two, I heard the shovel clang as it hit something hard. Jensen's eyes widened, and my heart skipped a beat. But then, something out of the corner of my eye caught my attention. Heading toward us were two men in a white golf cart.

"They're coming," I hissed, my body freezing where I stood.

The bench was surrounded by bushes, so the men couldn't see Jensen. Jensen pushed the small shovel underneath one of the bushes and frantically waved for me to hurry.

"Get over here," he commanded, taking a seat.

The men drew closer, so I calmly walked over to Jensen and sat beside him. He put his arm around me, his voice right by my ear.

"If we keep our feet together, it should hide the hole. Just act normal, okay?"

My back was drenched in sweat, and I could feel my

pulse in my throat. The cart was getting closer, the tires crunching on the gravel. Then, finally, the men slowly came up on us and I held my breath, trying to figure out what I would say to them.

With my grandmother's secret box not being on my property, did I have any rights to it? Probably not, but I wanted what was in it.

The men were only a few yards away, and I still held my breath. It wasn't until they passed us and gave us a nod of acknowledgment that I finally allowed myself to suck in a gasp of much-needed air.

"Oh, thank God," I said, clutching my chest.

Jensen stood and watched them disappear out of sight. "Do you think they suspected anything?" he wondered.

"I hope not," I said, kneeling on the ground to see into the hole. "Either way, let's get what we came for and get out of here."

There appeared to be a long, dark green rectangular box that looked like something soldiers would store ammo in during a war.

Jensen brushed away all the dirt and pulled out the box; a lock kept the latch closed. I wanted to open it then and there, but we needed to leave.

Quickly, I slid the box into my purse and helped Jensen fill the hole. It only took a few seconds, and once we were done, you couldn't tell the ground had been disturbed.

After taking one last look at my grandmother's and T's bench, Jensen and I walked the one-mile path back to the garden entrance.

What kind of secrets were going to be revealed once I opened the box?

When we returned to Jensen's Bronco, he opened my door and smiled. "Do you want to open it out here or wait until we get home?"

The box was quite heavy in my purse, but I knew there was no better place than home. I didn't want to rush when looking through everything.

"Home," I said, hopping in my seat.

Jensen chuckled. "Can you last that long?"

My fingers were itching to open the lock, but I was excited by the anticipation building up inside me. "I don't know," I said, winking at him. "Now get in and let's go."

I had a feeling T's love letters would be nothing compared to what was in the box. My grandmother's mystery was about to end.

THE SECOND WE ARRIVED HOME, Jensen and I sat on the floor of the back deck with the box between us. My fingers trembled as I swiped the numbers on the lock to the correct ones.

When I pulled on the lock, it gave way and I carefully took it off the latch. I took a deep breath and counted to five, steadying my nerves, before exhaling slowly.

I looked over at Jensen and he smiled. "You ready?"

I laughed. "I'm not sure."

The box was sealed tight, so it took a little effort to pry the lid. Once it was open, I couldn't tear my gaze away. Jensen and I both looked inside simultaneously, his eyes lit up with wonder. The box was waterproof, which was a good thing. There were pictures, a diary, and even a large brown envelope filled with what had to be two inches worth of paper.

Jensen sat back and motioned toward the box. "I'm going to let you take the reins on this. Take your time."

The first thing I grabbed was the diary; it belonged to my grandmother. Inside were her accounts of everyday life back when she was sixteen. After skimming through several entries, it was clear her parents wanted her to marry into wealth.

"What is she saying?" Jensen asked curiously.

I searched through more dates, and there was nothing about the mysterious T yet. I looked over at Jensen and sighed.

"Basically, her parents wanted her to marry for wealth. My grandfather came from money."

Jensen nodded. "I wonder what happened to T if she ended it by marrying someone else."

The diary was massive, so it was going to take me days to read every single entry. However, it didn't take long to get to the good stuff.

"Here we go," I exclaimed excitedly, grinning at Jensen. "Listen to this."

May 23, 19XX

Today is a day I will never forget. It was a day of discovery and emotion that I will forever look back on fondly. I had gone out to the pier, the same place I had visited a hundred times before. But this time was different; I was met by someone special. He's a young man I've known for many years but had never really spoken to until now.

As I locked eyes with him for the first time, my heart felt like it had been set on fire. He had grown over the years and was far more handsome than I had ever imagined. As we talked, I began to see him for who he really was: kind, caring, and full of life. His presence lit up the pier, and I felt like I was in a dream.

For what seemed to be an eternity, we conversed until the sun dipped below the horizon. I never wanted that moment to end, but eventually, it did. I left the pier with a newfound appreciation for life, and I fell in love at the same time.

I'm not sure what will come from this, but I'm excited to find out.

I WAS HOPING I'd find out what T stood for, but my grandmother didn't mention anything until much later. There were so many entries about their secret rendezvous on the pier and how they'd meet at Airlie Gardens. Their love was forbidden, but they wanted to be with each other.

When I got to my grandmother's last entry, it was as if I could feel all the pain in her words. I couldn't even read it out loud to Jensen.

December 25, 19XX

Today was supposed to be the day Thomas declared his love for me to my parents. He was going to ask for my hand in marriage. I had everything planned. He was going to show up, dressed in his best, and show my parents that he was worthy of me. Sadly, my parents had other plans. The dinner wasn't just me and my family, they'd invited the Holts. I knew the second Arthur Holt walked through the door of my house that my father had plans for us. My parents wanted me to marry for money, but I didn't think they would put the prospect of marriage in my face. I should've known they had something up their sleeves when they started spending time with the Holts.

Arthur is a handsome man, someone I know I can be happy with. He's sweet, funny, and very caring. If I had met him sooner, maybe things would be different. Thomas is who I love, though. Luckily, I caught him in the front yard before he could reach my door, but I wasn't the only one out there. My father saw us together, and I'd never seen him so angry; it terrified me. He told Thomas that I could never be his, that he was a lowly fisherman who couldn't give me the life I deserved. I wanted to defy my parents and follow my heart, but I loved them. It was either them or Thomas. That was the choice my father gave me. I didn't want to lose my family. The hurt on Thomas's face when my father sent him away is something I'll never be able to erase from my mind. I watched in horror as he walked away, his shoulders hunched and his head down. The rest of the evening was a blur. I couldn't eat, breathe, or even think, because I knew tonight was the last time I'd ever see Thomas. My family was going to make sure of it.

I RUBBED my aching chest and met Jensen's gaze. "T stands for Thomas," I said.

It was good to finally have a name to go with the letter. Jensen's eyes narrowed curiously as he focused on the diary.

"Did she give his last name anywhere?"

I shrugged. "Not in the entries I read, but I'm sure it's somewhere. Why?"

He reached for the diary, and I gave it to him. "This Thomas guy was a fisherman, right?"

"Yeah," I answered, wondering where he was headed with the questions.

He flipped through the diary and then reached into the box where he pulled out a stack of photos. The second his eyes widened, I knew he'd found something.

"What is it?" I asked, leaning toward him.

He turned one of the photos around and pointed at the man standing beside my grandmother. My heart stopped the second I looked at the man's face; it was as if I was staring at a picture of Jensen.

"Oh my God," I breathed.

A sad sigh escaped his lips, and he ran his thumb lightly across the photograph before turning it back around to look at it again.

"That's my grandfather, Everleigh. Thomas McLean."

I could feel the world spinning around me as I looked from Jensen to the photo and back again. Jensen's grandfather was the man my grandmother had written about in her diary. He was the man she had been in love with.

My grandmother's words in her letter to me finally made sense. She'd written that the world wouldn't have aligned for me if things had worked out for her and Thomas. It meant that Jensen and I wouldn't be together.

I reached over and placed a hand on Jensen's. "I'm sorry my great-grandparents didn't approve of him. I have no doubt your grandfather was an amazing man."

I didn't know much about him, nor did Jensen since he never met him. His grandfather had died at sea when Jensen's father was a little boy. McLean Charters ended up going to Thomas's brother, Matthew, and it was he who had helped bring Jensen's father into the fishing business.

Matthew was going to pass down McLean Charters to his sons if he ever had any, but he was given just girls. That was how the business went to Jensen's father.

Jensen set the picture down with the others and sighed. "I wish I could've met him."

Nodding, I looked at all the photos and smiled. "Me too."

I reached into the box and pulled out the large brown envelope and a newspaper clipping. It was Thomas's obituary.

My heart hurt for the man in the photo.

He had eventually married and had Jensen's father, but it made me wonder if his heart still belonged to my grandmother at that time.

"He was so young," I said, tracing my finger over the date Thomas had died. He was twenty-eight years old.

Jensen nodded. "Yes, he was. Hopefully, he's proud of what my dad and I have done with the business."

A sad smile spread across my face. "I have no doubt."

Jensen tapped a finger on the large envelope. "What do you think this is?"

"There's no telling," I said, sliding my finger underneath the flap to open it. Whatever it was, there were a lot of papers. However, when I slid out what was inside, my breath caught in my lungs. "Oh my God."

"What is it?" Jensen asked, anticipation in his voice.

My mouth gaped as I stared at the words on the cover sheet; it was a manuscript . . . and it was written by my grandmother. I recognized the title immediately. *One Day* by Rachel Holt. Then below her name were the words: *written under Ellen Thomas.*

Clasping a hand over my mouth, I gasped. "I can't believe this." Tears filled my eyes as I passed it to Jensen. "I'll be right back."

I raced inside to what used to be the old library. There were hundreds of books lined on the built-in bookshelves. My fingers skimmed quickly over the titles, and when I finally found the one I was looking for, I hastily pulled it off the shelf. It felt like my heart was about to burst out of my chest.

Ellen Thomas was my grandmother's pseudonym; it made perfect sense. Ellen was her middle name and Thomas was the man she loved.

With trembling fingers, I opened the book to a page in the middle just as a wave of tears fell down my cheeks. I only read a few words, but the main characters were Rachel and Thomas. It was their love story.

Clutching the book to my chest, I hurried back outside. "Look," I said, handing it to Jensen. "My grandmother wrote the story and had it published. Nyla found that blurry picture inside of it. I can't believe I didn't think to read the book."

Jensen flipped through the pages, his eyes lit with awe.

"Your grandmother had a ton of secrets, but I never would've guessed they'd have been as extravagant as this." He handed the book back to me, and I held it to my heart. "If you want all the answers, I bet you'll find them in there," he said, nodding at the book.

Excitement coursed through my body. "Oh, I have no doubt. I plan on reading it, starting right now."

Jensen chuckled and got to his feet. "I can't wait to hear all about it."

He kissed the top of my head and went inside, leaving me with the sound of the waves crashing on the shore. I climbed into my grandmother's favorite rocking chair and opened the book to page one.

Was there going to be a happy ending, one that was different to how their real-life love affair ended?

I was about to find out.

34

EVERLEIGH

TWO WEEKS LATER

Today was the day.

As I stared out the glass door toward the ocean, I could see everyone gathered on the sand, waiting for me. Jensen was already out there with Seth by his side.

Nyla walked up to me, dressed in the crimson bridesmaid's gown I'd picked out for her; her gaze was transfixed on the picture-perfect view. The sky was the prettiest shade of bluish-purple, and the clouds in the distance were cast in a pink and orange glow thanks to the setting sun. I couldn't have asked for better weather on my wedding day.

"How are you feeling?" Nyla asked.

A smile spread across my face. "Good." I turned to her and winked. "Maybe just a bit nauseous."

She giggled. "When are you going to tell everyone?"

Butterflies fluttered in my stomach. My grandmother wasn't the only one who could keep secrets; I had one of my own.

"Today," I promised, grinning wide. "I don't think I can wait any longer."

Movement outside caught my attention, and I watched as my father started up the walkway toward the house; it was almost time.

Nyla gasped and grabbed my hands. "You never got the chance to tell me what happened in your grandmother's book. I want to know what happened."

When I first started reading it, I was so engrossed in the story that I barely ate until I finished it. I'd never laughed and cried so hard in my life. The love story between my grandmother and Thomas was tragic and full of passion, but the story *did* have a happy ending.

I thought maybe my grandmother would've had her characters end up together, but the book turned out to be the exact same as her real life. Thomas married another woman, and Rachel found love again with the man her parents wanted her to marry.

It was nice to see that she had no regrets and was happy with her life.

However, the part in the book where Thomas died at sea was the most heart-wrenching chapter I'd ever read in any book. I could feel my grandmother's pain and agony over his loss. I firmly believe that writing the book was my grandmother's way of healing.

In the end, everything turned out the way it was supposed to. I explained all of that to Nyla and she clutched her chest.

"Do you mind if I read it?"

"Not at all," I said, trying to keep from crying.

Every time I talked about the book, my whole body was filled with emotions. Nyla wrapped her arms around me and hugged me gently.

"Thank you for letting me share this amazing day with you. I thank God every day that you were brought into my life."

She let me go and I grabbed her hands. "I feel the same about you. When Jensen and I get back from our honeymoon, you and I are going to change things around at the clinic." I squeezed her hands. "We're going to make it our own."

She nodded quickly, trying her best not to cry. "Sounds good to me."

My father's footsteps pounded up the stairs and he appeared at the glass door, his eyes widening when he noticed me in my wedding gown.

Lips trembling, he opened the door. "Oh, honey, you look so beautiful." He held out his arm. "Are you ready?"

Nyla stepped past him so she could make her way down first. I linked my arm with his and kissed his cheek.

"Yes, I'm ready. Let's go."

THE SETTING SUN shone its last rays on the beach, casting a golden-orange hue on the sand and illuminating the waves as they crashed against the shore. Jensen and I stood facing each other; he looked at me with such love and affection in his eyes that my heart nearly burst with joy.

I wore a simple white dress that flowed in the breeze,

and my hair was pulled back in an elegant braid. Jensen wore khaki pants and a white button-down shirt; he looked as handsome as ever.

We had waited for this moment for so long, and finally, here we were, about to say our *I do's*.

I took in every detail of the idyllic setting: the smell of the ocean in the air, the sound of the seagulls, and the warmth of Jensen's hand as he held mine.

"Do you, Jensen, take this woman to be your lawfully wedded wife?" asked the officiant.

"I do," he replied, his voice full of emotion.

"And do you, Everleigh, take this man to be your lawfully wedded husband?"

"I do," I said, my voice shaking slightly. "More than anything."

As we exchanged our vows, my eyes never left Jensen's. I felt like the luckiest woman in the world to marry the man of my dreams on this beautiful beach that was our home.

Once the officiant announced us as husband and wife, we shared a tender kiss. Then, as we turned to walk down the aisle toward the dunes, I couldn't help but feel a little nervous. I was about to tell him my secret; it was the perfect time.

"Jensen, there's something I need to tell you," I said, my voice barely above a whisper.

Everyone was still on the beach, which gave us a few minutes alone. My heart raced as I stopped and stood in front of him.

"Are you okay?" Jensen asked, his voice etched with concern.

It took all I had to contain my delight. "I'm more than

okay. I found out something a few days ago and wanted to wait until today to tell you. Guess you can call it a wedding present to us both."

Jensen's brow furrowed in confusion, but a smile played at the corners of his lips. "Okay, now you've got me curious. What is it?"

I took a deep breath and looked deeply into his eyes. "I'm pregnant," I said, biting my lip in anticipation of his response.

Jensen's eyes widened for a moment before a huge grin spread across his face. "Are you serious?" he asked, his voice full of excitement.

I nodded, tears of joy starting to prick at the corners of my eyes. "Yes, I'm serious."

Jensen pulled me into a tight embrace, lifting me off the ground and spinning me around. "This is amazing," he said, his voice filled with wonder. "We're going to have a baby!"

I laughed, tears streaming down my face. "Yes, we are."

As Jensen set me back on my feet, we both looked at the ocean stretching out before us. It was the perfect moment, the perfect day, the perfect news.

Jensen cupped my cheeks in his warm hands and gently kissed my lips, his grayish-blue eyes never leaving mine.

"This is just the beginning, Everleigh. I know it took us a long time to get here, but I'm ready to see where our path takes us. And now, with a baby on the way, we'll have even more fun adventures."

"Are you ready for that?" I asked teasingly.

He chuckled and kissed me again. "You better believe it."

. . .

THE END

Nyla's book is next! Be sure to check out her story, Beginnings by the Sea!

OAK ISLAND SERIES

Hide Away by the Sea
Beginnings by the Sea

More to come!

SNEAK PEEK AT NYLA'S STORY

BEGINNINGS BY THE SEA

From NYT bestselling author LP Dover comes a gripping tale of secrets, lies, and... love.

After her marriage failed, Nyla Clark started a new life in the charming town of Oak Island, NC. With her medical practice thriving and a new man in her life, everything seems perfect.

But Cohen Sumner, her handsome new beau, has a secret.

From the moment he saw Nyla, Cohen ached for her. He was willing to risk everything to be with her, even if it meant concealing the shocking truth.

The new couple is getting closer by the day until Nyla's ex-husband, Miles Henley, unexpectedly comes to town. Looking into his beautiful eyes, she's forced to confront feelings she thought she left behind in Boston.

Yet the complications don't end there. When Cohen and Miles come face-to-face, Nyla learns that the truth Cohen kept hidden links them all together in a way she never imagined.

Now, Nyla has a choice to make. Will she risk everything to rekindle a lost love? Or stay with the man who would do anything to be with her?

ABOUT THE AUTHOR

New York Times and *USA Today* bestselling author L. P. Dover is a southern belle living in North Carolina with her husband and two beautiful girls. Everything's sweeter in the South has always been her mantra and she lives by it, whether it's with her writing or in her everyday life. Maybe that's why she's seriously addicted to chocolate.

Dover has written countless novels in several different genres, including a children's book with her daughter. Her favorite to write is romantic suspense, but she's also found a passion in romantic comedy. She loves to make people laugh which is why you'll never see her without a smile on her face.

You can find L.P. Dover at www.lpdover.com.

ALSO BY L.P. DOVER

SECOND CHANCES SERIES

Love's Second Chance

Trusting You

What He Wants (Trusting You Prequel)

Meant for Me

Fighting for Love

Intercepting Love

Catching Summer

Defending Hayden

Last Chance

Intended for Bristol

ARMED & DANGEROUS SERIES

No Limit

Roped In

High-Sided

CIRCLE OF JUSTICE SERIES

Trigger

Target

Aim

In the Crossfire

ARMED & DANGEROUS/CIRCLE OF JUSTICE CROSSOVER SERIES

Dangerous Game

Dangerous Betrayals

Book 3 - TBD

Book 4 – TBD

GLOVES OFF SERIES

A Fighter's Desire – Part One

A Fighter's Desire – Part Two

Tyler's Undoing

Ryley's Revenge

Winter Kiss: Ryley and Ash

Paxton's Promise

Camden's Redemption

Kyle's Return

GLOVES OFF - NEXT GENERATION SERIES

Craving the Fight

Taking the Fight

Wanting the Fight

Desiring the Fight

Longing for the Fight

Loving the Fight

Needing the Fight

Ending the Fight

SOCIETY X SERIES W/HEIDI MCLAUGHLIN

Dark Room

Viewing Room

Play Room

FOREVER FAE SERIES

Forever Fae

Betrayals of Spring

Summer of Frost

Reign of Ice

LAND OF THE FAE SERIES

Winter of the Shadow Fae

Spring of the Cursed Fae

Summer of the Siren Fae

TBA

TBA

ROYAL SHIFTERS SERIES

Turn of the Moon

Resisting the Moon

Rise of the Moon

Unleashed by the Moon

Bound by the Moon

Claimed by the Moon

Taken Under the Moon

Awakened by the Moon

BREAKAWAY SERIES

Hard Stick

Blocked

Playmaker

Off the Ice

STANDALONE NOVELS

The Truth About Secrets

Love, Lies & Deception

Going for the Hole

Anonymous

Love, Again

Fairytale Confessions

THE DATING SERIES W/HEIDI MCLAUGHLIN

A Date for New Year's

A Date with an Admirer

A Date for Good Luck

A Date for the Hunt

A Date for Good Luck

A Date for the Derby

A Date to Play Fore

A Date with a Foodie

A Date for the Fair

A Date for the Regatta

A Date for the Masquerade

A Date with a Turkey

A Date with an Elf

CHRISTMAS NOVELS

It Must've Been the Mistletoe

Snowflake Lane Inn

Christmas With You

MOONLIGHT AND ALEENA SERIES W/ANNA-GRACE DOVER

Moonlight and Aleena: A Tale of Two Friends

Made in the USA
Middletown, DE
02 November 2024

63756171R00179